I0675467

Free U'tanse

Henry Melton

Free U'tanse

Henry Melton

Wire Rim Books
Hutto, Texas

WRB

This is a work of fiction. Names, events and locations, if they exist elsewhere, are used here fictitiously and any resemblance to real persons, places or events is entirely coincidental.

Free U'tanse © 2015 by Henry Melton
All Rights Reserved

Printing History
First Edition: April 2015
ISBN 978-1-935236-60-3

ePub ISBN 978-1-935236-61-0
Kindle ISBN 978-1-935236-62-7

Website of Henry Melton
www.HenryMelton.com

Character images © 2015 by Djamila Knopf
http://shilesque.deviantart.com/

Printed in the United States of America

Wire Rim Books
www.wirerimbooks.com

Acknowledgements

I want to thank Jonathan Andrews, Jim Dunn, Linda Elliott, Mike Lynch, and Tom Stock for helping me with my grammatical blindness. Just seeing the other world isn't enough, I need to report it with clarity as well.

Contents

Appendix

Western Ko

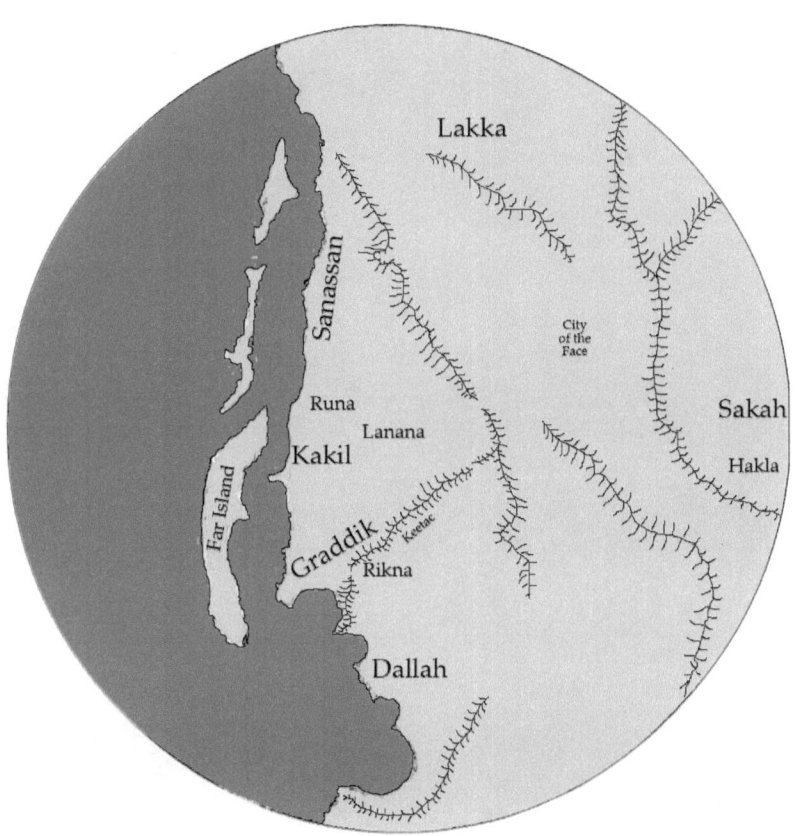

Who We Are

With every new generation of the U'tanse, the story of Earth, the Home world where we came from, seems more a myth and less historical. It doesn't help that our entire record of that time, when we were "humans," came from the writings of one man. But we have to believe the Book is all true. The story is simple, even if the details are elaborate.

After thousands of years of being nothing more than a red star in the sky of Earth, Betelgeuse had the last say. It was getting old, as stars go. For all of human history and more, it had been a giant, bloated up and just hanging on.

Then, the star collapsed and exploded into a supernova—not a tidy one. There were lobes and flares in this gigantic eruption. One of those flares just happened to be aimed at a much smaller star, Sol, the parent star of the planet called Earth.

Human technology back then was based on tiny structures called semi-conductors, and they fried under the onslaught of powerful electromagnetic pulses. Then, high velocity particles blasted that atmosphere, bathing the planet in sickening radiation. Many died, but as the Star faded, people learned to stay out of the star light and were poised for survival and recovery.

It could have been much worse. The Cerik were circling the planet in their starship, waiting for the humans to sicken. They are predators and it was as natural as breathing for them to wait in hiding until their prey were weakened and distressed. If it had not been for our ancestors, the first of the U'tanse, all of Earth and all of the humans would have been prey for the chase.

Free U'tanse

Abe and Sharon, Father and Mother to us all, fought the Cerik for all of humankind, and they won, at the cost of their own freedom.

That is the great secret we share, behind our telepathic blocks and our acts of servitude to our Cerik masters. Two U'tanse defeated a Cerik clan, and we have inherited all of their power. Someday when the time is right, the U'tanse will move, and we shall reclaim our freedom.

Taking a Break

Joshua glanced around the room. Ash and his little sister Veronica had settled down for a nap. The other cuties were in their playpen. Sylvia, the woman officially in charge of the nursery for that shift, had begun cleaning the floor. There was no better time. Making sure his *ineda* was tight and no one could catch any hint of his thoughts, he waited until Sylvia's back was turned and slipped out into the corridor.

His clairvoyance wasn't in the same class as his father's, but he could tell that there was no one coming his way. He raced out into the curving corridor and took the tight spiral walkway down two levels. Not for the first time, he wondered if there was a faster way to move around the various levels and branches of the Base. The place was ancient, built long before the U'tanse were captured from Earth and brought to Ko. The Delense had carved the hidden complex into the stone mountain, at best guess, several thousand years before the Arrival. It was, in many ways, unlike any other burrow on the planet.

Joshua put out his hand and touched the inner wall of the spiral for stability as he ran. He'd seen drawings of the Delense—not with his physical eyes, though. There was a drawing at one of the U'tanse Homes owned by one of the Cerik Names. The Delense were larger than he was and walked on all four legs. This twisty passage was probably the fastest way down for them. It was pure industrial Delense design, with no allowances made for their Cerik masters and certainly none for the bipedal humans.

He paused where the spiral joined the dock level, staying out of sight. Around the corner, in the supply room, he could sense someone stacking some boxes. *Robert*. It was the submarine pilot. *Good*. He wouldn't be long. Joshua eased out onto the dock and crouched behind some transport barrels. Closing his eyes, he waited. It was a good time to scan the Base. Four levels up, near the maproom, his father Cyclops sat motionless in his private office. He was likely using his superior *sight* to scan the planet for activities of the Cerik. That was what he did most days.

His mother Debbie was on the second level, over in the gardens, talking with some of the other women. He suspected she was handing out the work schedules. He hoped she stayed distracted, at least until he was gone. If she realized he was taking a break from cutie duty again, she'd send someone to stop him. Her clairvoyance wasn't as detailed and reliable as his father's, but when she flashed on something, she tended to act on it.

Heavy relays clicked and the dock level went dark. Robert's footsteps started moving off into the distance. The whole Base was in energy conservation mode. Most of the time, the hydroelectric power plant up in the hills gave them energy to spare, but they'd had to recharge the boat and the submarine both in the past month and the reserves were depleted. Mother's gardens came first, and then lights for the corridors. Almost everybody who had the *sight* was used to walking in the dark, but not all of them were gifted that way. Barker was a tenner, the one-in-ten males bred without psychic abilities, so he had no clairvoyance to help, and he wasn't happy about the situation. Debbie had given him access to one of their hand-held lights, but the man grumbled about the situation constantly. The others who really needed light kept to the lighted work areas or constantly had to turn the lights on and off wherever they went.

Once Joshua was sure the dock level was deserted, he felt his way over to the supply room and fished out his breather and leathers. They were still stashed in the tote bag in the corner where he'd left them. He gave them a sniff. Good enough. He peeled off tunic and shoes, added them to the tote, squeezed out most of the air and then tied it off tight. Padding over to the edge of the dock, he tossed his bag into the water and jumped in after it.

The smooth bulk of the submarine was in his way, but pulling the tote by its lanyard, he swam around it and made for the tunnel.

4

Daylight from the outside illuminated the opening down below the surface. He charged his lungs with several breaths and made the underwater passage. The breather had never been designed for use in the water, and as he made the short swim to the beach, he wondered what it would take to make one that did—air tanks for one thing. But that would take a harness to hold them. The complexity of the job evaded him. He'd think about it later. He was good at coming up with ideas, but he needed someone with the mind of a tenner to help him work out the details.

On shore, he ducked under the branches of a tree to dress. The chance of a Cerik flying overhead in a boat and seeing him was infinitesimal, but he'd been raised to be cautious anyway. With the breather to filter his air and leathers to protect most of his skin from airburn, he relaxed. He was free.

That's what they called him—a free U'tanse. Since he was a baby, every time the Base rescued someone new and introductions were made, his parents called him that—the first freeborn U'tanse. He was nearly an adult, so they shouldn't be upset when he made an occasional break for freedom, should they?

He was barely a quarter of the way up to the ledge overlooking the bay when the seam on his leggings ripped. He sighed, scaring away one of the little beasts that hid among the rubble on the slope. The one time he neglected to bring his sewing kit was the time he needed it. At least he brought the lotion.

The rest of the climb wasn't too bad. It was a hot day and the leathers didn't allow his body to sweat like it should. That was another bad design. U'tanse lived all their lives indoors, in the tunnels with filtered air. It didn't seem to him that enough thought had been given to dealing with extremes of the weather.

There was a small glade of trees at the top of the cliff. He picked up a nice large stone and moved it to the best shade tree. He peeled off the leggings, feeling the sea breeze provide a welcome relief from the heat, even as the chemicals in the air acted like a mild acid on his skin. He could tolerate the air burn for a while, but it was best to limit it. Fishing a squeeze pouch of lotion out of the side pocket, he applied a protective layer to the leg under the ripped seam and then dressed again.

Protected against the airburn, sitting in the shade, he closed his eyes and let his mind roam the planet.

Graddik clan was close, at least to his *sight*. If he had to walk there, it might take days. The Name's Perch was on a rock outcropping near the coastline, with the various *tetka* who served him lived in their own groves surrounding it, although Joshua had never spent the time to learn which dance held which function. The Cerik clans were confusing. He learned more by riding the thoughts of those U'tanse who had to deal with the masters directly than by trying to watch the actions of the predators himself.

His main interest was a short distance, at least by boat, from the Perch, in a re-made Delense burrow near the river. The Graddik Home was where all the U'tanse slaves owned by that clan lived. He scanned the tunnels and saw how many people were in their cells, or by the *ooro* tanks, or down by the bath. He often found girls down at the water. Today, while there were women there, there was no one his age. It was mid-day and everyone was working. In previous mental visits, he'd seen several girls he would love to have at the Base. This attempt, he couldn't even ogle them remotely.

"It's a fact of our existence here," his father had explained to him a couple of years earlier. He'd complained that there were no girls his age to play with. "We rescue workers abandoned by their Cerik owners. Since these workers are exclusively men, and often older men, that's why there are so many gray-haired guys like me. We also take on Festival girls, but while young, they're all older than you. Right now it's a lonely time. Just be patient for a little while longer, and you'll find many interesting girls arriving that are just your age."

He had patience, but that didn't keep him from seeking out some private time and looking out at the world. Some of the girls he watched as they bathed just might be the ones that showed up at the Base some day. Not that he told anyone what he did. He was very grateful he'd been trained in *ineda* from a very young age. Maybe his parents would understand, but it wasn't anything he wanted to share.

His mind flickered northwards to Kakil's Home. It was a much larger place, and he was happy to see Samson walking the ramp down to the bath with his buddy George. They were both several years older than Joshua, but one thing he'd noticed early on. Girls flocked around Samson.

Samson's Swim

Samson shrugged in his tunic. It was too tight across his shoulders and the fabric was irritating.

George poked him with his elbow. "I suppose you miss the baths, eh?"

A nod was all the question was worth as Samson suppressed the tension in his arm. George was a good friend, but he didn't realize how instincts could change since he'd started working with the Cerik all the time. A casual poke among U'tanse was one thing. It was a challenge to battle among his Cerik warrior buddies.

But I suppose I need this time back Home. I've got to keep both sides of my life in balance.

He unclenched his fist. George was a tenner and probably never noticed his surge of hostility. Maybe that was why he was so comfortable with the guy. He knew George wasn't trying to read his mind, trying to see if he was a monster inside.

They reached the changing room and Samson realized he really did miss the baths. The tunic he kept for Home use went on the shelf, and he winced as George stared at the new scar across his left side.

George shook his head. "It's tough there at the Perch!"

"Oh, not so bad. I was just a little slow that time. A *ralak* from Lanana deliberately ignored my *ruff* and took a slash at me. I couldn't kill him since he was on business there, but that didn't stop me from leaving him with a nice bubbling slash of his own to remember me by."

They headed to the water. George asked, "What's your *ruff* sound like? I hear the pilots down at the loading bay all the time."

Samson smiled, and then rumbled from his chest, slow and drawn out, "Errrrah!"

Both guys looked over at the bench where several girls were watching them, giggling and shivering. George sighed, "I never get this much attention on my own."

Samson, standing over two feet taller than his friend, with shoulders so wide no tunic fit quite right, could just tilt his head in sympathy.

. . .

Joshua, silently riding Samson's thoughts, appreciated the girls through the giant's eyes. While he could clairvoyantly see the girls directly, sharing the man's vision via telepathy was so much more vivid. Samson could bring down a solid *ineda* if he wanted—Joshua had been blocked out before—but the warrior lived among Cerik. Being close to the Name meant a telepathic block was dangerously suspicious. Samson was comfortable being open to a world of telepaths. He was who he was, and never tried to hide it.

In contrast, Joshua had rarely tried to taste George's thoughts. The tenner would probably be comfortable at home at the Base. He couldn't read thoughts anyway, so he wouldn't miss the constant beat of other minds.

The girls, however, were a mix, their thoughts a swirl of noise like winds or the waves. It was clear they'd raced down to the water to be there once they heard Samson was coming. Not all girls dreamed about him, but there were enough who did. Seeing him in the flesh gave them tingles.

As Joshua attempted to sample their thoughts, he felt a flush of his own as two of them considered swimming out to join Samson in more than conversation. But three of the girls were there for different kinds of shivers. If they dreamed of Samson, those dreams were probably nightmares. The scars fascinated and horrified them, and even more than that, his fingers and toes.

He's not even a U'tanse. He's a mutation, a monster, intruded an unblocked thought. With a nervous glance, one of the girls broke off eye contact and tightened her *ineda*.

Others had probably had similar thoughts, ones they kept quiet.

As Samson and George swam off in different directions, one girl turned to the others, "I don't know why they let him come here. He's dangerous. You know he's killed a Cerik! He could kill any of us in an instant, and I don't even think the Name would do anything about it."

There was a murmur of voices. One struggled to make herself heard. "Pen, you just like the tingle when he looks your way. He's no monster!"

"But you see his hands! Six fingers on each, and the same with his toes. That isn't normal."

The girl to her right giggled, "How did you get close enough to count?"

"Nobody should be that big."

"Luckily, you weren't in charge," said his defender. "He wasn't a random or a mutation. I looked up the records. His parents petitioned the elders to optimize his genes for size and strength. When his extra digits appeared, they searched the Book and found stories of giants just like him. He's pure U'tanse, pure human, the size and the extra fingers have always been in our genetic heritage. Personally, I like the idea of having a man around who has killed two Cerik."

"Omelia wants a big baby of her own," chided one of the others.

Just loud enough to be heard, a smug voice said, "She needs a man she won't smother in her bed."

Omelia said nothing, her mind tight and her face grim, but she got to her feet and left the smaller girls behind as she stepped down into the water and swam away.

The others turned to more gossip. Joshua detached from their minds and returned to his shaded overlook. Girls, even naked girls, were not so interesting when they cut at each other like that.

But was Samson still swimming alone? Guiltily, he peeked.

. . .

The thrill of the water as he pushed hard with his arms was pure bliss. He could never get any swimming done when he was on duty at the Perch. There was a creek that wound through the clan's grounds. There was even a pool deep enough to swim, but it would embarrass the Name if he tried to use it. Cerik hated the water. In the traditional tales he'd overheard, the aversion to mud and water was a common theme in the legends of the Cerik. During the time when they hunted the Delense as prey, those swimming, burrowing and very intelligent creatures could only survive by living in burrows surrounded by water and sticking to the muddy swamps where the Cerik wouldn't follow.

It was hard enough for Samson to maintain his status as a *rettik* without appearing to be any more of a prey that he had to. His grandfather, Scar, established what could be done as both a slave and a warrior. A Name would accept any warrior as a *rettik*—his right eye—if he were lethal enough and showed no weakness. His father, Goliath, followed in Scar's footsteps, with one kill of his own, up until the day when an opponent proved faster in a challenge. Samson was just lucky that Elehadi, one of the most powerful of the Names, had bought him from Graddik and transferred him to the Kakil Home.

Across the planet, there were U'tanse in attendance to all of the Names, but few became warriors. Samson felt the burden of his position. He must be the best right-eye for his Name. He must prove to all the Cerik that U'tanse were worthy not only as keepers of beasts and maintainers of the technology, but also as sharp claws in service to the clans.

He paused in his strokes, and in the dim light of the baths, he raised his hand before his eyes and looked at it carefully. He'd caught a whiff of the girls' thoughts. Six fingers. Twice the three claws of the Cerik. He'd already gotten some approving comments from his fellow warriors. Twice-three was less disturbing than five, to their minds.

The gauntlets he wore at the Perch were modified from his father's. Segmented armor covered his hands, with the outside edge tapered to a blade. He wondered what it would be like to have new ones, designed to mimic the three-clawed hands of the Cerik. He spread his fingers, toying with the idea—one for the thumb, his three strongest fingers for the power claw in the center, and the outer two for the third.

What would it take to get something like that made for him? U'tanse were great at building things—not him—but his cousins had those skills. He could ask the Name to order them made, but getting a favor from the Name had its costs. Working the U'tanse political side was difficult as well. He'd have to think about it. Perhaps George could help him out.

In the distance, Samson could hear someone swimming toward him. He grinned. The girls were fun, but he honestly didn't care for any fragile weaklings. If she wanted him, she'd have to hunt him down.

Samson's *ineda* snapped shut, and Joshua lost the connection among the noise of all the other thoughts in the world.

...

Oh well. Joshua looked across the bay. Storm clouds were coming, and the stone mountain that hid the Base was like a magnet for lightning strikes. Time to head home. He stretched and set his feet down the trail. It was time to review his excuses for abandoning cutie duty.

Everyone had been taking naps—almost everyone. Sylvia had been there and she'd never abandon them to be on their own. The other mothers came by all the time to check on them as well. It had been the perfect time.

Mother would buy it or not. He kept his eyes on the trail. If he injured himself, it would set his freedom back.

Veronica's face came to mind. His little sister wasn't anything like those gossipy girls. But was it because she didn't have any other girls her age to play with? She spent all her time with Ash. In her own way, she was suffering the same lonely life he did. She was the firstborn free U'tanse girl. Mother had been a pioneer. No one knew how quickly *ineda* could be taught to a cutie. Even in the first years when there were several Festival girls at the Base, no one had been willing to risk a pregnancy when there was a chance the babies, and then cuties, would have to spend years locked in a room where they could never see anything that could compromise the secrecy of the Free U'tanse.

But Joshua was born, and the irrational fear that he would grow up damaged by the security measures proved groundless. Tenners grew up isolated as well. Freeborn had their own problems. *But we are sane, in our own way.*

Monitor Duty

Joshua opened the door to the maproom and leaned forward to tap the light switch positioned just lower than his knee level. Cyclops arrived a moment later.

"Go ahead and sit down," his father said. "This is a working meeting. You're not in trouble this time."

Joshua relaxed just a little and found a chair as far from the center of the big table as possible. Others came in, bringing the number up to eight. Cyclops took the head position, the blindfold he always wore making him look a bit more regal than anyone else could manage. Several people were looking at the new kid.

Cyclops said, "Before we start, I'm including Joshua in today's meeting because it seems that cutie duty isn't sufficiently taxing the boy's energy. I would like everyone to recheck his *ineda* and give me warning if you find any leakage."

Joshua tapped his teeth together quietly, knowing everyone was suddenly trying to read his thoughts.

Robert chuckled, "It's my experience that since he learned *ineda*, no one can find him—especially when there's work to be done."

Others laughed as well.

Cyclops nodded. "Okay, then if there is no objection… Joshua, get map number twelve and spread it out on the table. For all of us, and not just the boy, remember that our task here is to stay ahead of Cerik activity. Any leaks, even in your dreams, could be catastrophic."

Joshua was already out of his chair, finding a clearly labeled rack of maps. He pulled number twelve and unrolled it onto the table. It was pasted together from four smaller sheets of the light-brown *shash* reed paper and was as wide as he was tall, nearly square and lined with details. It was a world map, with all the clan boundaries marked. Rivers were marked in a blue-colored ink. In fact, there were more colors than he'd seen on any one paper before. Mountain ranges had a rusty color. Clan perches were marked in black. The Homes were in a dark green. They had to be using imported inks.

The boundary lines between clans were clearly marked with charcoal lines, and frequently rubbed out.

The Base wasn't marked, but there was a dirty smudge on the paper, where fingerprints had casually left their own indicator.

Cyclops pointed to the Kakil clan region. "Elehadi is clearly planning a new push."

Across the table, Comfort was scribbling on paper. Joshua realized she was writing down what Cyclops was saying. Had she written what his father had said about him, too? He hadn't realized she was so quick with the pen. He'd seen her in the nursery a few weeks earlier, familiarizing herself with the place. Her son was due in another three months.

One by one, from Cyclops's right, each of the people reported what they had sensed with their clairvoyance or telepathy what U'tanse or Cerik were doing in the Kakil area. Joshua's mind raced. Should he report what he knew about Samson? Was it stuff they already knew? Would he be in trouble for poking around in the man's thoughts?

But when Hugo finished his report on the flights of the boats in and out of Kakil, Mark on Joshua's right, started immediately with his report. He had been monitoring how well the former Runa Home was dealing with all the changes Elehadi had imposed after he had killed the Runa Name and taken over those lands and holdings. Runa's possessions included all the Runa U'tanse.

Joshua's miff at not getting a say vanished as Mark detailed how Elehadi was making arrangements to increase the number of Festival girls to be sent away during the next West Coast Festival. Joshua made a mental note: *I'll need to visit the Runa Home the next chance I get and see who we're talking about.*

Cyclops spoke again. "We're not the only ones trying to read Elehadi's intentions. All the Names in the western regions are feeling Kakil's claws pointed in their direction. With the Face coming up, we'll need to be ready for anything."

The meeting continued for another hour, reviewing all the clans. Most of the people had nothing new to report. There were some deaths among the Cerik, but from the U'tanse view, nothing had changed. One by one, people started leaving. Cyclops spoke quietly with a couple of the people, and Joshua made no attempt to listen in. He had enough to think about as it was.

Eventually, his father said, "Joshua, roll up the map carefully and put it away."

"Okay." He hesitated, finally remembering which side was the inside of the roll. He worked carefully, not wanting to disturb the paste job on the paper. Finally he stowed it in its bin.

Cyclops said, "If a meeting lasts much longer than this, head down to the kitchen and get a tray of bread and drinks. Probably we'll all be too busy to think about it, so you'll have to remember."

"Umm. Okay."

The blindfold turned his way, "Do you have a question?"

Joshua hesitated. "Maybe. What do I do if I have something to say?"

His father shrugged. "Tell me—or just speak up."

There was a moment of silence. "I just know a few things about Samson."

"Samson bar Goliath of Kakil?"

"Right. Him. It's nothing much. I just know that he traded slashes with a *ralak* from Lanana a few days ago. The cut is still healing."

"This was at the Kakil Perch?"

Joshua had to think carefully, remembering the overtones of Samson's memory. He nodded. "Pretty sure."

"What else do you know about him?"

There was a lot, but most of what he knew was useless detail. "He's thinking of making a new set of gauntlets that will make his hands look more like Cerik claws."

His father frowned. "Is this something urgent he's planning?"

"Not really. He's just playing with designs. Why?"

"There is a lot of speculation about him. Many of the Homes' elders worry that he's become more Cerik than U'tanse. They fear his loyalties are more with his masters than with his cousins. He was the first U'tanse bought for his skill as a warrior, and doesn't seem to have many connections at the Kakil Home."

Joshua nodded. "He worries about staying balanced. He wants U'tanse warriors to be valuable to the Names."

"That still doesn't tell us anything about what he would do if confronted by an order to kill U'tanse."

Joshua leaned back slightly. "You think that would happen?"

"Imagine if the Names discovered the Base here. They'd send warriors to capture or kill us. Given the current value of a slave, more likely they'd kill us all. Suppose Elehadi sent Samson with those warriors. What would he do?"

After a moment, Joshua just shook his head. "I couldn't tell."

"Tell me, why have you been monitoring Samson?"

Joshua lowered his head, "Uh. Well, he's big and strong."

"And you're not?"

"Yes."

"You do know you'll grow larger, don't you? You should be as tall as I am; probably stronger, too. I've been less active since my eyes were destroyed."

Joshua nodded. He wasn't about to mention the real reason he visited Samson's mind.

Cyclops said, "Still, if you're comfortable monitoring him without being detected, then I'd advise you to continue. Samson works very closely with Elehadi and you know how interested we are in him. Any hint about what Kakil's Name is about to do will be valuable. If you find out anything, tell me immediately. Don't wait for a meeting."

Joshua smiled. "I will."

"Okay then, please make sure the maproom is tidy, then turn off the lights when you leave."

The people had left a number of dirt tracks, leaf debris, and charcoal stick shavings. He cleaned all that, then took the opportunity to peek into all the shelves and storage bins. The maps had probably all been drawn here. There were rolls of paper, marking pens, ink pots, and straight-edge boards. He found the blue inkpot, and noticed how tightly it was sealed.

The maps, what he could tell from peeking into the rolls without spreading them out on the table, were everything from world maps, to detailed maps of the Perches and Homes. There was even one with some dots on it that made no sense.

He was confident that if he were called to produce a map in the next meeting, that he'd find it quickly. He reached down and tapped the light switch. Instinctively, he sensed the location of all the chairs and obstacles with his mind.

With the darkness, he realized how silent the place was. Everyone was off to their alternate jobs; cooking, gardening, carpentry, etc.

His alternate job was keeping Ash and Veronica out of trouble, and comforting the crying cuties. That could wait a little bit, couldn't it?

He sat down in one of the chairs, relishing the dark. He had his father's approval to scan Samson. Why not now? He could also see what the Runa girls looked like.

A long time ago, when he was first stretching his mind out beyond the Base, he found it much easier to read a person when he knew where they were. Over time, he'd built his own mental map of the closer clans and the Homes they owned. He didn't know all of them, and maybe he should. He could use the map to help stretch his clairvoyant perception into places he'd ignored before. If he remembered, Runa had been north of Kakil, along the coastline.

After a moment of concentration, he felt drawn to a river valley. There was an increase in the noise of many minds creating a feel—a shifting tide of life. Focusing, he found the burned ashes of the Runa Perch. The *dlathe* tree grove used to have a wooden platform where none but the Name could rest, overseeing his Second, his *rettik* and the lesser names of the *tetka* of his clan. In a normal succession, the Second would kill his *La* and become the Name himself, taking over the Perch.

Apparently, when Elehadi of Kakil killed the Name of Runa, he also destroyed the *hurru*, the actual Perch of Runa. He absorbed the Runa lands and possessions into Kakil.

Looking around, there were other burned out places in the clan's grounds. Walking about, or resting in *erdan*, were warriors and Cerik workers. There were even a few U'tanse. The Runa grounds had spread out over the whole delta, with groves for several thousand Cerik, and killing pens for their prey. Runa had several wide, fenced-in pastures for runners. It must have been a thriving place before it had been conquered. Now it felt... neglected. There was no energy to the place. The courtyard where boats landed and where runners could be herded aboard for sale to other clans was deserted. There was a cliff facing the ocean, and scavengers scuttled about on its rocks, cleaning any flesh still remaining on the dead.

Joshua didn't share Samson's admiration for the Cerik, but he didn't have any interest in the dead ones either. He needed to find the Runa Home. Homes needed water, fresh water. He stretched his view up the river. He found it.

It was a U'tanse Home, just like the others he'd seen. A rounded Delense burrow that, over the generations, had become more square-shaped as the human taste in engineering and repair made the place more livable.

The feel of the Runa Home had changed as well because of the conquest. Joshua could quickly taste an undercurrent of fear in the people's lives. In a real sense, they missed their Runa overlord and feared what this new Name would do to them. The word had arrived that triple the number of girls would be going off to Festival, and only a few would come to replace them.

This was not the time to see how pretty they were. No one was in a mood to smile. Joshua felt repelled by the place. Optimism and joy were gone.

Yellow Alert

Samson stood guard, one of several warriors posted on the perimeter of Elehadi's private hunting grove. His orders were simple: kill anyone who attempted to enter the grove—anyone other than Elehadi and Stakka, the Name's first telepath. From the gossip, the other *rettik* thought it was unusual for the Name to put so much trust in a telepath. Usually it was the Name and the Second who formed the leading pair. But that wasn't Samson's problem. His duty was to follow orders—exactly; not that anyone in the area was anxious to visit the grove. Elehadi didn't need any excuse to have anyone killed. Most often, he'd do it himself just to keep his claws sharp.

Barely at the limit of his vision, off to his right, he could see another guard waiting in *erdan*. In the other direction was another, but from his post, the one to the left was hidden by a large tree trunk. Nine warriors provided the barricade while Elehadi was "hunting".

I wish I could achieve erdan, *like a Cerik. Standing watch, my thoughts are too noisy.*

Joshua, riding Samson's thoughts silently, had a different opinion. It was helpful to listen in to his idle 'noise'. Since he'd gotten the order to follow Samson's thoughts a few days ago, he'd gotten quite comfortable, fitting silently into the flow of the warrior's thoughts.

Samson lifted his breather and smelled the breeze. A moment of raw Ko air wouldn't kill him, and he felt the need to sniff for any betraying scents. There was something, but it was barely detectable through the filters. He brought all his senses to maximum. There was a scrape of a twig.

His clairvoyance wasn't as good as many of the U'tanse, but although his Cerik buddies had excellent hearing and smelling, none of them had *sight* like the U'tanse.

Ah, there you are. It was a *hatsen* in the underbrush, probably doing some hunting of its own. A dozen paces would put it in range, but other than the joy of the chase, he couldn't do anything with it. Cerik could eat it. Cerik could eat almost anything. But it was poisonous to U'tanse. Not to mention that leaving his post could be fatal as well.

Another rustle of the tangled vegetation on the floor of the grove came from behind him—inside the protected area. Silently, Samson pivoted and saw Stakka approach.

Samson watched motionless, well aware that the telepath was probably reading his every thought. He made no effort to bring up his *ineda*. It was the telepath's right to monitor his thoughts. Instead, as he always did, he watched the Cerik carefully, cataloging in his mind every weak point in Stakka's armored hide, listing every possible way his U'tanse skills and weapons could kill him.

The telepath moved past, on his way back to the Perch, only showing that he had read Samson's thoughts by the distance he kept between them.

Satisfied at the bare hint of respect, Samson waited only a few seconds more before Elehadi also appeared, only this time with no betraying hint of his motion over the ground. The Name was a supreme hunter. He would not have reached his position otherwise. Samson remained motionless.

<U'tanse,> came the sharp growl.

Samson knelt in place and lowered his gaze.

There was another string of harsh vowels and hissing. Joshua had never learned Cerik, but he caught the meaning out of Samson's mind.

<Make preparation to leave for your burrow in two days. Return when the Face is complete.>

Samson tapped his heels together, a practice he'd gotten from his father, an emulation of a warrior's rattle of hind claws.

Elehadi moved off rapidly though the trees, leaving no hint of his passage.

Think of it as an extra vacation. No U'tanse has ever been allowed at the Face. He couldn't have brought me along. But there was regret in his thoughts.

Joshua disconnected from Samson's thoughts, feeling his own body tensed in the chair.

Elehadi and Stakka were in secret conference before the Face. He should tell that to Cyclops.

...

Joshua walked the garden rows beside his mother, picking the little purple sadapples she was experimenting with. It was a native Cerik plant, ignored by the Cerik and other U'tanse families, but Robert brought a few back from one of his excursions, claiming the Uuaa, another slave race, would occasionally eat them. Debbie was the chief gardner and had a whole chamber dedicated to native plants. They needed different lighting and air. The first generation of the sadapples had been bitter and unusable for anything other than mulch, but she had been adjusting the water and running the air at a fifty/fifty mix of filtered to raw. The fruit still had to be pulped and treated with vinegar, but as a paste, it could be baked into a filling bread.

She said, "You know, you are sort of related to Samson."

"Oh? What do you mean, sort of?"

She brought out her shears and trimmed a dead branch. "When I was very young, I was orphaned. My father had been ... killed in a boat accident, and my mother was slaughtered in a Cerik attack. Scar became my father, watching out over me until I came of age."

"And Goliath was his son."

She nodded. "He was a big guy, and timid around me, but I thought of him as a big brother. I guess that makes Samson your cousin—sort of."

Joshua put his mind around it. "So, you grew up with Scar. Do you know the Cerik language?"

"Oh yes. I picked up some from him, but I learned a lot more over the years in my monitoring duties. I suppose we should teach you as well. It takes time."

They picked some more fruit. Joshua asked, "Did Goliath have six fingers?"

"No. He had rather standard genetics, like his father. However, he adjusted his growth hormones. It's like forcing your body to heal, only pushing the pituitary gland to adjust the production a specific complex chemical. It's dangerous, in case you're getting any ideas. Just like girls getting fertility training, boys who want to grow bigger really need a mentor to help them learn the right way to do it. Here at the Base, there's really no need for big strong warriors. If we have to fight the Cerik, then we've failed already."

He'd heard her say that before, and he understood. If the Cerik ever learned of them, they could destroy even the deeply buried tunnels and everyone in them. They had done it before, when conquering the other slave races. An overloaded power storage cell could vaporize tons of rock. They'd even fine-tuned the process they called *flick*. They could drop a specially prepared power cell from a boat and turn the area into molten slag.

The people living in the Base were free U'tanse, but they could not protect themselves. They didn't have the technology. They didn't have the numbers. All they had was secrecy and their ability to spy on the Cerik.

A low-pitched chime rang through the tunnels. Joshua checked the bell room in the upper level connected to the main air filter system. Clairvoyance was as common as telepathy, but varied widely among people. All women and most men were trained to monitor the cells of their bodies for healing and for careful control of fertility. Gifted ones like Cyclops could see details at will, anywhere on the planet. Debbie had flashes of insight, details of everything around her for miles, but it was rarely under her control. Joshua was not in his father's class, but he could direct his *sight* better than most.

"Cyclops rang the bell," he reported. "A yellow flag."

Debbie said, "You'd better go then."

He set down his reed basket and ran for the spiral. A yellow flag meant there was a problem at the factory. All available workers should head to the dock.

For a community of telepaths, the Base was particularly handicapped when it came to raising an alarm. Even if the place were on fire, with people dying, it would be too hazardous to lift *ineda* and call for help. Thus, the bell. Someone with *sight* would see which flag was posted and pass the word to the tenners and those whose clairvoyance was limited.

At the dock, Paul was loading workers into the submarine. "Chemical spill! Cleanup crew will need suits and breathers. We're leaving in five minutes."

Joshua elbowed his way into the supply room and started suiting up.

Hugo put his hand on his shoulder. "No, Joshua, stay put. Not this one."

"I can do it!"

"Not in that suit. It's falling apart."

"I can fix it! I've got the kit right here."

"No time. Sorry."

Joshua, still half into his leather suit, watched the others get into the submarine. As it submerged, he scanned the hidden factory burrowed into another mountain on the opposite side of the bay. There were people working there already. On the surface, he could sense animals moving away from hidden vents that were now puffing out poisonous vapors.

"Joshua," it was Rachael, wheeling a bed down to the dock. "Get dressed, you need to take care of the cuties. The rest of us have to be on healer duty."

He focused more carefully at the workers at the factory. Yes, two of them were being carried in carts toward the emergency doors.

He gave no argument. At least he was useful for something.

Nursery Duty

Veronica dashed through the door, took a sharp turn and nearly knocked Joshua over.

"Hey, Very, watch it!" He had a grip on her thin wrist, but she was slippery and almost got free.

She whispered, "Ash is chasing me. I've got to go."

He relented and let her slip free, watching her dash into the maze room.

The nursery took up five rooms connected like a pentagram. The four babies had one room to themselves, although there was plenty of room for more. When a baby was mobile enough to deliberately ignore a call to stop running away, they were deemed a cutie, and moved to the cutie barracks. Ash and Veronica were the oldest, with Sam, Gurlie, and Olive a few years younger. Until they passed their *ineda* qualifications, they never left the cluster of rooms and never knew anything about what made them unique on the planet, as free U'tanse.

The maze room was Joshua's idea, after growing up alone with only the little ones and an occasional Festival girl willing to play chase-and-hide with him. When he'd graduated to the outside and discovered all the other people who lived in the Base—vibrant, alive people who just managed to hide their every thought, he talked Old Dennis the carpenter into the idea.

Veronica dashed into the maze of adult-high fence lines draped with *shash* to hide the view. Her frantic thoughts bubbled and flickered as she fought the excitement of the chase and tried to get a handle on what little *ineda* she'd been taught. Ash raced to follow, knowing Joshua was in the way before he came into view, swerving wide to miss him. Ash was trying to control his own thoughts as well so he'd have a better chance of sneaking up on her.

Joshua used his *sight* to follow them for a moment. If they developed clairvoyance like his, the maze would be useless in chase-and-hide, but it would still be serving its purpose, developing cuties' mental skills.

He had to take care of all the children today. Grellin was two levels up, surrounded by the women healers as they worked, hoping to repair his lungs. They had him unconscious until he could handle the pain. Bernard was waiting his turn, doing his best to repair the burned flesh on his arm on his own until one of the more experienced healers was available to help.

It wasn't an accident the best healers were usually on child care rotation. He'd broken an arm and several bones in his right foot when he was growing up. He just hoped none of his charges broke anything while he was on duty. He knew enough to work on his own airburns, but he'd never studied real healing seriously.

A brief scan of the Base showed several people hurrying up to the maproom. He should have been there, but the accident threw everyone's duty schedules off.

An outraged wail came from the babies. He sighed and hurried to see what was wrong. A sniff told him immediately. Little Shelly needed changing.

...

It was a frustrating day. The Face was here, and Joshua was missing it. His attempt to locate the City of the Face, somewhere deep in the continent, was a bust. None of the cuties gave him the free time to hunt for it—not that he'd be able to understand what was going on. He didn't know Cerik, but maybe he could tap into some unblocked thoughts.

Scanning the maproom wasn't any good either. He could see people working, but they were all blocked, and his *sight* was no good for listening in to conversations. Rumor was that some rare individuals could *hear*, clairaudience, but he didn't know anyone with that ability.

Sylvia showed up late in the day with fish. He rounded up the cuties and went through the hunt for bones with them all. She fed the babies.

She was only a few years older than Joshua. She'd arrived as a Festival girl all the way from Tenthonad on the east coast and had her pick of older men. Her Timothy was starting to crawl and she came by more often than most of the mothers to check on her first born.

Joshua moved close to her and whispered, "What's the news?" Officially, gossip was off limits in the nursery, where a cutie might overhear something sensitive.

She turned her head to the left to see how close the cuties were, but they were all chatting over by the food table. She spoke quietly, "The Face has started. All the Names had a bloodletting ceremony where they swore to avoid killing each other for the duration of the event. It's over for the day. The Names are just wandering about, admiring the special *hurru* they built in the City. The real events, the rotating feasts, will be starting early, before dawn our time."

She shifted Timothy in her arms. "You know, I'm not on transcription duty until nearly noon tomorrow. Would you like me to come by and give you a few hours off to listen in?"

"That would be great! I've been looking forward to the Face since I was cleared to visit the maproom."

She laughed. "I got that impression. Okay, I'll come by as soon as I can."

. . .

Most days, Joshua slept in the cell he'd taken over when he got his permission to leave the nursery. But since he was on duty even at night until more nursery workers could make the time, he had to sleep where he could hear the little ones. Ash had stolen his old bed, and he couldn't blame the kid. Still, he had to rummage through the stores for padding to make a new one. Too many of them were stuffed with *shash*, but finally, a squeeze located one that was quiet and soft rather than crunchy sounding. He set up a pallet and covers near the babies. Once he darkened the room and tucked little arms and legs under their blankets, he settled down, listening to the quiet arguments among the cuties.

He hadn't expected to sleep long, but it was a surprise to find Ash shaking his arm.

"What is it?"

Ash bubbled worry in his unblocked thoughts and his frown was clear to see even in the dim light.

"It's Very. She's hurting."

He scanned his sister's thoughts, walking over to her bed. She'd started building a *shash* fence around her bed, complaining about the noise of the other cuties. When Joshua opened the little door she'd made, he saw her turning and whimpering in her sleep.

"Veronica."

She shook her head, eyes still closed.

He shook her shoulder. "Wake up."

He sensed a bit of her swirling nightmare; cuties were holding knives—cuties were being cut open by a giant monster figure in the dark. It dissipated as she gasped and cried out. "It hurts!"

He held her close. Her thin frame shook.

"Josh. It was horrible."

"It's over now. It was just a bad dream."

She shook her head. "No, it was real."

He couldn't dismiss her insistence. Everyone had different sensitivities.

"I'll check with Mother in the morning. I only caught a little of it. Cuties fighting a monster with knives. Was there more?"

She hesitated. "Maybe. I don't know. They were hurting. He was cutting them apart. But there was something else … I don't know what it was."

Veronica pulled herself upright and crossed her arms across her chest tightly. He let his hand rest lightly on her back. He said, "Are you okay?"

She nodded. "I don't think I'll go back to sleep. Can I go sit with the babies?"

"Sure. I'd be happy for the help."

Ash had been waiting silently in the shadows. When he saw her get up, he headed back to his bed.

Escape from the Nursery

Joshua found Samson's thoughts, but the giant was sleeping, his arm forming a pillow for someone. He was dreaming of Omelia, so Joshua assumed that it was her. It was still early morning, so he hopped lightly through other minds at Kakil Home. No one was aware of any attack on cuties, and something like that would spread through the telepathic community like an explosion no matter where in the world it happened.

He shifted his concentration over to clairvoyance and his *sight* told him that although some of the Home elders were up and working, no one was particularly worried. They seemed to be in a meeting. He wouldn't be surprised if Kakil's U'tanse community had its own system of monitoring the Face. Any big decisions made by the Cerik affected their slaves as well.

George was also up and active, his *ineda* firm as ever. He was hunched over, intent, scribbling something on paper, but Joshua's *sight* wasn't any good at seeing details like text. Sometimes he could actually see the shapes, but they didn't make any sense. That must be how the Cerik see text—just random squiggly shapes.

"Joshua."

He blinked, his mind fully back in the nursery. It was Sylvia. She had a sleepy Timothy in her arms. "Couldn't Veronica sleep?" She tilted her head over to where the little girl was dozing, still sitting in her chair.

"Nightmares last night."

Sylvia nodded. "She's always had them. I'd hoped she would grow out of it." She looked back at him. "You should wash up before you go to the maproom."

"Okay." He stood up, feeling stiff.

There was an artificial river carved by the Delense into the granite as a chain of waterfall pools from the upper levels through the heart of the rock down to the dock level. The Builders had been even more water-loving than the U'tanse, so each level had a bath pool large enough for a swim, but the lower ones were largest. But none were as large as those in most Homes. Those burrows usually had sprawling one-level mazes alongside a river, now roofed over to keep in the filtered air.

As he stripped and lapped the pool a couple of times, he wondered what the lost pool of Dallah had been like. Several of the Base elders were survivors of a quake that had collapsed those tunnels and they occasionally chatted about their old Home. The pool must have been at sea level if they had escaped via submarine. Had it been salty? Joshua preferred swimming in fresh water.

The kitchen was near the lower-level pool, and he could smell rice cakes being toasted. He dried off and found a tray ready for maproom workers. He volunteered to take it up, swiping a couple of the sweetcakes for himself.

There were five people working. Cyclops was speaking quietly, listing Cerik clan names. Comfort was writing them down. Joshua wheeled the cart in and set the tray on the vacant end of the map table. Hugo snagged a cake for himself and poured a water.

Joshua wheeled the empty cart out of the way. He might need it later. But for now, he moved close to his mother. She set her ledger down and whispered, "I thought you were on cutie duty."

He nodded and flicked his fingers, inviting her to the door. They moved out into the corridor.

"Sylvia is giving me a break. What's going on?"

"We're still a little while from the first Face hunt, so your father is looking over details the other Homes have collected."

"Reading their logs?"

"Yes."

Joshua sighed. "I wish I could do that. One of the guys I'm monitoring was working on something and I couldn't read a line."

"It's a rare gift." She smiled. "So you're monitoring the Homes regularly now?"

"Just a few people. I don't even know where most of them are."

"Checking out the girls?"

He flushed. "Sometimes."

"Don't worry about it. I slurked on the boys when I was your age."

"I don't like listening in on the girls. They're weird."

His mother said nothing, but her grin was irritating.

"Um?"

"Yes?" she asked.

"Has there been any alert concerning an attack on cuties?"

She frowned, "No. Where did you hear that?"

"Nowhere. Veronica had a nightmare. I just wanted to make sure it wasn't a leak she picked up."

Debbie shook her head. "Nothing like that. I wouldn't worry about it. Nightmares happen, and interpreting dreams can be a lost cause."

Hugo appeared at the door. "Sakah's opening the gates."

She hurried back inside. Joshua followed her, staying out of everyone's way.

Cyclops said, "Sakah won the first feast in the sticks-and-pebbles yesterday."

Hugo said, "Sanassan's right eye is thinking Sakah won the draw because he brought *shillee* for the hunt. And ... they're off."

Cyclops chuckled. "There are more than forty Names in the hunt. The way the *shillee* are running, several of the Cerik have already stumbled into each other. A couple of accidental slashes, but no one is calling oath-breaker, not yet. Not in a *shillee* chase."

Debbie added, "Several of the smaller clan Names are watching from the perching stones. Half of them are regretting waiting out this chase, the others are happy to avoid the more powerful Names out on the blood field."

Joshua followed the commentary and wished he could find the place himself. Everyone was locked down, so he couldn't ride their thoughts. But even filtered through words, the event was exciting. Comfort was copying down everything at a frantic pace.

The chase ended a few minutes later with all the lizards ripped apart and devoured. It was a successful first feast. The Sakah Name watched over the event from the blood Perch and waited for the challenges.

There were few. Only a Name who participated in the feast could bring up a grievance, and Sakah's territory was deep in the middle of the continent. He had a few small neighbor clans in his mountain valley and Hakla's traditional claim for more of the valley's lands was brought up. As usual, a plea for more lands was ignored.

Sylvia tugged on Joshua's arm. They hurried out into the corridor.

"What are you doing here?" he asked.

She looked worried. "I can't find Ash and Veronica. I looked everywhere in the nursery rooms."

"Did you check the maze?"

"Yes! They started a chase-and-hide game and I lost track of them."

"Who's watching the babies?"

"Olive and Gurlie."

He sighed. "Olive has probably already forgotten what she's supposed to be doing. Go back and relieve them. I'll find Ash and Very."

They split at the spiral. Sylvia headed straight down to the nursery. Joshua wanted to make absolutely sure that the escapees couldn't reach the more sensitive areas of the Base—places like the maproom, or the docks. To do that, he'd need to use his clairvoyance to check every single room, level by level. His mother could sometimes use her flash *sight* to become aware of every place at once, and he was tempted to get her help, but the Face wouldn't pause for them.

He put his hand on the stone wall and focused his perception on the stone itself, gradually widening the field of his awareness until it was as large as he could make it. He moved it through the level, winding through every work room, storage cell, and bedroom. When he was confident the cuties were not there, he moved his attention to the next level below.

A few minutes later, his heart pounding, he located them at last, not too far from the nursery over in the gardens, on the same level. As he raced down the spiral and zeroed in on them, it was clear what they were up to. They'd found the strawberry patch, and had hidden themselves between the rows of barrels, snacking on the ripe, red fruit. As he padded closer, walking quietly on the balls of his feet, he could hear them giggling.

They were still hiding their thoughts fairly well, maybe better than he did at their age. Still, it was up to the elders to decide when cuties could be released from the nursery.

He reviewed what they could have seen on their escape route, and there wasn't anything too out of the ordinary. Every Home had nurseries, corridors, and gardens. Ash and Veronica had never been told where they lived. They got the same bedtime stories of the founders Abe and Sharon, Sue bar Carl and the Cerik who ate her, and stories that mentioned other Homes. As far as the cuties knew, this was just a Home like all the others. When he was younger, he'd never even thought to ask the name of the place where he lived. They didn't know they were free U'tanse, because—other than the awareness of Cerik monsters in the world—they didn't know about slavery. All they knew was their rooms and the people who took care of them.

But now, earlier than planned, they'd gotten a glimpse of what was outside of the nursery. If all they remembered was unrestricted strawberries, that might tempt them to try it again.

"Ah, ha! There you are!"

There was a spike of fear from both of them as his shout broke their *ineda*. Ash was quick to get a mental chant going. Veronica was worried about what would happen to them.

He loomed over the barrels. His sister tried to hide her stained fingers.

As Ash tried to stand, Joshua pointed his finger, "You just stay put! I'll tell you when you can get to your feet."

Joshua tried to remember what it was like to be really angry. He wanted that to show on his face, not the relief of finding them in a relatively safe place.

Veronica pointed to Ash, "It was his idea! He saw the lock codes. I didn't want to come."

Ash looked at her as if she'd become some other person.

Joshua crossed his arms. "And he made you eat those strawberries."

Her eyes widened. "Ah..."

"The both of you thought you deserved those strawberries more than everyone else. More than Sam, or Gurlie, or Olive? More than Sylvia or Rachael?"

Ash was looking stubborn. Veronica began leaking tears.

"Debbie is going to have some words to say when she discovers you broke into her garden like wild beasts and destroyed her strawberry harvest. What else did you mess up?"

Joshua thought he was being clever—not that there were any wild beasts in the garden—other than a few fingernail-sized creepers who came in with the *shash* harvest and managed to survive the filtered air. But he liked the idea that there might be beasts lurking around the corner. It might keep them from being too adventurous the next time.

Veronica was leaking enough distress that Sylvia was sure to know that they had been found. Joshua didn't feel competent to just take them back to the nursery and declare the event over. Certainly they'd need to change the lock code on the nursery, but he really wanted one of the elders to take over and make sure the cuties were properly scolded.

But they were all busy. It was up to him.

"Ash, Veronica, you wanted to see the garden? Okay, I'll show you what real garden duty is. Stand up. Now pick up all the stems and broken leaves you've left on the ground. Yes, all of them."

He quickly found two mulch bags and set them to picking up every dropped leaf in the garden. After that, they were treated to the joys of fertilizer blending.

"Is that poo?"

"Yes, Veronica. What did you think we did with it?"

"Ooo. Yuck!"

Sadapple picking, and a life lesson in not eating every fruit you see, was in process when Debbie arrived, all frown and glare. His mother tapped her fingers, staring at the tired and dirty cuties.

"Joshua, go take care of the door lock codes. I'll deal with these two."

He was happy to leave. Maybe he should have just sent them back to the nursery, but if he was left in charge of them, he had to make decisions on his own.

Tension at the Face

Rachael showed up the next morning with a friend, Bernard. Joshua showed the man around the nursery, catching glimpses of his wrapped arm when he wasn't looking. He seemed to be doing well, keeping the pain under control.

"We had an escape yesterday," Joshua explained. "Ash managed to sneak a peek of someone using the lock code on the door, so make sure you hide the control pad when you use it."

He chuckled. "I've gotten the whole speech about nursery security, but they never talked about the lock. I guess I'd have tried to break out at that age myself."

Joshua looked around. "You have to be conscious of listening ears. I guess it was a lot easier when I was the only cutie around. If we were somewhere else, I'd be asking questions about your factory job, but it'll have to wait."

"Yeah." Bernard brushed his whiskers, then shrugged. "I may not have much to talk about." He looked back to the other room where Sylvia and Rachael were feeding the babies. "But it's nice to be here in the Base where there are more women to look at. Personally, I'm counting the days until the next Festival."

Joshua laughed with him, but he had to face the reality that when the next group of Festival girls arrived, the Base would still be short of available women. There was no guarantee that any of them would be interested in a guy as young as he was.

Shortly, Bernard was back with the others, learning how to bounce Little Shelley on his knee with only one free arm to keep her stable. Joshua was released to his maproom duties.

. . .

One of his duties as the youngest guy in the maproom was to collect and organize the log sheets. Comfort and Lincy took alternate shifts copying down everything that was said, but at times, they were working so fast they couldn't do more than grab a new sheet and let the full ones lay scattered on the table.

Joshua took the sheets, lettered the date and sequence on a vacant corner, and stacked them neatly. During the slow times between the feasts, he took the opportunity to catch up on the events he'd missed. He wasn't the only one. No one was on duty full time, although Cyclops sometimes slept in his chair.

There were over two hundred clans, although perhaps half were small and were not able to host feast hunts of their own. Many had been transported to the City of the Face by their more powerful neighbors. Joshua had never heard of most of them. If a clan was too small to have its own boat, then with rare exceptions, the Name owned no U'tanse either. A U'tanse Home was expensive to maintain.

Even so, there were three to five feast hunts per day, depending on how long the Name held court afterward.

Joshua asked, "Does that mean the Face runs for weeks?"

Cyclops shrugged. "It depends. The more powerful clans tend to win the supposedly random sticks-and-pebbles and get their feasts early. When there's only smaller clans left, the bigger clans leave early. Hunts with rare animals or neighboring clans that have grievances they want to air can keep the Face running longer, but the last few times, it fell apart after about a week. It's a loss of prestige for a Name to have to abandon his feast hunt, but it's common."

"It sounds rude."

His father laughed. "That's the Cerik for you. What you call rude is just a different *ruff* for them. Their whole culture is based on challenges and calculated insults. And I suspect the Face has grown too large."

"What do you mean?"

"I don't know the history, but if feels to me like the Cerik population is growing. Sometimes, workers just leave and form their own clan, if they can get away with stealing a few females. Maybe the Face was designed for fewer numbers. Maybe there were smaller regional Faces back before they had boats that could travel across the continent, but that's just speculation."

Joshua frowned. "You know, one of the guys I'm monitoring, George at Kakil, is trying to get his friend Samson to collect Cerik history tales."

"Oh? Why?"

"I don't know, but he seems persistent. Samson is putting him off. He doesn't want to upset his Name."

Cyclops nodded. "Makes sense. Being a U'tanse warrior is risky enough as it is, but if your George does collect any history tales, let me know. There's mention of them in the Book, but we have too little information about Cerik history."

...

Joshua went by his private cell to change clothes. It was frustrating to be back sleeping in the nursery, but he had to keep up with his extra duties.

He frowned when Bernard showed up again for the morning shift, although it was plain the man was just waiting for Rachael to show up.

I ought to tell him that she is planning to have a baby with Paul. But he wouldn't pay any attention to me. I'm still a cutie as far as he's concerned.

He heard some of the adults gripe about how much better it was in the old Home where few people used *ineda* and you were constantly tapped into the rumor stream. Everyone knew when couples formed, and there was none of this uncomfortable uncertainty he felt sure Bernard was suffering.

Still, it wouldn't last long. The man's arm was nearly healed and he would probably head back across the bay to work at the factory again. The workers lived in the facilities there, although they depended on the gardens at the Base to keep their diet more varied than just the fish they caught in the hidden inlet that led to the factory dock.

He picked up the food cart and made another delivery to the maproom. There were more people today. He picked up the log sheets and scanned them. The Lanana feast was going poorly. The Name had purchased several *lo sendt*, half-sized runners, to be prey from the Lakka clan. It turned out that they were undernourished, kept in pens for too long.

Elehadi, the Name of Kakil took loud exception to the poor prey. They were too easy to catch and tasted too much like kept prey, rather than wild runners. The Lanana Name on the blood Perch made his gripe about the Lakka, but ultimately the failure was his.

Cyclops said, "Kakil took over Runa not long ago, and Lanana is their neighbor to the east. Get any information you can on the tension between Kakil and Lanana. Elehadi made the same sort of complaints against Runa at a previous Face, before he attacked them."

Hugo said, "Lanana's Second has ordered one of his *rettik* to quietly go back to their boat and send a shouter message to alert the border scouts."

Debbie reported, "Graddik's Name is watching the spectacle carefully. Both Kakil and Lanana are on his northern border and if Elehadi makes a move too soon, Graddik is prepared to call him an oath-breaker for violating the *katche*. Graddik knows the other clans are reading his mind, too."

"Joshua," his father said, "you've been scanning Kakil and Runa. Check them again now. Look for any signs of warriors collecting either at their borders with Lanana or at the Kakil boat landing areas. See if Elehadi has any current invasion preparations."

Surprised he was given an active role, he nodded. His heart was beating rapidly as he pulled up a chair and directed his *sight* toward Kakil.

Cyclops wasn't done giving orders. "Rock, it's past time to get the semaphore working at Lanana's Home. Get a messenger in place."

"The boat is still undercharged."

"Drain the tub's charge. Tell Lander to put the transport projects on hold."

Joshua wished he understood what was going on, but he had a job to do. He tried to filter out all the other conversations.

Kakil's territory was large. Elehadi had been expanding for as long as Joshua could remember. From what he'd been told, it had always been a large clan, but now it was growing even bigger, absorbing several of the smaller nomadic clans that had shared the grazing lands that ranged from the west coast to the western mountain range. Now, apparently, it was taking on more established clans.

Joshua had no problem locating the Kakil Perch where the Name usually resided, but Cyclops had wanted him to look farther afield. Just like he'd done before when he searched for Runa, he expanded the range of his *sight* and began moving his focus in a widening spiral, trying to understand what his clairvoyance was revealing.

The Perch felt particularly vacant. Usually, the Name's top assistants were there, but now many of them were off at the Face as part of his party. The warrior huts where he'd often found Samson were still populated, however most of the favored warriors were dozing, showing no sign of being on duty.

Nearby was the landing area where Kakil's fleet of a dozen or so boats rested. Surely some were gone to the Face, but there wasn't much activity around the others.

He moved on. While the Perch was the heart of the Name's operations, the clan occupied a much wider range. They were all predators, and over time, pens were built to hold prey. Large irregular circles dotted the plains, surrounded by huts for the workers. There was activity in some, as Cerik chased down runners. Occasionally, he could see U'tanse in their leathers, managing the herds.

It seemed peaceful, as much as any Cerik community was peaceful. Still, he kept looking.

Then he saw something he hadn't noticed before. There were three large circular pits. Hundreds of animals were confined inside. Surrounding the pits were dozens of Cerik—workers or warriors, he couldn't tell.

There was something very strange about these animals. They didn't move like runners, and they were confined too tightly to be grazing animals.

Then he spotted some workers near one of the pits. They rolled a cart piled with five runner carcasses up to the edge and dumped them in. Some of the animals attempted to jump out, but they weren't built for it.

But they were definitely predators or scavengers, because more individuals collected around the meat and began tearing the bodies apart.

Joshua felt something was wrong. This wasn't anything he'd seen before. Blinking, he returned his focus to the maproom.

"Cyclops, I don't see a military build-up in Kakil, but I saw something strange."

His father asked, "What is it?"

"There's these pits, filled with animals. There seem to be more guards around them than I would have expected. They're about half the size of the Cerik and they're definitely meat-eaters."

Several people in the room started laughing. Even Cyclops had a smile. "Don't worry about them. Those are just the Cerik females."

Jawbone

Cyclops gave him the quick explanation.

"Just like Cerik can't read, their females don't even have language. They are so different, they don't look like the same species to us. They herd their females like their prey animals. Their bodies are smaller and shaped differently, and they can't jump. That's why larger clans use those pits. Male cubs with their larger hind legs eventually learn to jump out, and only then are they taught the Cerik culture. That's also why the Cerik have never cared to deal with U'tanse women. Their own females have no intelligence. Few of the Cerik have ever made the mental stretch to consider our women as individuals.

"Only the Name and his top level people are allowed to breed. That's why there are guards around the pit—to keep lower level workers from trying to sneak in.

"But that's a good call noticing the collection of guards. Keep looking, especially around the boats and at border locations."

Having the adults all laugh at him was irritating—but nobody had told him about the Cerik females before! He was happy to be able to report, "There's no activity at the Kakil boat field."

Struggling to ignore the heat in his face, he closed his eyes and sent his mind back to Kakil.

Just to check for himself, because he couldn't really believe it, he read the thoughts of some of the Cerik females. It was strong, basic stuff; visual images of sisters to be kicked aside to gain quicker access to food, the scent of dominant females and the scent of her own cubs. Joshua couldn't connect very closely—it was alien, animalistic. He had to agree. He'd never class them as intelligent.

Pulling away, he was suddenly grateful for Veronica, Olive, Gurlie, and even Little Shelley—the females in his life whose minds were open to him. They felt so normal. Even those girls from remote Homes who seemed so weird to him—that was comfortably familiar. How horrible would it be to share a species with a sex who seemed really alien, just animals?

...

The Face continued with no explosion. Lanana's feast ended and the crowd moved on to Dallah's hunt. By the end of the day, there had been only three feasts.

Joshua reported that he found no buildup of warriors anywhere in Kakil. There seemed to be more in Runa than he expected, but there was no organized activity.

Cyclops suggested it was just a remnant of the Runa invasion. "At the time, we were all puzzled at Kakil's bloodthirsty actions. In addition to the slaughter of the Runa Name, all the cubs were killed, and most of the females. But it was business as usual among the clans. It hasn't even been mentioned at the Face.

"We were fearful for the Runa Home, but Elehadi had a plan all along. He moved about a quarter of his workers and warriors into Runa fields, and demoted all the Runa to manage the runner herds. He then began a program of trading U'tanse who used to be the Runa herd managers to other clans for a fewer number that were more skilled in engineering.

"In the end, he had fewer U'tanse to feed. Festival by Festival, he's also been reducing the female population by trading them off. No one quite knows what his long-term plan is, but he's definitely an expansionary Name, and I'm sure he's not done."

Hugo mumbled, "As long as he leaves Lanana alone."

Joshua asked, "What's special about Lanana?"

Cyclops turned his head, as if he were sniffing the wind. Joshua knew what that meant. He made sure his own *ineda* was strong.

"Lanana is the gateway for the products we produce in our factory. Nobody, not even the U'tanse elders at the Homes, can know that the Base, as a community of free U'tanse, exists. Yet, we need to trade. Certainly no Name would trade with us, his first impulse would be to track us down and destroy us. The Face would unite to rid the planet of free U'tanse.

"So for years we traded only a few things secretly during the Festivals. Then, some years ago, Lanana's Name was killed and his Second took over. This new Name relied more on his U'tanse to organize and schedule his trades. It was a profitable move for him, because the Lanana Home became something of a west coast warehouse for goods originally acquired from east coast clans. Much of the trade for east coast goods goes through Lanana instead, and Lanana's boats are responsible for much of the shipping across the continent.

"With trade negotiations no longer face to face between Names, we managed to become a minor supplier ourselves. Sometimes when a Clan orders metal goods or chemicals, instead of coming from Getterin or Goladen, it comes from us instead."

Joshua frowned, "So people at Lanana know about us?"

"Not really. Back when your mother was a Festival girl, the elders were told that we were a secret Home, organized as a cooperation between two or more unknown clans."

"How could that work?"

Cyclops shrugged, "It was at least believable. From the very first days of the U'tanse, there were promises made that a new Home would be created with no less than twenty-seven people. Smaller clans couldn't afford the expense of setting up a Home, so the story is that some smaller clans combined the expense to gain the benefit of U'tanse ownership. Since it was technically in violation of the oaths, the clans had to keep it a secret."

Hugo said, "It's a fantasy, but Cerik scheme and make secret plans all the time, so people believe it. We're the 'Secret Home' and since we provide nice things like the red air-filter powder that works better than their Home-grown stuff, nobody wants to look too closely."

Cyclops nodded, "Since all our trade is channeled through Lanana, we were sweating the Kakil challenge. If Elehadi invaded, then we'd need to warn our close trading partners and make sure there was nothing that could lead the Name back to us."

Hugo added, "We're still sweating it. He's an erratic Name, powerful and dangerous."

. . .

Samson rubbed the polishing cloth carefully around the jawbone, making sure that he didn't accidentally dislodge the leathery tissue around the sharp bone spikes the beast used as teeth.

"A month or so ago, my friend in the next hut over found this *haeka* stalking the mating pits while he was on guard duty. Instead of killing it, he snared it in his *dul* and turned it loose in my hut while I was sleeping." He chuckled.

Omelia ran her finger cautiously along the sharp edges of the large teeth. "He was your friend?"

"Sure. That's what friends do. Anyway, I was sleeping in just my leathers and a breather. I didn't have my gauntlets—no weapons. Believe me, it was quite a shock to wake up with a crazed beast this large coming at you."

She shivered. "What did you do?"

"Well, my first instinct was to punch it, right in the face. That stunned it for a second—long enough for me to roll to my feet."

"And then?"

He had a thoughtful look. "You know, I have a famous name, right out of the Book. When my father told me that, when I was still living back at Graddik, I went to the library and read the story for myself."

She put her hand on his arm. "I think I've heard it before. I haven't read the Book though."

Samson shook his head. "He was some kind of supernatural strong man. That part I liked. As a man, not so much. He was a jerk who trusted the wrong woman." He grinned at her.

She wrinkled her upper lip to show her teeth. "I don't care for that. But what does this have to do with your *haeka*?"

"Well, this Samson was attacked by a mythical earth beast called a lion. He killed it by ripping the jaws open. I had nothing but my hands and I was not going to run away from the *haeka* and be laughed at by my friends. So, I got under its left forepaw and put my knee as close to its head as possible and gripped its jaw. It was tough, and I've got these scars on my palm, but I did it—ripped the jaw free."

"They were watching?"

He laughed, "Sure. Good sport. I tasted the blood, but it was bitter and already hardening. I spit it out and said, <You know this tastes horrible to me. Next time let me choose my own night-time snack.> Then I tossed most of the carcass out and let them eat it. But I kept the jawbone. It makes a nice decoration."

Omelia didn't understand the Cerik language, but she was riding his thoughts as he told the story, seeing the images, and so she understood his playful insult. She laughed with him.

Joshua, following both their open thoughts even caught a hint of the bitterness of the beast's blood in those vivid memories.

She took Samson's hand and ran her finger across the scar lines. "I could heal these scars for you."

He let her hold his hand. "I could have healed them, too. You have to be pretty good at healing in my job. No, I kept the scars on purpose. It makes for better storytelling."

She smiled. "You want to tell it to your children."

He smiled back, "And my grandchildren, if I get the chance."

But then he frowned. "Someone is calling me."

Joshua tried to trace the telepathic interruption, but he just got Samson's reaction. Someone there in the Kakil Home had formed a strong image of Samson in his head to attract him. The message was clear, once Samson tracked it back to that unknown person.

"You wanted to be notified when Elehadi left the Face. He's heading back."

Samson turned to Omelia. "It looks like my vacation is over. It's time for me to pack up."

She hugged him. "I'll be waiting for you."

Joshua felt torn, he wanted to be with the other monitors if things were happening, but he was scheduled to show up at the nursery. A quick look at the maproom showed people a little more active than usual. In the end, duty called, and he dressed in his softest tunic for child care, but his mind was still following Samson.

The giant was on the move, already in his leathers and walking toward the main entrance. Walking hunched over to fit his height through the corridors, he attracted the attention of people everywhere.

"Hey, Samson." George came up running, and fell into step beside him. "I hear you're going back to the Perch."

"Hey, runt. Yeah, gotta be back on duty as soon as possible. I'm trying to beat the boat."

"I won't slow you down. I was just wondering… have you given any thought to asking about the Cerik tales?"

Samson wondered what had gotten into George. He'd never paid much attention to the Cerik before.

"I'll keep my ears open. The Name won't appreciate being pestered. Have you given any thought to my improved gauntlet?"

George nodded, "Actually, I have. I showed your sketch and handprint to Easton over in fabrication. Of course, he wants to change the design. Some kind of steel ribs that join halfway up your forearm. I told him you'd talk it over with him."

"Sounds okay. Thank you. But it will have to wait until I get another break." He thought to himself, *I guess this is what politics is all about.* "I'll do what I can about the fables."

"That's great." They walked a few more paces before George asked, "Did you make a holder for that jawbone? Are you going to wear it? Why?"

"Sometimes Cerik wear decorations—the bloodier the better. I'm sure I can fight without this getting in the way." He tapped the long tapered bone fastened to the left side of his chest, opposite where he wore his breather while indoors.

He reached for the breather. "Unless you want to run with me all the way to the Perch, I guess I'll say goodbye for now."

George chuckled. "See you next time."

Samson hesitated and punched him lightly on the shoulder. He opened the main doorway just wide enough to slip through and started his run.

Invasion

Samson ran at a brisk pace, but not a flat-out sprint. His top speed could never match the bounding pace of a Cerik in pursuit, but he had more endurance. His father had mentioned that, and he was a normal five-fingered giant. It was their lung capacity, the man had speculated. The U'tanse had a more flexible body than the Cerik, with their subdermal armor plates, and maybe that allowed for more air with each breath.

The normal breather mask had never been good enough, not for a warrior's demands. Samson's was three times the size of a typical U'tanse air filtering mask, with dual filter canisters. On his face, in proportion, it didn't look too outlandish. People paid more attention to the gleaming sharp blades on his gauntlets or the tightly stitched repairs where he'd been slashed by an opponent. Now, he was sure, their eyes would be drawn to the jawbone strapped to the side of his chest.

The distance between the Kakil Home and the Perch was a two-hour walk, but he needed to be there sooner. In emergencies, he could call for a boat to come pick him up, but that would attract undesirable attention. So he ran.

Two-thirds of the way to the Perch, he picked up a recurring thought among others of the Cerik warriors. The word had gone out to gather at the boat landing area. There was some mild anticipation. The Name traditionally gave grand orders from the Perch itself. Elehadi had sometimes given his from the open door of his boat. Samson shifted course.

...

Joshua focussed on the chaos around him. "Sylvia, I've got to deliver a message. Sorry."

She looked at the three crying infants and glared at him. "You just showed up for your shift, and now you leave?" She sighed and dismissed him with a wave of her hand. "You haven't been paying attention as it is. Get back when you can."

He nodded and started the walk back to the maproom. Something was happening at Kakil, and he needed to report it.

. . .

Samson approached the cluster of warriors, noting that even though they never gathered in bunches like U'tanse, preferring to shout at each other rather than whisper, they spread apart even wider as he approached. He had no illusion it was due to respect. His friends had made it clear that, especially after he'd exerted himself, like with the run from the Home, he stank.

He wished to be able to say the same of them, but in their climb to become the premier predators of Ko, Cerik had the benefit of only a faint body odor of their own. In his case, the sweat trapped under his leathers cooked to a ripe aroma. He was just lucky U'tanse chemistry was sufficiently different from the major prey species that he didn't smell tempting.

He arrived just in time. The Name's boat settled at a colorfully marked landing pad. Oddly, the two other boats that had made up Kakil's party to the Face hovered in the distance, their buzzing noise urging everyone to gather a little closer to the boat so they could hear the Name's orders better.

Elehadi appeared in the open door. He paused and scanned the assembled warriors. It seemed to Samson that his gaze paused on him for a moment, but from the other's thoughts, it was a common impression.

<The Face is over. I wish to look over my lands. All of you, follow me.> He turned back into the boat and the door closed behind him.

With a moment's puzzlement, members of the Rear Talon dance hurried rapidly to power up the other boats in the landing area. Warriors followed, with some jostling, to find a boat that wasn't already filled. Samson got on the third boat to lift. It turned to follow the slowly moving leader. There were few enough Cerik telepaths that only a few of the boats had them. Cerik telepaths were rarely warriors.

After a moment's hesitation, Samson decided to share what he knew with the warriors resting in the dark beside him.

<The Name has ordered the boat to head toward the north.>

There was some murmur. The gossip had been that Elehadi would attack Lanana and those lands were to the northwest.

...

Joshua said, "The convoy of boats is shifting to the north. Gossip says Lanana."

Hugo agreed. "That's what I would expect."

Cyclops said, "Dangerous. The Name of Lanana is still at the Face. He's planning to attend feasts for another two days. If Elehadi attacks Lanana while its Name is still at the Face, Kakil would have broken the *katche*. I'm not sure Elehadi can take the risk. All of the other clans could join up against him."

Joshua said, "They are traveling very slowly ... another course correction, westward."

Debbie reported, "Lanana warriors on the ground are sending shouter message to their commander. They see eighteen boats, flying in a row, heading straight toward them. Now flying overhead."

Cyclops shook his head. "Still flying slow, they're deep into Lanana territory now, but they don't appear to be aimed at the Perch."

"Samson has reported to the warriors flying with him that they have passed the Lanana Perch. The warriors are confused. Samson has touched the thoughts of the warriors he knows, and everyone is uneasy. He doesn't want to risk checking Elehadi's thoughts. Samson's own *ineda* is down on purpose and he's deliberately keeping his own speculations to a minimum."

Cyclops said, "Checking the Face. Rumor of Elehadi's actions are the main topic. Half a dozen Names are abandoning their plans and heading back to their boats—they're all western clans."

Hugo asked, "Could this just be for show? Rattling his claws?"

No one answered him.

Joshua said, "Course correction. The boats have sped up to normal cruise speed. They're approaching the western mountains. Whoa. I felt that. All the boats are turning to the right, following the mountain peaks."

Cyclops nodded. "Sharp turn. Boats heading south. Now taking the southwest branch of the range."

Hugo grumbled. "Not good."

Joshua looked at the map spread out on the table. It wasn't marked, but the Base was near where that mountain range ran into the sea. Elehadi could be heading straight for them. But then again, he could change course at any time. Graddik was north of the mountain range, several smaller clans were on the southern flank.

...

Samson flinched. He spoke to his fellow warriors.

<The Name has ordered his boat to land at the Rikna Perch.>

There was an ease of tension. No one understood what the Name's plan was, but there was action coming—action that warriors understood.

...

Rikna! The target passed from telepath to telepath all across the planet. Unfortunately, the Name of Rikna had no telepath in his party. He had been one of the Names spooked to leave the Face early. When the the news arrived, sent to his boat in flight, the Name suddenly realized how badly he'd been tricked.

Cyclops shook his head. "Once Rikna's party was in the air and out of range of the City of the Face, then the Name and his lands were no longer protected by the *katche*. Elehadi's telepath had to have been watching his every move. He gave no explicit order until Rikna was clear of the blood oath."

Hugo asked, "Should we notify our people at Lanana that they're safe?"

Cyclops was quiet for a moment. Then he shook his head. "Their elders probably know by now Elehadi's flyover was just a false signal, or perhaps a political statement that he considers Lanana under his claw. Save the semaphore for emergencies."

Joshua hadn't been told what a semaphore was, but now wasn't the time to ask. Samson should have his full attention.

...

Samson's boat landed and all warriors spilled out in a practiced fan. More boats were landing all around them and the Rikna's landing zone was already overfilled.

Elehadi was on top of his boat, shouting orders. Samson was sent with a party of two Cerik to what looked to be a large stone hut on top of a nearby hill. The Cerik quickly outdistanced him, but he knew he could catch up with them. They were sprinters, but he could keep up his pace for hours.

The one in front, decorated with a string of broken Cerik foreclaws clattering against the hard plates of his chest, gave him a quick glance, expecting a challenge. Samson gave him no sign, calling him "Necklace" in his thoughts. The Cerik was ambitious, Samson knew, and had his eye on the Second position, should the opportunity present itself. And that made him particularly alert to challenges from everyone around him.

I may have to take him out, if he challenges me. He'd never show submission to anyone but the Name, but his position among the warriors was a cliff walk, as dangerous to act too aggressive as it was to be too submissive. It was worse now. In spite of the scent of blood in the air, anyone who neglected Elehadi's orders to pursue a personal challenge wouldn't be permitted to live. In battle, he was compelled to ignore minor threats.

There was a scream of defiance from the top of the hill.

Joshua felt a shiver, and it was his own. Samson's thoughts were calm, tactical, as he lightly touched the thoughts of the ones in the hut. There were more minds up there than the three telepaths they were ordered to kill. The senior telepath sensed Samson, and but then quickly realized the U'tanse wasn't his greatest threat.

Necklace smashed though the thin entrance gate of the hut and landed in the pile of rubble. The defenders had scattered, sensing his approach, but the hut appeared to be just a protected front end to a wide crevasse in a stone butte, almost a corral. A number of workers had retreated to the defensible hilltop position when the attacking boats had appeared in the sky. Many were cubs. *Sad. No cub will live today.*

It was almost a rule of conquest. When a Name lost his life, the victor took out the young ones the loser had sired. A cub attempted to escape downhill, and ran straight into the second Kakil attacker. The half-sized youngster was no match for the warrior. Samson coming up behind saw the slash of a claw and the Rikna cub tumbled down the slope, bloody and already in his death throes. Samson nicknamed his other partner "Cubslash".

Samson leapt over the body, already choosing his opponent. The senior telepath was already in battle with Necklace at the left side of the cluttered space, fighting for his life. There were tables and partitions, probably used for training, that had been hurriedly piled as a crude barricade. Samson took one flying step up onto a table and landed just outside slashing range of the Rikna who looked most fit. There was a howl behind him as Cubslash took out the another cub. He was taking out the easiest prey first.

The defender was fast, leaping to Samson's side and reaching out with a wide swipe of his talons. More opponents clustered in the other direction.

No! He couldn't let himself be surrounded. The Rikna, although just workers, outnumbered them. He grabbed a broken timber from the barricade and swung it completely around, clipping his primary opponent and giving the others pause. Cerik battled with their own claws. Weapons were not instinctive.

And he was U'tanse. One who fought. That was rare.

Samson made the most of their delay, moving inside the claws of the first defender and jabbing the sharp blade that made up the side of his gauntlet precisely where the two chest plates met. Cerik blood bubbled and hissed in the air.

He wasn't down. The wound might be fatal, but it wasn't quickly so. Samson parried a returning swipe. The defender was shaken and his weakness gave Samson the opening to wedge the timber and trip him. Knee on his back, Samson forced the metal blade just under the neck plate that protected a Cerik's head, and severed a nerve. The giant predator shook, but could not make his arms and legs move. He would die on his face.

The U'tanse bellowed, <Who's next!>

To his right, Cubslash had a third or fourth cub dying on the ground. Necklace was taking on two defenders at once. The survivors were backed up against the broken rock that made up the back wall. Two of them rushed Samson.

They weren't warriors. One was early to the fight and took a smack to the side of his head with the timber. The other was smaller, weaker, and Samson got under the Cerik's leap and threw him across the barricade, tripping up one of Necklaces opponents. With both down, the Necklace jumped on top, slashing the eyes of first one, and then the other. Briefly, he glanced at Samson, whether in annoyance or gratitude, he couldn't tell.

But they both had one remaining opponent, and the instant connection was gone.

In the back, the four remaining survivors, knelt face down on the ground in classic Cerik submission.

In Samson's head, he heard Stakka, Elehadi's telepath, send him a message, <**U'tanse, the Name orders that you may not receive *uuka*.**>

Gritting his teeth, angry, Samson drove his gauntlet blade hard into the eyesocket of his remaining opponent. He shouted to his battle companions, gesturing toward the back wall.

<The Name has ordered that I may not receive *uuka*.>

It was bitter to watch as Necklace and Cubslash went to growl the customary threats over the surrendering workers, and received the survivors' promise of everlasting obedience.

Destroy the Perch

Joshua was shaken, both by the intensity of Samson's anger and by the realization that he had not been the only person monitoring the U'tanse warrior. In spite of all the coordination that the battle required, Elehadi, through his telepath, was keeping a close watch on his U'tanse warrior.

And I'm sure there were others, many others. How many U'tanse had vicariously lived through Samson's fight. How many had felt what it was like to kill a Cerik?

Joshua felt Samson's surge of battle-lust. He understood it, but it made his stomach feel queasy. Samson lived for that. Joshua respected his skill. He understood his choice to be a warrior, and all that involved. He didn't have to sympathize with it.

For the first time, he had doubts about his decision to monitor the heroic giant. Samson hadn't felt more than the briefest regrets about the deaths of all those cubs. And those battle deaths weren't intellectual numbers either, tallies of his prowess; he relished his kills.

Those girls who called him a monster—were they right?

...

"I don't understand it, but the Rikna Name does know that Kakil has already taken his lands." Debbie shook her head, "In spite of that, he's still heading to his Perch at top speed."

"He is a Name." Hugo shrugged. "That means he's won every battle he's ever fought in his struggle to get to the top. Maybe he's that confident he can take out Elehadi in single combat and reverse the situation."

She listened to Hugo's suggestion, but she shook her head. "Maybe. He's all rage and bloodlust. His pilot fears for his own life. It may be a hard landing, just to avoid slowing down."

Cyclops said, "It doesn't matter. He's lost everything. His Name is far more important than his life."

Debbie gripped the edge of the table, her fingers white with pressure. "Here it comes!"

Cyclops narrated, "The Rikna boat came in fast, bounced twice, and slammed broadside against two of the Kakil boats. There's damage, but the door opens, and Rikna's Name is out in a bound, heading for his Perch."

Debbie shook her head. "The pilot is trapped. He's got a broken arm. The rest of the Rikna party are getting to their feet. But …" She blinked and broke her telepathic connection to the pilot. "Kakil warriors are streaming in. I don't want to feel to him die."

Joshua listened to the events as members of the Base team touched various minds and Cyclops sometimes used his *sight* to get a broad picture of the action. Joshua still checked on Samson. Once the hilltop fight was done and *uuka* taken, his party, now down to just Necklace and himself, moved on to take other strongholds.

"Samson has heard that the cubs in the pit have all been killed."

Cyclops sighed. "That's it for Rikna. Hugo, what do we know about the Rikna U'tanse? How big is the Home?"

. . .

Samson heard Elehadi's battle cry, loud and distinctive, even from the next ridgeline over. He paused in his run, as did Necklace. Maybe some prey would escape, but he had to watch this.

They climbed the next hill. There, the view slightly dulled by a ground haze and drifting smoke, the Name of Rikna raced to challenge the Name of Kakil. The figures moved fast, blurring together as they merged to strike and then separated to gain traction for their next leap. Delayed by distance there was the slap of hard leather against leather as their blows shook the air.

They merged again, and then there was motion all around. The mental shouts reached him before the sound of their cheers as the Kakil warriors celebrated Elehadi's *ssitt* as he ate the eyes ripped out of Rikna's former Name.

He enjoyed the moment's rest. But the battle was over. No one would fight for a dead Name. All they had to do was line them up and let Necklace take the *uuka*.

Barely had they begun to walk down the slope when Samson felt a familiar call. **<U'tanse, come to the Rikna Perch.>**

He growled at the warrior at his side, <I have been summoned to the Perch. You'll have to take the rest of them without me.>

Necklace snarled, <I never needed any help from you anyway.>

Samson turned and headed back to the landing area. He was satisfied. Necklace had been a good battle partner.

...

Elehadi was testing the captured *hurru*, moving his rear talons uneasily on the main beam. Samson, as he approached, could see battle wounds, quickly scabbed over and ignored, as befitted a Name. Only a telepath could feel his pain, and Samson was wise enough to give his master's discomfort no thought.

As he approached, he bent low, tapping his heels together.

He could feel the Name's gaze, and he knew the smell of Cerik blood on his leathers was somewhere in Elehadi's thoughts. Samson stayed motionless.

After a moment, the commanding voice said, <U'tanse, I have a task for you.>

Samson rose, his head still down, his shoulders bent forward. He shouted, <For your Name.>

<I am offended by this inferior Perch. Destroy it for me.> He moved off to the stones beside it with an easy bound.

Samson raised his head, examining the structure built of large *dlathe* tree trunks. It was braced against the stones of the hilltop so that the single main perching log was higher than any ground around it. The whole thing outweighed him several times over. There was no way he could lift it, and the way the logs were notched together gave it a solidity that certainly had withstood storms and quakes for years, perhaps for generations.

He tested his strength against the main log, and it had no give to it.

There was a whisper in his head. Some unknown U'tanse engineer watching behind his eyes said, **"Unlock the upper left support."**

Samson could see what the man said. He moved into the structure of the Perch, stepping between the rock outcroppings until he found a place to stand. He knelt down low, locked both arms around one of the support beams and lifted, his legs straining with the effort. At first there was nothing to see, but he could feel it. There was a gap, barely enough to let air in between the interlocked timbers. He set it back down, knowing it was slightly misaligned. He took a deeper breath, shifted his legs and lifted again. This time, the logs were visibly disconnected. But it wasn't enough. A third lift, and when he released, the upper log shifted a few inches, no longer in the notch cut for it. There was a creak of timbers elsewhere in the structure.

He didn't need help to see where the next weak point was. It was complaining. Forcing his gauntlet blade into a point where the timber was compressing and bending, a second log snapped free. The pressure whipped it hard against another, shattering it. Samson reached in and twisted, freeing a medium-sized log nearly as long as he was tall.

He had a lever now. With his pry bar, he worked across the upper tier, breaking the timbers free of their anchor points that had connected them to solid granite. The noise, as the Perch's own weight was distorting the platform into a tangle of twisting logs, suddenly peaked, and the conglomeration began rolling down the slope. Pieces began flying off as timber struck stone. Warriors and workers who had crept closer to see what he was doing now had to jump free with all their speed to keep from becoming mangled with the rubble. Stones were knocked free, adding to the avalanche.

Behind him, Elehadi's *pree* announced his satisfaction.

Samson's heart thundered in his chest and his arms and legs quivered from the exertion. His breath whooshed through the breather's filters. He was tempted to take it off, just for a moment. But that was his body's instinct, not his brain's. Now was not the time to pour poison into his lungs.

There was a low voice. Stakka growled low near the Name. Both turned their eyes on the U'tanse.

<Soon, all the Rikna will have given *uuka*. At that time, the U'tanse must give their pledge.> Elehadi waved his claw. <You should go prepare them. You know how to speak their language.>

Then he turned his back to talk to Stakka. Samson had been dismissed.

Joshua felt the puzzlement bubble up in the Samson's mind. But the order had been given, so he began the trek down the slope. He would need to find a U'tanse to lead him to the Home.

I'm not an elder, nor a messenger. I'm just a warrior. Will they listen to me?

Prepare for *Uuka*

Joshua sat in the chair, his legs pulled up to his chest, his arms wrapped around them, rocking slightly as he listened to all the voices around him. Cyclops was relaying the activities of the Name of Graddik, and at the same time, conferring with Hugo on gathering all they knew about the U'tanse of Rikna.

Rikna was a small-to-medium-sized clan, with a U'tanse Home that handled most of their *chitchit* export business. It had little economic importance.

Graddik was a large clan, and had been watching the expansion of Kakil on its northern border with concern. And now, just over the mountains, its southern neighbor had fallen. Effectively, Kakil had placed Graddik in a *dul*—just a like a prey in the hunter's sack. Had this action been a reaction to the Graddik Name's threat to denounce Elehadi to the Face? Or had this been Kakil's expansion plan all along?

Hurriedly, Graddik was making trades with other clans near and far. There was no defense against an attack ferried by boats, just as Kakil used against Rikna. Whereas Rikna's Name and his chief warriors had been uselessly trapped in the air on their flight back from the Face, Graddik had more than a dozen boats of its own, and an attack force he could send to Kakil if Elehadi attempted an invasion like that again.

The Name of Graddik left his mind open and readable as he planned a potential retaliation invasion of Kakil. He wanted Elehadi to know that all of Kakil's females and cubs would be quickly slaughtered if he crossed the line into Graddik territory.

And so, boats were being purchased with Graddik's runners and Graddik's store of old Delense devices. His warriors might have to do their own hunting in the mountains, rather than feed off the penned runner herds, but perhaps they had been getting too soft anyway.

Joshua kept a loose connection with Samson, knowing he'd taken time to wash the blood off his leathers on the way to the Rikna Home. After a while, he announced, "Samson has arrived at the Home. They were expecting him and the elders were waiting at the door."

. . .

The elder reached out and took him by the arm, probably not the wisest thing to do to a warrior with battle still in his veins. Samson, however, had a lifetime of resisting what his instincts told him to do. He followed inside and noted the door being closed and sealed behind him.

There were six of the elders waiting to talk to him.

"Please, have a seat. Our corridors are too low for you. As soon as we knew you were coming, we made arrangements." What was obviously a storage room near the entrance had been set with several chairs and a table with drinks. One of the chairs was very large, probably meant for two.

Samson touched the speaker's mind. He was Dario, definitely one of the elders, but young enough to only have a touch of gray. He checked the others, and reluctantly, they dropped their *ineda*. Fear and uncertainty filled the room. Eyes flickered to the *haeka* jawbone strapped to his chest.

Dario asked, "What's going on? There was nothing, and then death and destruction started happening all around."

Samson nodded. "Elehadi, the Name of Kakil, has killed the Name of Rikna and taken his lands and property, and that includes all of his U'tanse."

Elizabeth, with graying hair down to her shoulders, asked, "But why? What caused this?"

Samson spread his hands, "No one knows the plans of Elehadi. That he chose Rikna to capture was a surprise to us all. However, this is the way of the Cerik." He reached for the large mug on the table and tasted. It was a fruit drink, and he finished it quickly.

He cleared his throat. "I have been sent here as a translator, I suppose. Elehadi's telepath will be listening to my thoughts as you speak. You need to make ready for the Name's approach, when he feels ready to come here."

Their fear spiked, both when he said their conversation was being monitored, and when they realized the Name would visit.

Samson explained, "Right now, all of the captured Rikna are giving *uuka*, their promise of loyalty to their new Name. When that is complete, he will come for your oath as well."

Eyes shifted to an older man, Roger, when he asked, "How is this to be done? Shall I speak for the Home?"

Samson shook his head. "I will be corrected if I am wrong, but Elehadi will want the oath from all of you—not just the elders, but everyone."

"We don't have breathers for everyone," Kathy said. "Is he coming inside?"

Samson waited a moment for Stakka to send him a clarification, but when nothing happened, he said, "The Name is only concerned with the traditional Cerik workforce. I feel that what he would expect would be every male of age. I suggest you include every woman in a leadership position as well. It will be a mass oath, not one by one."

Samson paused, then added, "It may be that he will require a blood oath. Whether via stigmata or blades, everyone should be prepared."

Kathy grumbled, "So we'll need to heal wounds as well as airburn."

Samson nodded, "Yes. I'm sure you know what he has already done to insure the loyalty of his Cerik captives."

Several of them shuddered. The death cries of all the cubs had ripped through every telepath.

Kathy said, "But that...."

Roger interrupted, "Kathy! I'll explain the realities of Cerik conquest later. Now is not the time!"

She paled, lowered her head and nodded. Loud complaints against their masters while being monitored was not wise.

Dario asked, "What will the Name want from us? Rikna isn't a large Home. We've mainly provided technical support for the clan, herding for their runners, and small animals for trade."

Samson shook his head. "As I said, I have no idea what his plans are. I do know that you should realize that the Rikna clan is extinct. These lands are just the Rikna areas of the Kakil now. Whatever Elehadi asks, for whatever reason, do it quickly."

Roger said, "Fordan, Elizabeth, I think we should pay attention to what the man just said. Go now and get everyone ready. Kathy, perhaps you should go help Elizabeth."

With just three of the elders left, Roger asked, "Samson, we know just a little of what happened to the Runa Home when that clan was taken over. Honestly, we weren't paying much attention. Were you dealing with them?"

"No, not directly." Samson offered a smile. "I am young, and I have not been in service as a warrior for very long. This translation job is new for me and unexpected. But the Name is to be obeyed, not questioned."

The elder nodded. "I understand. It had been our hope, with the previous Name of Rikna, to dam the creek that flows from between the two nearest peaks and create a swampy area to raise *dakka*, and add them to the animals we trade. Do you think Elehadi would be open to such a plan?"

Samson just shook his head. "You're asking a warrior things that are beyond him. I'm not your expert. Ask those elders of the other clans. Ask Kakil Home, ask Runa Home. But I would focus my entire energies on getting through this change first, before you worry about other projects.

"I feel you want me to tell you that everything will be okay. I don't know that it will be. When the Name wants more from you, he will tell you."

They were clearly disappointed, but he had no more than guesses about when the oath ceremony would happen, and even less information about their future. They brought him more food and drink, for which he was grateful. Now it was just a matter of waiting.

...

Cyclops said, "The east coast Homes are giving up for the night. Elders are telling their assistants to wake them when Elehadi comes to take the oath."

Joshua woke, embarrassed that he'd dozed off in his maproom chair. Quickly he checked on Samson, but the warrior was taking advantage of the rest to catch up with his sleep as well.

He caught himself before he asked his father what was going on. He could check for himself, couldn't he?

Rikna was a land of fires. He could feel them, as well as see them. The Cerik weren't a technological people, in spite of their flying boats and spaceships. Ko had no great turn of the seasons as was described in the Book, and so Cerik were quite comfortable sleeping in the open, seeking protection only for the storms. Those fires weren't for nighttime warmth.

Everyone was up and awake. In spite of the words of *uuka*, the forces of Elehadi weren't willing to trust their captives, not with the battle only a few hours in the past. There was no moon in the night sky, so torches, bonfires, and a few smoldering buildings lit the area.

Joshua found the Name, perched on top of his boat, holding court. One by one, the most important of the Rikna dances came before him, making their own oaths, often ceremonially bleeding their loyalty. Elehadi roared and shouted, and the feelings of being a supreme ruler spread out from him. Everyone was getting the full treatment.

Probably, the captive U'tanse were far from his thoughts.

Joshua stood up from his uncomfortable seat. "I will maintain my monitoring." Cyclops nodded. The man was probably more worn out by the ordeal than he was.

When Joshua saw the empty food cart, he felt an unbearable weariness. He had intended to head to his bed, but this was one task he couldn't put off. He wheeled it down to the kitchen and put together easy-to-eat snacks and refilled the drink container. He wheeled it back up to the maproom where the night shift workers were noisily grateful.

Only then did he collapse on his bed. Sleep was difficult at first, with the memories of the cries of cubs being cut down by uncaring warriors drifting through his dreams.

Bleed the Oath

"Joshua. Wake up."

He blinked and saw the faint image of Sylvia, wrapped in her gown.

"What is it?"

"They need you at the maproom."

He checked the time the way he usually did, using his *sight* to see the sky above the Base. It was night, but the moon had risen above the horizon, splotched with a streak of red. Three months ago, at closest approach, the moon had cracked and lava oozed, getting more visible every month. He was told that happened every few years.

But if it was still night, or early morning, then something was happening in Rikna. As he stumbled out and headed up the spiral, he checked on Samson. The warrior was being woken by the elders.

Only Debbie and Hugo were on night shift.

As he entered, his mother said, "Monitor Samson. Talk clearly. I'll be transcribing and I don't write as fast as Comfort."

He nodded, gulping down a cup of water. "He's already outside the Home. The U'tanse are being lined up to follow him out. The ones with breathers are already finding places in the meadow in front of the Home. The rest are waiting inside, staying in filtered air until the Name is in sight."

He heard the scribble as she wrote down what he said, but he was seeing the events to the northeast. It was becoming easier to block out events in the maproom and concentrate exclusively on the scene in Rikna.

"The elders gave the word that everyone who wasn't taking care of the babies and cuties should participate. There's some as young as me lined up. There's a lot of fear bubbling off of them. The knives distributed among them increases their uneasiness."

. . .

Samson breathed the cool air, watching the flickering torch light as Elehadi's party came closer. Behind him, he could hear more of the U'tanse start to funnel through the entrance out into the night. There were whispers and mumbles and whimpers from stubbed toes. Not everyone had taken the time to get dressed for the outdoors.

He glanced back and winced as he saw them lining up in rows of twenty. It was a natural number for U'tanse, but not for the Cerik, who thought in multiples of three.

As the Name approached, Samson walked forward and joined the party of the conquerors. Elehadi looked at him as he lined up on the Name's right side.

<Which of these speaks for the whole?>

Samson was sure that Roger knew Cerik, but it would be a mistake if the elder spoke without being ordered to. He shouted out to the man, "Roger, take three steps forward!"

Elehadi sniffed the air. As loud as it was, it was an insult, but whether directed at Roger or the whole crowd of a hundred and sixty-something, Samson couldn't tell. As far as he knew, the Name never dealt with the U'tanse directly. His position as a favored warrior was the lone exception.

Roger was elderly and stooped over, his breather dangling from his belt. Even to human-kind, he wasn't imposing. Then, perhaps reading his thoughts, Roger straightened himself up.

Elehadi said, speaking to Samson, <U'tanse, you take the *uuka* from them.>

Samson showed no uncertainty in his bearing, but his mind raced. He knew the words, in Cerik, but only a fraction of the Rikna U'tanse would be able to say them, even with coaching. He'd have to do it in U'tanse.

He strode to the crowd, facing Roger. He yelled, loud enough so everyone could hear.

"The Name of Rikna has fallen, and your lives now belong to your new Name, Elehadi of Kakil." He paused, making up a new script for this audience. "Your expression of loyalty is more important than you know. No dissent, no expression of fondness for the dead one can be tolerated. If the Name is dissatisfied, he'll order you killed right here, and I'll step in to do it myself as a kindness to you!

"In a moment, I'll ask you to say the following, 'I pledge my life to Elehadi of Kakil and his *rettik*. I will obey you with my life and my blood.' And when you say this, scream it out with all the breath you can muster. I mean it. Your lives are in the balance."

He looked them over, and saw the necessary fear in their eyes. "Now start, when I raise my hand." He saw fidgeting and people breathing in. He raised his hand.

It started rough, but Roger yelled so loud Samson was afraid he'd hurt himself. The others joined in. Samson tipped his fingers higher, and they put even more noise into the pledge. As ragged voices dwindled off on the word "blood", Samson stood motionless, waiting for Elehadi's reaction behind him.

With a gruff voice nearly as loud as all of them together, the Name shouted, <Bleed!>

Samson repeated the order, "Bleed, now!"

There was a shiver through the crowd as people pulled out knives and sliced along their forearms. There were far too few knives, so they were passed to the next one over and the action was repeated. Whimpers of pain and weeping dotted the assembly. Those on the front row, and several people in other rows, merely held up their forearm and blood started appearing on the skin with no blade needed. Since the first generation, the stigmata skill had been learned among those who needed to deal with their Cerik overlords directly. After a moment, everyone held up a bleeding arm.

Elehadi snorted, satisfied, but hardly impressed. He spoke to Samson, <Get these back to work. Take a mid-day boat back to the Perch.>

The Cerik party turned back toward the former Rikna Perch, the light beyond the hills still glowing from the flames.

Samson nodded to Roger, "It's done. You can get back inside."

Roger coughed, and it was clear the outside air had affected him. "Nobody died tonight. Thank you."

"Rikna Cerik died. Quite a few of them. You were very lucky. Elehadi was in a good mood."

Roger just nodded, slipped his breather back on, and joined the stream of people trying to go back into the Home. They'd had to open the entrance wide, even both of the airlock doors, just to allow so many people to pass through quickly. Even the ones who had stayed inside would be dealing with contaminated air for a while.

Kathy came up to Samson, as the crowd thinned out. She asked, "Is it true, what you said? Would you have killed U'tanse?"

Samson didn't look down to meet her eye. "I have little use for *ineda*. Should I lie, it would catch up with me. Did you sense that I lied?"

She shook her head.

He continued evenly, "I meant exactly what I said. Cerik enjoy the kill and once they started, more would die than necessary."

She started to say more, but kept her tongue, and her thoughts were hidden under *ineda*. She went inside.

After all had cleared, Samson noticed Dario waiting at the door for him. There was more to be said, and the Name had meant for him to stay a little longer. He sighed and walked toward the door, smelling the whiff of U'tanse blood that stained the ground.

...

Joshua shifted his attention back to the maproom. From the look on his mother's face, he knew something was wrong.

"What did I miss?"

She looked unsettled. "Hugo was monitoring one of Elehadi's rettiks. After they walked away, the Name said that there were more U'tanse than he'd thought. Too many U'tanse."

Joshua knew that couldn't be a good sign. "It was the elders. They thought they should get as many people out there for the oath as possible. Samson didn't ask for that many. They should have just had the males.

Maybe the Name thought they were all males, with the same number of females inside the Home."

"Maybe. It's hard to guess what he was thinking. Elehadi has never based his power on the U'tanse like some clans have. Although Kakil Home population of U'tanse has been relatively stable, he's been actively shrinking the Runa population."

Joshua was puzzled, "Why? As I understand it, slaves are supposed to be resources. The more slaves, the richer you can become."

She smiled at him. It was practically a quote from the lessons she'd given him when he left the nursery and was told the truth about the U'tanse and their place on the world Ko.

"It's complex. For one thing, the Cerik don't own slaves. The Names own slaves. It's extremely rare for a U'tanse to be owned by anyone who isn't the Name of a Clan."

Cyclops walked into the room. "I wish I could have been in on this conversation from the start."

Joshua said, "Elehadi thinks he has too many U'tanse."

He asked, "The oath went okay?"

"Yes. But Rikna padded the group with every available person and the Name thinks he has too many."

He sighed. "The Runa problem, only more so." He sat down at the map table and picked up the notes Debbie had been writing. Joshua let a smile creep up onto his face. These were his parents, but he knew it was strange—a blindfolded man with no eyes reading the logs of the night shift.

After a few minutes, Cyclops said, "I've heard people say Elehadi is old-fashioned, perhaps longing for a different time. Before the U'tanse, sometimes one clan would capture another and use them as slaves. It certainly looks like he's doing the same thing."

Joshua asked, "But if he had Cerik doing all the herding and other slave tasks, then what would become of the U'tanse?"

Understand the Cerik

Veronica whimpered, tossing and turning in her bed. Joshua hesitated a moment and then shook her arm.

"Wakey. It's morning."

Her eyes came wide open, looking at him and then grabbing at his arm. "Josh! You're okay!"

He chuckled, peeling her hand loose. "Yes, I'm fine. How are you?"

She was clearly confused. "But... I saw you. Flying through the air! You looked terrified."

He shook his head slowly. "Nope. No flying. The only thing I'm scared of is you, right now. Go on, get up. I'm sure the women could use some help with the babies."

She shifted her focus. "Um. Okay. Is that man gone?"

"Bernard? Yes, his arm has healed. He's gone back to work."

"Oh? Where?"

Joshua tried to look stern. "You know the rules. When your *ineda* is solid, then you'll learn more stuff. When I caught you in the strawberries, yours fell apart."

She crossed her arms. "I don't know how you can expect to hold onto your *ineda* when someone snaps at you like that. It shook me up."

He shook his head. "That's the most important time. That's why there's so many different techniques. If you get startled again, just think about the taste of strawberries—really hard. Keep it going until you get your block back up."

His sister's eyes went all dreamy. "Those were really good."

He could feel the hint of their flavor seeping out through her thoughts.

"Practice it. You're going to want a strong *ineda* before too long, and for more reasons than just hiding from me."

She wrinkled her nose and got up. "I'd rather play with Little Shelly than listen to more of your lessons."

He was happy to see Veronica go, her nightmare forgotten. But he needed to catch a little more sleep. It had been a long night.

...

Samson settled into the shallows on the far edge of the Kakil bath, near the outflow so the stink of his skin and the blood he was attempting to wash off wouldn't contaminate the waters.

The others kept their distance from him, and that was fine. As much as the Rikna U'tanse suffered from their little cuts, he had his own to deal with. No one knew of his injuries, because he'd learned to block them out of his mind, but his leathers wouldn't stop a Cerik's claw—only his own agility could save him. Most times, it was enough. But twice during the battles, a razor-sharp claw-tip had drawn blood. The one on his arm was a little deeper than the line on his ribs. His trained healing abilities had allowed him to close the wounds and stop the bleeding, but real healing took time.

Omelia swam quietly up to where he rested. "Let me work on that."

He smiled in the darkness. "I gave off enough 'Leave me alone' thoughts that I was sure everyone got the message."

She giggled. "I was sure you didn't mean me. Now lie back and relax. Let me do the healing."

He settled back, tilting his head a little so the water wouldn't cover his left ear. Her hands traced the line on his arm. A thought came, but he dismissed it quickly.

Her laugh was calm and cheerful. "Don't worry. I'll leave a scar line."

He relaxed a little more.

She worked silently, but then after a moment, she asked, "What did Bruce want to talk about?"

He grumbled in the dark. The gossip moved fast, even relaying the momentary conversation he'd had with the primary leader of the Kakil

U'tanse while passing in the corridor. "That was stupid, even for an elder. I told him I was being monitored and talking to him under *ineda* would look suspicious to Stakka. He just smiled and said that of course, there would be nothing disloyal to the Name discussed—as if his assurances would be believed by any Cerik."

"But you did it."

"Well, yes. He's an elder. I live here at this Home. How could I do anything else?"

"Is there anything you can share with me?"

He sighed. "There was nothing that needed *ineda* anyway. He told me that a lot of people were upset by all the killing and even more were shocked when I told the Rikna that I would kill U'tanse if the Name ordered it. If they are so easily offended, then they shouldn't watch. What did they think was going to happen? Cerik battle to the death, and when clan attacks clan, the cubs are the first to go."

"Why is that?" She sounded a little timid, as if afraid of offending him.

"The cubs?"

"Yes."

He was quiet for a moment, putting together thoughts he'd never spoken aloud. "Cerik are different. They think different. Their whole biology is different. Only a few males ever reproduce—only the Names and in large clans, the lesser names as well. The drive in every Cerik to achieve status and have a Name is more than just pride. It's the key to having descendants. In some ways, the Cerik clan is like a hive, with females that do little more than breed and only the best, most successful males providing the genes for the line. They don't think about it like that, but it shows up in everything they do.

"There's little value in an individual Cerik life, not like it is with a U'tanse. With us, every death isn't just the end of one soul, it's the extinction of every descendant we might have had. With an ordinary Cerik, death is just the end of a life that would have had no ... reach beyond itself anyway."

She mumbled, "Except the Names, I guess."

"Yes! And that's how they think. The Name is revered, worshipped even. He's the embodiment of the clan, of the future of the whole clan. For a Second to consider making his move, to attack his Name, he has to be very sure of himself and very sure he's going to win."

She stroked the line on his chest. "That explains the arrogance. In his head, a Name is more important than everyone else. He is the clan."

Samson put his hand on her waist as she worked. "Which brings us back to the cubs. Wiping out a new generation is a direct attack on the Name. Yes, it leaves him with deep rage, but it also takes out his heart. A Name would never express any affection for his cubs, but working up close with Elehadi, I could see it in the way he made arrangements for the breeding pit and the cubs. They are his future, and he knows it on a deep, instinctual level.

"And when Elehadi conquers another clan, he breaks the Perch and wipes out the genetic line of the former Name. That says all the survivors are now his workers and part of the Kakil clan."

She said, "But surely, there are mature survivors that were descendants of the Name that was killed. The former bloodline isn't totally gone."

"Have you seen what Elehadi does with the survivors? Warriors become workers. Workers are sent out into the fields to tend the herds—slave duty, in effect. Those survivors have their lives, but it will be a long, hard struggle to lift themselves up to the status of the Kakil."

He pulled Omelia closer and kissed her.

…

Joshua tingled with the second-hand, rising tide of lust. Any other day, he'd stay connected, slurking, but the ideas he'd just heard were churning in his head. He disconnected and walked back to the nursery.

High-pitched squeals of laughter brought a smile to his face as entered the rooms that had formed his entire world for the first years of his life. Little runners dashed by, paying as little attention to him as furniture. Little runners that could grow up to become anything, even the Fathers and Mothers of new worlds, perhaps.

Cerik didn't understand this. They couldn't, or rather they had no interest in understanding anything so deeply U'tanse.

In every Home, attached to every major clan, there were rooms like this filled with laughing and crying little bundles of the future.

Something Samson said gave him the shivers. If Elehadi was turning captive Cerik into slaves, that meant the former herders of those clans, the U'tanse workers, were now all out of a job.

How long would the Name afford to keep them fed and protected in their Homes if they weren't doing any work?

"Joshua!" Veronica saw him and came running. He was puzzled until she ran up and wrapped him in a hug, her little head buried against his stomach.

Awkwardly, he put his arms around her shaking shoulders. There was no doubt about it. Something was very wrong with his little sister. She never did this.

Distress in the Air

All the children were a little on edge. Joshua felt it himself. There was uncertainty in the air. Joshua could feel a wave of queasy unease from the Rikna Home as all those telepathic U'tanse fed on each others' fears.

The babies and cuties, telepathic themselves, probably had no idea where this feeling was coming from, but it was strong enough to creep into their heads.

Had this happened before, when Runa was conquered? He didn't remember, but maybe he had been distracted by other things. Certainly he wasn't so directly involved back then.

He forced a smile on his face. If he didn't say anything about it, probably the kids would never remember it either.

"Hey, Ash! Show me what you've got." The boy looked up from his sketches. Hesitantly, he showed the charcoal drawings.

It took a second for Joshua to recognize the blobs for what they were. "Strawberries. And the pots."

Ash beamed. He pointed with his blackened fingertips. "I tried to show the seeds, can you tell? I wish I had colors."

Joshua chuckled. "You left the seeds blank."

"Right, I filled in everywhere except the spots."

"Be sure to save these. Your mother will want to see them."

Ash frowned. "Maybe the next ones. These aren't good enough. Say, when you take out the trash, does it go back into the garden?"

He nodded. "Right. Back into the mulch."

Ash grinned, "So my strawberries go back to the real ones."

"I'll make sure they do."

. . .

The routine chores, from changing the babies, to breaking up squabbles, to reading stories about Quaky the Underground Troll and Jojo the Fish to the little ones, was a pleasant break from his own worries about the Cerik invasion. But when Comfort arrived to take over his duties, even she was looking a little worried, her hand resting on her belly. Was the little one growing inside her also feeling it?

He was glad to let her take over the nursery, and he rushed to get up to the maproom.

Hugo looked up when he arrived with a snack cart. One shake of the man's head and a touch of his finger to his lips stopped Joshua at the door. Inside, Cyclops was motionless in the pose he'd come to know as his father's meditation. He was trying to do something that required his full concentration.

Joshua waited, and a couple of minutes later, he saw his father shift positions, and he knew it was safe to bring the cart into the room.

Cyclops gestured to the others: Hugo, Debbie, and Lincy. "No luck. I don't even know why I try. When Elehadi and Stakka go into that private grove, I can't get a thing. They sit in that meadow where no one can hear or see them, and when they come out, no one is prepared for what they have planned."

Hugo said, "We could use a *listener*."

Cyclops chuckled, "While I agree, there's no use hoping for a talent like that to drop into our ranks. I haven't heard a whisper of one. It was on the list of psychic talents in the Book, so I have to believe clairaudience is possible, but either that set of genes is missing in our ancestors, or we haven't discovered the way to trigger it."

Debbie said, "Nobody thinks reading text via *sight* is possible either."

He nodded. "Let's keep it that way. I'd hate for the Homes to start writing all their logs in code, just to keep me out."

Joshua thought about that project George was working on so intensely. He'd been preoccupied with Samson and the Rikna invasion. He'd need to check on the tenner again when he had time.

Lincy was faithfully scribbling down her log entries. Debbie reached for a mug from the cart. She asked, "Joshua, what have you heard from Samson?"

"He's still waiting for word from the Name. He's staying out of sight as much as possible. He's not very popular right now."

She nodded. "Anything else?"

Joshua hesitated before saying, "Everyone in our nursery is on edge. They're feeling the fear."

His mother frowned. "Has anyone said anything about it?"

He shook his head. "No, and I'm trying to ignore it, too. They might not even realize the dread is coming from somewhere else."

"Probably best."

Cyclops stood up. "I need to take a break. Have someone come get me if something happens."

After he had left, Debbie said to the others, "I'll be the one to wake him. He's been running without sleep for too long."

Joshua stayed on duty for the next few hours. Telepathic communication between the Homes mentioned the contagious fear in their ranks as well. He took note of some of the ways others were dealing with their frightened children. There were games, extra chores, and swimming races. Not all of those things would work at the Base, but it gave him some ideas to try.

When Hugo left the maproom, Joshua was surprised to see Bernard show up as a replacement.

"Rachael told me to come back from the factory so she could check my healing progress, so I did." The man winked at him.

When Joshua only nodded, Bernard frowned and whispered, "Don't you like me, kid?"

Debbie was ignoring their low voices at the end of the table. He gave a polite smile. "Oh, you're okay."

He didn't want to get into his own feelings right now. He didn't know why he disliked the man. Veronica had some reservations too, but maybe he was reading too much into his sister's reactions. She hadn't actually said anything bad about him.

Bernard bumped his elbow. "Hey, maybe you can come over to the factory some time. I'll show you around."

Debbie asked, "Bernard, you told me you came from Graddik."

"Yes. Robert rescued me when I was caught in the forest fire along the coast."

Joshua raised his eyebrows. "I didn't know about that. You've been in two fires?"

He looked embarrassed, "Bad luck, I guess. When I jumped off the cliff into the surf to avoid the flames, the Cerik pilot who had ferried us over to fight the flames just wrote me off as dead. I would have been, too. The current off the point pulled me south far too fast to swim. I didn't know what to think when something big came up under me. I grabbed at a metal ring on the hull and clung there for my life until Robert opened the hatch and tapped his forehead."

Joshua wondered what they would do if they every tried to rescue someone who didn't know how to block their thoughts. Toss them back in?

Debbie looked toward the ceiling, "I came from Graddik originally. Who were your parents?"

The man looked embarrassed, "Um. I ..."

She waved her hand. "No, that's okay. It was an improper question. We all have family to protect. I just had old memories come back to visit."

Joshua looked at Bernard with a new eye. If his mother was asking about his parents, then she thought of him as a younger man. How old was he? Joshua had been thinking of him as old, an adult. He had a beard. He was a factory worker, and a lot of those guys were as old as his parents.

Debbie assigned Bernard to find a *rettik* serving Graddik's Name and listen in on his thoughts. Any hint as to Graddik's defense plans would be useful. Even if Kakil wasn't ready to take on Graddik immediately, there was a real chance that Graddik might move quickly to make a punishing reply to this latest insult. The Base needed a clear view of what could happen, and what preparations to make. If a war broke out within hiking distance of where they were hidden, major changes might have to be enforced on a moment's notice.

...

Samson heard Stakka calling him.

<U'tanse. The Name calls you to his Perch.>

He rolled out of bed and pulled his leathers from where they were hung. Omelia asked, "What's happening?"

"I'm being called. It has to be urgent. When Stakka calls me telepathically, it usually is."

She reached for his customized breather and checked the level of the chemicals in both of the side-mounted filters. He would have preferred doing that himself, but he surprised himself and said nothing. He guessed he trusted her.

She smiled and handed him the breather. "I'm not Delilah." She must have tracked down the story and read it herself.

He smiled back. "I know." He secured his straps and fastened the jawbone in place. "I don't know when I'll be back."

"I will know."

They touched fingers for a moment, and then he was gone, moving through the corridors rapidly, hunched over to keep from hitting his head on the ceiling.

Joshua told his mother what was happening. She fumed a moment, then stalked out of the room to wake Cyclops.

Samson felt a moment of relief when he left the entrance to the Kakil Home. Standing straight, breathing through the filters, seeing the sunlight—these things had become normal to him as he worked for the Name. Hiding from his own blood, shaking off their disapproval—it was a bitter thing. He could feel their frowns as he passed them by in the corridors. Didn't they know he was doing all of the U'tanse a service by showing the Cerik just how valuable they could be?

He could feel Omelia's thoughts touch his, and he let his tension ease. He stepped off into an easy run, heading toward the Perch.

. . .

Kneeling down, tapping his shoes, he waited for the Name to acknowledge his presence.

<You will deal with the Rikna U'tanse. I have too many of your kind.>

Samson felt a twist in his stomach. What did he mean?

<For your Name.> He paused, then composed a question. <Do you wish me to find places for them to work?>

Elehadi snorted impatiently. <I have all the U'tanse I need in Kakil and Runa. Sell the Rikna to the other clans if you wish, but I have no desire to buy energy cells for their Home. Close it down.>

Samson clicked the taps on his heels. <I will need a boat, and some time to make the sales.>

The Name gestured dismissal with his claws. <You may have a boat. Return here at the New Moon.>

Samson thought, *Six days. What can I do in six days?* But he said, <For your Name.> He backed out of Elehadi's presence and began to walk briskly toward the boats.

Shut Them Down

Cyclops said, "You weren't the only one following Samson. The word has spread through all the Homes. But I need your perspective. What was he thinking? What was he feeling?"

Joshua shook his head. "It was like a kick in the stomach. He'd been so confident he was making the Name consider U'tanse more valuable, and then he was told to dispose of them—his kind."

"So, what was Elehadi's exact words? Was it 'dispose of them'?"

"I don't know Cerik words. The meaning was something like 'get rid of them'. It was Samson who brought up selling them to other clans."

Cyclops thought for a moment. "I doubt Elehadi honestly thought he could order Samson to kill them all. One against hundreds isn't tactically reasonable. He might have phrased it bluntly on purpose, to see Samson's reaction."

Joshua shrugged. "The Name didn't give him any argument when he brought up the time needed to make the sales. He just said to come back at the New Moon."

Others were arriving and all the chairs around the map table were filling up.

Cyclops acknowledged them with a nod.

"You've heard the news. Elehadi is going to break up the Rikna Home—shut it down entirely. Samson is in charge of selling them all off to other clans, but we all know that can't be done. There will be leftovers. In the Cerik mind, the women and children don't count. It's hard enough to get the Festival girls exchanged. It would be impossible if we didn't have the Agreements of Tenthonad that all the clans promised to observe."

Bernard asked, "Why is he even bothering to shut it down? Surely the Rikna could turn a profit. They sell small mountain prey. Even I know that."

Joshua said, "Elehadi specifically mentioned the energy cost of keeping the Home running."

Hugo grunted. "That's how he thinks. He's always got plans within plans. Cutting off the energy import necessary to run the Home might be a strategic move against the Tenthonad clan itself. They're the primary energy suppliers for all of Ko."

Cyclops said, "Maybe. Here at the Base, we're the only U'tanse settlement that has its own source of energy, our hydroelectric turbines. Every Home out there has gardens that need earth-lights and air circulating plants, and plants to refresh the air-filtration chemicals. Some have their own factory systems. Homes are probably the biggest drain on energy that the Names have to support."

Hugo added, "Except the boats. And Elehadi's conquests have been so successful because he can move an army of warriors into place with his fleet of boats."

Robert asked, "How big is a Home's energy cell? How many boats could be powered by the Rikna storage cell?"

Cyclops waved his hand. "We're getting away from the most urgent problem. Elehadi is going to shut down Rikna. Some people will be sold off, but when the lights go dark and the filtered air stops, how many will be left to die in the burrows? And what can we do to rescue them?"

...

The Rikna elders were standing outside the main gate when the boat landed. Samson ducked through the boat's opening and gestured at the gate. "We can talk inside."

They went through the Home's airlock and sat at the same table they'd used on the day of the blood oath.

Samson stowed his breather at his belt and waited for all of the elders to do likewise. They would need to see each other's eyes as they talked.

They were waiting for him to speak first. He had been under *ineda* for most of the boat flight over. He couldn't trust anyone right now. Even the boat pilot seemed to be acting on other orders, choosing a high-altitude flight over Graddik lands.

He cleared his throat and lifted his *ineda*. He needed them to believe every word he said.

"I respect your position as elders of the Rikna Home. Under other circumstances, I would listen carefully to what you say and obey the orders you would give me.

"Circumstances have changed. You already know my orders, given by my Name, our Name. In a very short time, these burrows will go dark. The air will stop moving and go bad. Any U'tanse left inside will find no refuge, no help. Anyone left behind will die. I need your help to get as many of your people sold off to other clans as possible, and I need it to happen in a very short time.

"I have never done this task before. I will need your help to make it go smoothly."

Roger asked, "What do you need?"

Samson leaned forward. "Who are the U'tanse of Rikna? What are you good at? Make me a list of everyone. Tell me what each one does. I'll work with the Kakil *ralak* to pass the offer around to the Names of other clans. You will do the same through your telepathic contacts with the elders of other Homes. We need to make the workers of Rikna as desirable as possible, so that they will sell quickly."

Kathy spoke, "But what of the others? Not all of us are 'workers' in a way that a Cerik would understand. What will happen to the infants, and the elderly? What Name would make an offer for an old lady who washes clothes?"

Samson's face stayed impassive. "Until we make the offer, we can't know. Perhaps there are clans who would like their own Home of U'tanse, but have never been able to afford it. Perhaps others need to expand and will look on this situation as an opportunity.

"But to start, I need that list. Start now, give me fifty names to take back to Kakil in a couple of hours. I'll start converting this into offers Cerik can understand while you finish the process."

Kathy asked, "Why? Why is he doing this? We could work harder. We won't make any demands."

Samson's shoulders sagged. "The Name's plans are beyond me. And while I have made suggestions in the past, I have never been able to change his mind about anything. Your best chance for survival is to work hard within his plan. Give me a list. Think hard about what makes your people special."

...

Joshua shook his head, conscious of all the faces looking at him. "Samson doesn't believe he'll succeed. He's more comfortable with the Cerik than he is with his own kind. He actually understands the … simplicity of letting the useless U'tanse die. But in spite of that, he remembers his own days in the nursery and the kind women who looked after him and took care of him when he was always the outsider and the freak. He really wants to save everyone. He just doesn't think it will work."

Hugo said, "It won't. Samson knows how Cerik think better than all of us here. They'll sell some of the workers, but not enough."

"I've been listening in on the Rikna," said Debbie. "If they were fearful and uncertain before, it's much worse now. Everyone is starting to look at themselves as a product. 'Will I sell, or not?' And so many of them know that no Cerik would ever consider them. 'What is it like to suffocate? Or will my lungs burn out first?' Mothers are being torn up with worries for their children."

Comfort, scribbling the log notes as fast as she could, said, "The children should be our first priority." She spoke softly, to herself.

Cyclops said, "Comfort, could you please repeat what you said."

She looked up, startled. "Ah. I just said rescuing the children should be our first priority."

"And why is that?"

She looked uncertain, then straightened her shoulders a little. "It's obvious. If we can't rescue everyone, then we should get the children first."

Hugo said, "It might be easiest to get some of the children out. No Cerik would have any idea of how many there were. From their eyes, they're invisible. They won't notice that some are missing."

Robert said, "And they're physically small. We could pack more individuals into a boat. Ours is one of the smallest that were made."

Others started contributing ideas. They would have to land a boat near the Home, but out of sight of any of the Cerik. Someone would have to sneak into the Home, make arrangements with the Rikna and lead the children to the boat.

"We can't just send a message to the Rikna and have them send the children out?"

"How? We're all under *ineda*. They don't even know we exist. We have no way to signal them, and if someone were to break *ineda* to reach them, it would put the whole Base in jeopardy."

"Who will go? They might be seen outdoors, so it can't be a woman. A man would be mistaken for a Rikna U'tanse worker outside on a herding chore."

"Someone sneaky. Someone who is familiar with the outdoors."

Bernard added, "And definitely someone good with children. There's really only one candidate."

Joshua was startled as people started looking his way.

"Me?"

Debbie said, "No. It's too dangerous."

Joshua thought about it for a second. "Um. I wouldn't know what to do. Someone would have to tell me what to say."

Patrick, the boat pilot, nodded. "I can work with Joshua. He can keep his head."

Debbie looked over to Cyclops. Behind his eye bandages, Joshua's father looked impassive, like a statue.

Joshua took a breath. "Okay. I'll do it. Tell me what I need to do."

Sneak Into Rikna

"You can take off your breather if you wish," Patrick called back from his piloting position.

Joshua was clinging to the railing installed along the cargo bay walls. The boat had never been fitted with seats, and the way the boat was dodging through the trees, his fingers were white with tension. "I'm okay!" he yelled back.

He was still getting used to the new leathers. As soon as the decision to send him out on this mission was made, Robert pointed out that Joshua's leathers were gaping at the seams and ready to fall apart. He was hurriedly fitted into a new set, ones large enough that he could wear a tunic underneath.

The boat felt like it was falling, and he gripped even tighter.

"Sorry about that," Patrick said. "We're following the mountains between Rikna and Graddik territories. I'm trying to stay hidden from both sides. What's worse, I don't want anyone to hear us, and flying this low, the buzz is distinctive. I have to rely on every deep gully and steep cliff I can find."

Joshua swallowed a gulp and said, "It's fine. Just don't hit anything."

"Just another couple of minutes."

He shifted his grip on the railing. Everything was happening so fast. Samson had gotten his preliminary list of workers and headed back to Kakil. Cyclops thought they ought to take this window of time to slip him into place before Samson returned. With only a few days left, every hour was critical.

His father had taken a moment to talk to him in private. He took his hand. "Joshua, I'm proud that you're taking this risk, but I don't want you to push your limits. I want you back. You're very important to the Base, to all the Free U'tanse, and particularly, to me."

All those people—people who had smiled and dismissed him as a cutie just weeks ago—they were all counting on him to sneak in past the Cerik and rescue a bunch of children from certain death.

The buzzing noise shifted, they tilted, and then there was the crunch of touchdown.

"Come on, we've got to get this boat covered."

Patrick had shown him what to do before they left. The hatch opened, and hot, dry air puffed in. Patrick took one corner of the netting and Joshua took the other and they hauled it outside.

The only boat the Base owned, a smaller model, was a wide, flat oval, looking almost like an egg that had been half-buried in the ground. Patrick had landed between two enormous boulders, each much larger than the craft. Hurriedly, they dragged the netting over the boat and scrambled around, finding broken branches and small bushes to spread over the netting.

Patrick mumbled, "If they get close enough to smell us, it's all over, but if we can keep them from noticing us from a distance, it's the best we can do."

Joshua knew this. They were hiding from superb natural predators. No camouflage was likely to last very long. He had to get in, collect the children and get back before some wandering Cerik noticed the boat. He also knew what Patrick wasn't saying. If detected, he'd take off alone, leaving him behind. Under the best circumstances, the boat would be mistaken for a spy from some other clan.

Patrick knelt down in a natural shelter beneath the overhanging rocks. He pointed. "That's the direction of the Rikna Home, downhill. There's another ridge you'll have to cross, and then you should be able to see it. There's a rear entrance they use to access the *sendt* pens. Once you reach the pens, you should be okay, as long as you pretend to be just another U'tanse worker."

Joshua nodded, although he was still uncertain about everything. Even when Patrick and the other adults gave him confident-sounding instructions, he knew they were just guessing. He had to rely on his own *sight* and telepathy to get him inside, unobserved. And once inside… just hope he could encounter the right people.

And there was no reason for delay. Cerik were as lethal in the dark as in daylight. He might feel more stealthy once the sun went down, but it would be an illusion.

Patrick shook his hand, and Joshua was off, following a watercourse down the mountain. It wasn't too steep, and he was grateful for that. If everything went smoothly, he'd be leading a bunch of children back up this way.

The trickle of water bent to the west, but he kept going straight, finding an animal track over the ridge.

And there it was. Rikna Home looked like a wide mass of clay domes, molded together, spreading from a cliff on one side to a rubble pile from an old avalanche on the other. The Delense who built it originally hundreds of years before had used the structure to block in a large meadow, now containing a herd of *sendt*, the runners Cerik used as a staple prey.

He could feel the inhabitants under the domes, but just this moment, none appeared to be outside. He hurried down the path and went through the gate in the simple wire fence that kept the runners from escaping.

The airlock was clearly U'tanse design, an add-on to the original burrow. He slipped in through the outer door without too much of the unfiltered air mixing into the airlock chamber. There were wooden shelves lining the wall where other workers had left their leathers. It was perfect. He shed his and folded them carefully, putting them at the far left end, so he'd know which were his in a hurry.

He brushed the wrinkles from his tunic, gripped the paper he had folded up inside his suit, and entered the corridors of Rikna.

He didn't know which was the strongest impression, the fear coming from everyone in the burrow, or the strong animal stench coming from the leftmost branch of the tunnels. His *sight* showed extensive pens down that way where smaller animals were bred for trade with the other clans.

He took the right branch, toward the living areas. Almost immediately, he walked up to a man entering from a side branch.

"Who are you?" the man asked, frowning.

Joshua tapped his forehead, and held out his sheet of paper.

Puzzlement was quickly quenched as the man stiffened his *ineda* in response to the tap. He frowned at the text and then said, "Come with me."

Joshua followed for a few paces. The man opened the door to a work room. "Wait in here." He closed the door, taking Joshua's paper with him.

There was nothing else to do but have a seat on the bench. The paper requested a secret visit with one of the elders of the Home. As much as possible, he hoped to keep his presence hidden from everyone else. The fewer who knew he was there, the less chance someone would leak the information. Normal Homes were a noisy hive of telepathic exchange, not like the Base where everyone used *ineda* all the time.

The shelves were filled with a variety of tools. He recognized about half of them, the woodworking tools, knives, saws, hammers, and fasteners. There were also spools of twine and a number of leather items that made no sense to him.

A quick check with his *sight* showed his greeter was still hurrying through the corridors, hunting for an elder. That was actually good. If he'd made a telepathic call, the man could have found them quicker. He was taking the secrecy seriously.

Joshua let his mind drift, checking on Samson. The warrior was back at Kakil, boiling in frustration. He'd discovered just how hard it was to spread the word of the sale of the Rikna U'tanse.

The traditional way Names communicated with each other was via *ralak*, messengers sent in person to speak to the Name. Kakil's *ralak tetka* had members specializing in everything from arranging trades to formally challenging Names to battle. The sale of U'tanse was far down the priority list, and arranging for a boat trip to neighboring clans was difficult at the most peaceful of times. Now, with warriors on alert for possible retaliation for Kakil's invasion of Rikna, and the number of boats decreased by the crash when Rikna's Name landed, *ralak* could give Samson no promise of any formal visits to promote the sales.

Luckily, the Cerik hadn't been dependent on *ralak* visits for a long time. Names could count on two other ways to pass messages. When the Delense invented the boats, they included shouters, machines that could pass the words of the pilots from boat to boat, or from boat to the starships that still circled in the sky above—mostly empty, since Cerik exploration had lapsed. Even before the Delense extermination, Names had begun to use the shouters to send messages from their boats to boats of other clans. Arrangements had to be made so that someone was listening at the receiving end at the right time, so shouter communication was most common between clans that had trade arrangements already in place.

There was also a mystery. Shouter communication became weak and unreliable during the time around a Small Moon. Cross-continental shouter messages stopped altogether during that time.

Samson had just discovered this limitation, frustrated that even as his deadline approached, many of the East Coast clans would be out of communication, unable to finalize a sale offer.

But there was one last possibility. Cerik telepaths could communicate across clans easily, often exchanging gossip. But no one passed messages as a favor to another clan.

Samson feared that none of the Cerik methods would get the message out. Could he trust the U'tanse to push the information up to their masters fast enough?

Joshua heard footsteps and tensed, his attention returning to his current situation. There was a polite knock before the door opened. Two elders walked in. Joshua nodded. "Roger, Elizabeth. Greetings. You may call me Joshua."

Their *ineda* was complete. He stood, offering the limited bench seating to the elders. The door was closed and a latch he hadn't noticed before slid into place

Roger shook his head. "We can stand." He handed the document back and spoke softly. "You are offering protection to some of our children?"

Joshua whispered back. "Yes. About six is all I can handle in one trip. They will be kept safely, off the records of any clan."

Elizabeth asked, "So, are you able to make more trips? What about others—the elderly and workers who can't be sold?"

"Children are our first priority. This trip is very risky, and we'll have to see how it goes before we can plan others. Any hint that a rescue is happening can destroy any chances for more. Personally, I'd love to help everyone escape."

Roger nodded, "The children are our priority, too. Keeping this secret will be difficult. Parents will have to be told something. I also have to ask, are you working with a group? One young man can't handle six children. And how will you get them to safety? How far will they have to travel? Are you prepared to keep them fed and supply water and good air?"

Joshua smiled, "I was chosen for my ability to handle children. However, I couldn't handle six infants. There is a hike involved, and secrecy must be maintained. For part of the trip, any cuties with no *ineda* might need to be blindfolded. Part of it will be in outside air, however healers will be ready to take care of any airburn or lung damage. Airburn lotion would be useful, but not critical."

Roger and Elizabeth looked at each other. They didn't open their telepathy, but they'd obviously worked with each other long enough to just know what the other was thinking.

Roger sighed. "We have no choice, as risky as this seems. We'll prepare the children. You should stay put; out of sight. I'll have food and drink brought to you."

Elizabeth said, "I'll take care of that. The fewer people who know you're here, the safer for us all."

Cuties Escape

Samson wrote as small as he could on the back of a note Omelia had written him. He'd never thought to stock paper or writing supplies at his hut for when he was on duty, but the lists he was making were only for his own use. The *ralak* had excellent memories, but he wanted to give them a carefully phrased offer of the U'tanse for sale. And that needed a good description of their job skills.

And then he heard Stakka's call, <**U'tanse, come to the Perch.**>

He set aside his paper and walked out. His hut was near the Perch, but he hadn't expected to go back before the deadline. What had changed?

Elehadi was there waiting. He watched as Samson went through the abasement ritual. Then he spoke. <U'tanse, my telepath has given me distasteful news. There are thoughts coming from other clans, thoughts from your kind, thinking about stealing away some of my Rikna U'tanse.>

Samson bowed his head slightly, <I have not sensed this.>

<Perhaps Stakka is a better telepath than you.>

Samson made no protest. It might even be true. Instead, he said, <I will be speaking with the Rikna soon. Then I will know if any of your U'tanse harbor disloyal thoughts.>

Elehadi hissed. Then he said, <You will also place guards about their burrow. Any hints you detect will be sent to Stakka. I don't expect much for the sale of these worthless ones, but should any clan or their U'tanse think to steal from me, I will take action.>

Samson shouted, <For your Name.>

. . .

Joshua stood and peeked out the door. His greeter was casually lounging in the corridor. Joshua beckoned with his fingers. The man checked down the hallway and came to the door.

"Tell the elders, there will be guards coming very soon. I have to leave." The message was passed and Roger came hurrying back.

Joshua repeated what he had heard.

Roger nodded, "The children are coming in just minutes. You say the Name's telepath detected us?"

"I don't know. They detected 'thoughts' from other U'tanse. I don't even think it was us. Maybe some other Homes have been considering a rescue as well, and it leaked. In any case, with posted guards around this place, I don't think another rescue is possible. If we don't leave immediately, then I might not even be able to take this group out."

But there were footsteps coming down the corridor, and someone giggled.

Elizabeth led the group, carrying one infant. A girl about Joshua's age was carrying another in a sling. Four cuties followed, three girls and one boy.

It was a special game, he sensed from their thoughts. The infants were asleep, and the older girl was a blank. Her *ineda* was good, but he saw the stress on her face.

Elizabeth said, "This is Sally. She'll be taking care of the children."

Two infants, four cuties and Sally—that was seven, but he'd said 'about six' hadn't he. Joshua took a deep breath. He'd make it work.

Sally whispered to him. "The infants have been drugged. We have blindfolds."

He nodded, then speaking to the cuties, he said, "Hello, my name is Joshua. Are you ready?" The four responded, grinning and nodding.

They pulled out the sashes and knotted the bands around the eyes of the cuties. "Now the game goes like this—you'll hold hands as we lead you around. Listen to what we say, because there are obstacles to walk around. Feel the air and smell what you can, but you can't talk. Okay?"

They nodded. One girl said, "Yes." The others giggled.

Elizabeth said, "Pete." The greeter nodded, and led the way out the back airlock, holding the doors open. Joshua hurriedly grabbed his leathers and breather from where he'd stashed them. He slipped them on and then took the infant from Elizabeth and held it across his shoulder just as he had held Little Shelley not too many hours ago. He took the hand of one of the cuties and they linked up with Sally in the middle of the chain. With Pete to handle the doors, they were soon outdoors.

Pete put his finger to his lips and then waved them on while he headed the other direction. Joshua could see a worker in leathers walking their way, but still around the bend. Pete hurried to stall him.

There were no Cerik in the area. Their main danger was an innocent sighting and an unblocked thought by other U'tanse. Joshua set the pace and kept his eye out for the little ones, trying to make sure he didn't trip them up.

"Move around the rocks," he said, pulling a little hand to the left so they would avoid the obstacle. He steadied the warm, breathing bundle on his chest with his other hand.

The *sendt* near a water pond snorted and moved off as they approached. The little boy wrinked his nose and said, "Euew!" The little girls shushed him.

At the fence, Joshua held the gate and Sally led them through. After closing the fastener, he came back and took the little girl's hand again.

The hike had the cuties whimpering before they arrived. Sally's eyes widened as she saw the boat. "We're almost there," she said, "and I have drinks for us all." There was a weak cheer.

Patrick nodded when Joshua put his finger to his lips, but he had the hatch open for them. Sally helped each of the cuties to step up inside and let them drink from the bottle she carried.

"Can I take off the blindfold?" asked one of the girls.

"Not just yet. But you can sit down here." Sally had them lined up against the wall before they dozed off from the drug. Then she helped him move the sleeping infant he held over to the pallet with the other one.

Sally looked at the inside of the boat. "We could have brought more."

Joshua nodded, "But the plan was for me to have led all the children here by myself. I don't think I could have handled too many more."

She sighed. "You're right. But shouldn't we go back for more?"

He shook his head. "Just before we left, more Cerik guards were ordered to move into position around the Home. I don't know how long we have before they arrive."

Patrick said, "Then I'd better get out of here. Come help me with the net."

Together they pulled the netting free and spent a frustrating couple of minutes freeing the branches and brush from the web. Then, with the door closed, and Sally and Joshua braced to keep the sleeping children from sliding around. Joshua grabbed at the folded net. "Here, help me wrap them with this."

They tied the ends to the railing and made sure each of the little ones were secure, and then the boat lifted off with a buzz.

Patrick was a good clairvoyant. He had to be to avoid detection. He yelled back at them. "I'm going to risk a high altitude trip." They felt the sag of extra weight and the buzzing noise dropped in pitch as they gained altitude.

Sally gripped the railing. "I've never been on a boat before."

"I find it's best to just hang on and let Patrick do his thing."

The pilot said, "I don't think anyone noticed us. Boats are going to and from Rikna all the time now." He shifted their course.

"Where is your Home?" she asked.

Joshua shook his head. "There are new rules. Lots of things are secret. Until your *ineda* has been checked and those in charge are confident that you can keep your mind blocked all the time, many things will be hidden from you. I can't even tell you who we are."

She looked puzzled, and a little frightened, but nothing leaked past her block. Slowly, she nodded. "I understand. I didn't know there were any U'tanse who could fly a boat by themselves."

He shook his head sternly. "Don't even think about stuff like that. Don't think about where you are or what you're doing. Not now. Talk about other things. Who are you? What were you doing, oh, a month ago?"

She looked down at the scarred metal floor. "I'm nobody, really. I'm still a cutie, technically. I work in the animal pens and do my shift in the nursery. I'm Sally bar...."

He held up his hand. "Stop. You won't get family information from anyone, and no one expects it. There are reasons. You're just Sally now, although some people even change their names."

Her mouth was open. Then she said, "If you're wanting me to think about ordinary things, you're going to have to stop telling me how strange you are."

He smiled. "Okay. I'm ordinary. Tell me about these." He tilted his head toward the children.

She looked at the infants, a frown wrinkling her forehead. "The smallest one is Green, and her mother is having troubles. She had a bad accident tending the *hatsen*. One of the males bit her arm, and nearly took it off. When the news came, she knew no one would ever buy her, with her arm still healing."

A smile crept over her face as she continued. "The fat one is Buster. His mother is a brave one, but I guess she knows best. He laughs a lot. I hope he keeps it up, with his mother gone."

She pointed one by one at the cuties. "That's Jinger, Weelie, Karli, and of course, Kurtis, who's a handful."

He nodded. "Karli and Kurtis are holding hands."

"Brother and sister. Karli has always kept an eye out for her little brother. I'm not surprised both of them came together."

"Weelie?"

"She's a little artist. We had to order more paper for the nursery, just for her."

"I'll have to introduce her to Ash. He's the same way. Of course, he's a little older and tends to spend all his time with my sister, Veronica."

She chuckled. "Romantic conflicts in the nursery—I've seen a couple of those."

"And Jinger?" he asked.

Sally frowned. "If they'd asked me, I would have chosen someone else. She's always been with her friends, and none of them were included. She may have it rough for a while."

Patrick said, "Hang on, course change coming up."

Joshua gripped one hand on the railing and spread his other arm to protect as many of the unconscious bodies as he could. Sally duplicated his motions on the other side.

There were several hard shifts, and everyone slid several inches across the floor, but then the buzzing changed pitch and they were down.

"We're here."

There were noises outside. As the hatch opened, they could see factory workers hurriedly moving the camouflage shed on little wheels to hide the boat from the air.

Debbie hopped inside, followed quickly by Comfort and Hugo. Each person picked up one of the children and without a word, they walked the path down to the dock at the edge of the water.

Sally looked confused, but followed the ladies, holding on to Buster. Her eyes widened when she saw the long metal thing with an open hatch.

Joshua nodded and smiled. "No questions yet."

She gave him a long-suffering smile and followed Debbie as she carried her burden through the hatch into the strange tank.

It was tight quarters in the submarine, and Joshua had to stand, but the hatch closed and Robert piloted them underwater the short trip across the bay.

Everyone relaxed a little once they submerged. Everyone except for Sally. She reached out a hand and took Joshua's.

"It's okay," he said.

She nodded.

Cyclops was waiting at the dock inside the Base as they unloaded.

"Cerik guards were already arriving even before you took off. If you'd taken any longer to get airborne, you would have been trapped."

He turned his head, speaking to Sally. "I'm afraid we can't make another trip. Not unless something changes."

She nodded, her mouth open as she looked at the man with the bandage across his eyes. Joshua smiled. Her *ineda* didn't leak a bit.

Mistakes

Joshua was happy to let the ladies handle the care of the new visitors while he took the opportunity to doze off for the first time in over a day. Still, his brain couldn't quite settle down. His *sight* showed Sally talking to several of the adults, likely getting her *ineda* tested.

He closed his eyes and couldn't help but check on Samson.

Dario looked quite small, facing him across the table. "No, perhaps you and I can stay at this for long hours, but this trial has put a lot of stress on Roger." He hesitated, "If at all possible, he needs some rest. We need his wisdom, and waking him right now would put more stress on an already exhausted body."

Samson nodded. "Okay, I will talk with him later. But you have to know that the Name has been informed that other Homes have been planning some kind of rescue mission—an act that the Name sees as nothing more than theft of his property."

Dario's mind was open, and Samson could read his rise and fall of emotions as he considered what he was told. It was all news to him.

Dario nodded thoughtfully, "Well, I do know that I have been getting well-wishes from other Homes since the invasion. But, I don't know of any real plan for a rescue. How could that even be done? We're far too distant from any other clan to survive an overland trek. There's not that much air filtration powder in stock. And certainly no Name has ever let any of their U'tanse fly a boat."

Samson followed his logic. "Yes, it could only be done under the command of a Name. Still, it's not impossible for an ambitious leader to attempt to boost his own prestige by poaching on our Name's least secure lands. It would be, as Elehadi said, theft of his property, and his anger would be severe should anyone from Rikna join in this attack."

Samson leaned forward, and Dario bent back, reacting to the towering figure looming over him.

Samson lowered his voice to a whisper. "I know you've thought about it. Every prey caught in a *dul* wants to find a way out. But you should know what immediate, horrific, penalties will occur if the Name finds treachery from one who spoke the *uuka*. It wouldn't be just you, it would be your family, and to be honest, who in this place isn't your cousin? One infraction could make this whole effort to find buyers useless, because there just might not be any of you left to sell."

There was more said, but Joshua drifted off to sleep and didn't remember any of it.

. . .

The twitch in his ribs woke him. Or rather the poking. Joshua blinked and brushed away the little fingers that were making another attempt to put bruises on his side.

"Cut it out."

He focussed on Veronica, kneeling next to the pallet he'd set up in the nursery. "Josh," she whispered, "there are people here!"

He leaned upright and looked over to where several beds were hastily set out to handle the new cuties. The babies were probably over in the other room. It looked like Karli and Kurtis were awake. Sally was also wide awake, sitting with her back against the wall, a solemn expression on her face.

"Very, these are cousins come here from another place. You knew there were other people out there, didn't you?"

Her shoulders hunched inward. "Well, yes. But why are they here? Where did they come from?"

"How is your *ineda*?"

He felt the swirl of confusion in her head fade under as if a thick blanket dropped down over her.

"It's one of those?" she asked.

He nodded.

She sighed, and gripped his hand. "But who are they? Do you know them?"

He nodded. "I've met them. Let me get up and I'll introduce you."

He got to his feet and shook the wrinkles from his tunic. He hadn't taken any time to clean up. He still smelled like he'd taken a hike through the mountains.

Sally looked up as he approached. Karli and Kurtis glanced at her for reassurance.

"Good morning. I'd like you to meet my sister Veronica."

Sally stood and put on a smile. "It's good to meet you. Joshua said nice things about you yesterday."

Veronica was too timid to much more than give a little nod, her eyes wide at meeting someone so strange. When your whole world has been a handful of connected rooms, and the only people you meet have been there for as long as you can remember, any new person was strange. Joshua thought back. She'd kept her distance from Bernard, too.

Sally's smile grew a little larger and more genuine. She held out her hand. "Come, let me introduce you to Karli and Kurtis." She saw another body stirring. "And Weelie, once she gets her eyes open."

Joshua stayed put as the cuties exchanged their first words. No one was really comfortable, in spite of the warmth Sally was presenting. He leaned back and peeked in through the doorway that was half open to the babies. It looked like Comfort was in attendance.

Sally seemed to be doing a good job getting the cuties to open up and actually talk to each other, so he ducked through to check on Buster and Green.

Comfort looked up as he approached.

He whispered, "How are the newcomers?"

She nodded her head and whispered back. "They woke up just fine a couple of hours after you arrived. They were a little fussy, but I get the echo of their mothers' thoughts, calming them down."

"Tough for them."

Comfort nodded, her face strained. She'd been copying down all the log entries. She was well aware that those distant mothers faced suffocation or some other more bloody death in just days.

Debbie walked in. She put her hand on Joshua's shoulder. "Your father has been waiting for you to wake up. You should go talk to him."

He hoped his mother would stay and help get the cuties introduced to each other, and provide the necessary and difficult explanations to the youngsters who had no idea what was going on in the outside world.

He took an extra two minutes to swap out his tunic for the clean one and to drop the other into the laundry. He wished there was time for a bath, but he knew there wasn't.

Cyclops waved him to a chair as soon as he arrived.

"I'm hoping you've monitored Samson?"

"Before I fell asleep, I saw the meeting with Dario."

"Just Dario? Not Roger?"

"Dario made the plea that the elder was exhausted, and I think Samson believed it. Certainly Dario was wide open and had no idea of our visit."

Cyclops nodded. "But what did Samson say? I've just gotten gossip from other Homes. Nobody seems to admit to a rescue plan, and if Stakka has a whiff of our activity, it's very bad news. If we have a leak then we need to find it immediately and stop it before something even more critical gets out."

Joshua tried to remember what he had sensed before he had dozed off.

"Samson doesn't believe Stakka's report, although he doesn't let himself think that clearly. When he was talking to Dario, he was warning him not to make a future mistake. He was quick to believe that Dario was innocent of any current treachery against Elehadi."

Joshua outlined Samson's reasoning. The U'tanse were powerless, so any rescue had to be some plot by another Name.

Cyclops leaned back in his chair. "So it could be a mistake by Stakka, misreading people's desire to do something as a real active plot. I really want to believe this possibility."

Joshua shrugged. "I get the feeling they're pushing Samson into this role because they can't read U'tanse motives and thought processes very well. He's their translator. Stakka is reading Samson's every thought just like I am."

Hugo, who had been quietly listening, said, "Maybe it's a good thing they don't understand us. We've suffered long enough because we didn't understand the Cerik."

Cyclops looked his way. "What do you mean?"

Hugo looked toward the middle of the table, his shoulders hunched forward a little. "I probably shouldn't say this, but the first Father, Abe, made a mistake, trading himself, and his descendants into slavery."

Cyclops said, "We wouldn't have existed otherwise."

"Maybe. But look at where we are. The only freedom we have is to work in the shadows, living off the crumbs of the Cerik. Abe probably thought the Cerik would be like the human slave masters on the old Earth planet. You've read the book. He wrote plenty about human slave cultures. Maybe he thought that by now, the humans and the Cerik would have come to an agreement and we'd be living as equals. That certainly hasn't happened. It's actually getting worse, year by year. The big clans made their fortunes off of U'tanse and Delense technology, and then they shut down our expansion. You have to agree that all they want to do is cut our population down to a level that will sustain the big clans, and no more."

Cyclops nodded, "I have to agree on one point. They don't want many of us. Someday, they might want to wipe us all out in one massive purge, just like they did to the Delense. Too many of us, and that would be impossible. For now, it would be so easy. They could just stop all the power deliveries that run our air filtration machines, like Elehadi has threatened in Rikna. Let us suffocate."

Hugo shook his head. "That's not Cerik enough. They'd *flick* all the Homes."

Joshua disagreed, "No. They might threaten to *flick* the Homes, but they'd be waiting in hiding, with their claws sharp, as we ran out the door to escape. They like their killing more personal."

Hugo took in a breath. "You know, you're right. Cyclops, your boy is getting more than just tactical info from Samson's mind. He's getting to know how the Cerik think."

No Name

Sally looked up from her game with Weelie, Ash, and Veronica when Joshua walked back into the nursery. He saw her face shift from total focus on the cuties to showing a little reserve. He guessed she wanted to find a polite way to bow out of the game.

"Hey, Very, Ash, do you mind if I borrow Sally for a bit? I'm supposed to ask her some questions."

His sister frowned. "More secrets, I bet. She's just like you that way."

He raised an eyebrow. "And you know how to get around that."

She glared at him. Ash and Weelie looked questions at each other.

Sally stood up and followed him.

When they went toward the exit door, she said, "I was told I wouldn't be able to leave the nursery area until my *ineda* had been checked."

He nodded, grinning. "And I'm the guy doing the checking. You're my official task for the next few hours."

Carefully, he bent over the control pad next to the door, shielded it from sight, and tapped the circular dots in a memorized pattern. "I've got to be careful. Ash got the last lock code and escaped to the garden with Very in tow."

"Your sister is worried about you."

When he closed and locked the door behind them, he nodded. "She's been having nightmares. She's always had them, but they're worse now. I think it's spillover from the dread coming out of Rikna."

She sighed. "It was bad, like a fog in the corridors. You couldn't escape it."

He led her down the corridor. "I try to ignore it while I'm in the nursery. If I don't make a point of it, the little ones will forget it ever happened."

She looked at the walls. "This place looks strange. The nursery was painted, so I didn't notice. Are these stone walls?"

He nodded. "Rikna Home was a standard Delense burrow. They crafted them of mud and hardened them with some chemicals. For some reason, they built this place into solid rock. They licked these corridors into the granite."

"Licked them?"

He grinned. "I saw the machines. Old and falling apart, but you could see the tongues, eight of them, on a spinning shaft. The tongues were rough-surfaced and probably oozed some acid or something. I doubt we'd ever get them running again."

"I've never heard of anything like this before."

He shrugged. "The Delense were good at keeping secrets, too. The Cerik never knew about this place. One theory was that this is where they planned their attack. This is where they decided to make their break for freedom. They needed a place hidden from the Cerik. Their plan failed, and they were exterminated, but they left their secrets behind."

They entered the garden. For a quiet place to talk, the benches near the sadapples and overlooking the wheat was private enough.

She took the cup of water he offered and sipped. Then she shook her head. "You shouldn't be telling me this stuff."

"It wasn't my decision. Believe me, I'm too young to make that call. But you've had several people checking your *ineda* constantly since you first saw the boat. I've been told that your skills are good. You can keep it up constantly, effortlessly, like we do here.

"But do you have the motive, the will, to keep it up, or would you get tired of the routine and just let it slip? Cyclops said to tell you more."

"Cyclops?" She grinned. "The monster with one eye?"

He shook his head with a slight smile. "My father. You've seen him, I think. Tall man with a bandage wrapped around his head?"

Her mouth formed a little 'o'. "Sorry for calling him a monster. I didn't know."

Joshua chuckled. "No, that's fine. He named himself after the monster of the myth. It was his way to be free of his birth name. He is supposed to be dead, and any hint that he still lived would put his friends and relatives at risk from Cerik retaliation. A number of people have changed their names for the same reason."

Her forehead furrowed in thought, "I'm still missing something. Who are you people? My teacher had us memorize all the Homes and taught us which clans sold which products and such. I've never heard of a place like this."

He nodded. "That's how it's supposed to be. There are no Cerik here. We have no Name. We are free U'tanse, made up of the cast-offs. Almost everyone here was rescued after some Name left them for dead. At least the men. Most of the women went to Festival to be traded to another Home, and instead chose to come here."

Sally was silent. Joshua could tell that her *ineda* had tightened even more. He couldn't sense the vague hints of emotion like before. It was as if, telepathically, she didn't even exist.

She whispered, "Free U'tanse. What does that mean?"

Joshua looked across the garden, remembering all the times his mother had brought him here to work and to talk about things.

"I'm probably the worst person to answer that. I was born free—the first one, in fact. I've never known what it's like to live under the Cerik. I've been monitoring people in various Homes, but that's their lives, not mine."

"No Name." She tasted the idea.

"No. Now, I'm not saying we can do whatever we want. They'll still kill us on sight. We live inside a mountain, with no leaking thoughts to betray our existence. Maybe someday that will change, but not until we are more secure."

She looked him in the eyes. "Am I supposed to stay here?"

He was a little confused. "I don't know. What do you mean?"

She looked over at the sadapples, frowning at the purple fruit she'd probably never seen before and said, "Well, my family is all back at Rikna. My father is a *sendt* herder. Mother has a shift with the *hatsen*, and is one of the women's teachers. My older brother is studying Delense tech. I was on nursery duty when Elizabeth came in and started picking the cuties for this rescue. She's my grandmother, by the way."

Sally looked down at the floor. "She didn't explain anything. She just said to take care of the little ones, for as long as it took—and to stay under *ineda*. I didn't realize I was leaving home. I didn't know I'd never see my family again."

Joshua tried to imagine what she was feeling. What would he be thinking if he was off on a mystery task and knew that he'd never see his parents or Veronica again?

"That's tough. Can you read their thoughts?"

She shook her head. "Elizabeth must have talked to them before I got the chance. Both my parents are under *ineda*, and that's something they hardly ever use. Jack, my brother, doesn't know anything. From what I can get from him, he thinks I'm at one of the huts out in the *sendt* fields, doing some special task for grandmother."

She rubbed her face with both hands. "When we were talking about making several rescue runs, I was wondering how to get the word to them. And then, that was all shut down."

"I wouldn't give up hope. This place is made up of people who were given up for dead. The first thing we talked about when Kakil's invasion started was how to protect the U'tanse. We got in quickly, and because of that, we rescued you and the little ones."

She snapped, "Oh, don't be like that! I'm a little one, too, and you know it. I'm still a year away from passing the woman's test, and now, with my training impossible to complete, I'll be a cutie for even longer."

He nodded, "You know, that's an important point. Veronica is still years away from needing to get the women's training, and all the other women we have arrived from Festival, already trained. Nobody here has been mentoring new females. Still, there are several people I know who could do that kind of training. I'll bring that up with the others.

"But one thing—you aren't a cutie, not by our rules, anyway."

She looked confused. "What do you mean?"

"I'm not 'of age' by Home standards either," he said. "But here, I'm a man, not because of my body's development, but because I have a solid and reliable *ineda*."

He stretched his shoulders and looked out over the garden with a smile. "I guess I hadn't realized it. I've always been unique—the first free U'tanse.

The first of our cuties to be released from the nursery, and the first in the Base to step from the children's chores to real grown-up jobs. But that's how it works here."

He smiled at here. "And so have you. You've got an *ineda* that people can rely on. You've taken on an adult's task in caring for the Rikna little ones. People here will be expecting even more adult work from you. Getting your women's training is important. Everyone knows that. But don't call yourself a cutie anymore. No one else will."

Price Drop

Joshua gave his report when all eyes around the map table turned to him.

"Samson is seeing the same thing Debbie reported," he nodded toward his mother. "Only, he's seeing it through Cerik eyes. His offers to sell Rikna workers are coming back with insults. It's just Cerik negotiation over prices, but the way they do it is just short of a challenge to fight to the death. He has only five committed sales—three engineers and two small animal-breeders. Elehadi is getting only a few dozen *sendt* in return, and a shipment of trimmed *conek* logs."

There was a groan from several around the table. These were insulting prices indeed.

Hugo asked, "And Elehadi is going along with this?"

Joshua nodded. "Samson sent a messenger to Elehadi to see if he would agree to the terms. The Name told him to stop bothering him about details."

Lincy looked up from her scribbling and said, "Prices that low should increase the number of workers finding new Homes, shouldn't it?"

Cyclops nodded, a frown on his face. "It might help the current crisis, but if it triggers a world-wide drop in the value of a U'tanse, the Cerik will be increasingly reluctant to spend for expansion, or even to maintain their Homes at current levels. A drop in the value of an individual U'tanse life means that it'll be easier for an overseer to just let underperforming people die if they can be cheaply replaced."

He turned to Joshua. "How did Samson take the news?"

"He made no analysis. It was just the new rules to him. He sent shouter messages in reply to some other offers he had considered too low before, adjusting his position lower. What he's seeing from the Rikna elders is a list of nearly a hundred and fifty male and female workers, and offers coming in for ones and twos and threes. There's no way he'll find positions for all of them, even if he had more time."

Bernard to his right started his report. Graddik was not even considering buying any of the Rikna U'tanse, if it would in any way help Elehadi in his plans. The report from Lakka, however was more upbeat. They were considering purchasing several workers with *sendt* herding experience, if they came with their own gear—not that they were even thinking about bringing the families along.

Cyclops asked, "Is anyone getting any information from the smaller clans? At these prices, they could get the minimum twenty-seven to start a new Home for barely the transportation costs."

There was no response. The Base had more monitors than any of the Homes, but there were not enough skilled telepaths to peek into all the clans. Before the current crisis, Cyclops had been content to rely on each of the Homes to monitor their smaller neighbors. Now everyone had their attention turned on Kakil and Elehadi's actions.

Hugo said, "Not in answer to your question, but I've gotten a whiff of a new nomadic group. Someone raided the Rikna female pit and made off with a few. I got the feeling from the Kakil guards that they aren't too worried. In my opinion, Elehadi doesn't want any of the Rikna clan to remain. He just wants the land and the *sendt* herds for his own people. If the Rikna Cerik vanish into the mountains, he could care less."

Cyclops asked around, "Any confirmation?"

Joshua said, "Samson has to keep up with the activities of the guards around the Rikna Home. They are all Kakil. No Rikna is to be considered a warrior. When Samson takes a boat to Rikna, there's always more Kakil workers riding along with him, but when he flies back to Kakil, he's often the sole passenger."

Hugo asked, "The new Kakil, are they workers or warriors?"

"Mainly workers. The number of Kakil warriors in Rikna is actually dropping. Elehadi doesn't want to appear weak at his own Perch, so some boats are going back to Kakil for good, but they're only taking warriors, not workers."

Hugo tilted his head, as if he had a new idea.

Cyclops asked, "You have a thought?"

Hugo waved his hand, dismissing it. "Nothing. Just something I need to look into later."

...

Joshua relaxed in the bath on the third level. Nobody used this one, so it was his favorite place to stretch out and soak away the grime. It had been his favorite place to reach out and view the girls in distant Homes, too. Now, with all the urgency of the current crisis, he'd limited his monitoring to Samson and other important targets. Girls would have to wait.

What he really wanted to do was to sleep, hopefully with no dreams. Samson was working long hours, so he had to stay awake as well.

He closed his eyes, and with hardly any effort slipped into Samson's worries. He was on one of the smallest of the boats, one he'd started to use heavily, almost like his personal transportation.

The pilot had give him an assessing look. Samson knew exactly what the Rear Talon was thinking. Exhausted and days since his last workout, he looked like prey. If he hadn't been on Elehadi's mission, he'd have been worried.

The boat shifted. They were approaching Kakil Home. He wished there was time to see Omelia, but the job came first.

They came down and settled with a slight jar. The pilot was hardly in a mood to show consideration for his kind.

Samson shoved the hatch open. <Wait here.>

The pilot gave a barely audible *ruff.*

He entered the main entrance airlock and clipped his breather to his belt. **"I need to speak to the elder."** He directed the thought to Bruce.

He snagged a passing worker. "Get me something to eat."

"Uh, okay." The guy hurried off into the depths of the Home, irritation clearly oozing from his thoughts.

I can't worry about that. Standing in for the Name at Rikna quickly lost him potential friends. If they couldn't understand he was working hard to save lives, then it was their fault.

He found a bench and sat down, unsealing his leathers, to give his skin the chance to breathe. There was no time to go to his cell or to clean up.

The food, a plate of simple pastries, arrived first. He was chewing when Aarison, one of Bruce's assistants, arrived. He nodded. "Bruce is unavailable. What can I do for you?"

"I need the report I asked for—which clans are really serious about wanting Rikna, and which can I ignore."

The man didn't meet his eye, "There are problems. The other Homes have reservations about using U'tanse telepaths to provide trading information for one clan at the expense of another. Each Home has their own Name to protect."

Samson sniffed, looking at the pastry as if it had suddenly spoiled. "I suppose I should tell the Rikna that the other Homes are too busy to help them right now, then."

"No!" Aarison said. "It's not like that at all. You know Elehadi is running some plan against the other clans. Everybody knows that. The instant you asked for that report, the word went out between the Cerik telepaths and orders came down to avoid helping Kakil."

Samson tossed the half-eaten food back onto the plate and looked him in the eye. "And here I thought every U'tanse would band together to help those in need. This isn't something hard for you. I'd do it myself if I had the time and skills, but I need someone who already knows the minds to touch."

"You want Home to spy on Home? That's a hard thing to ask."

"No. I want Elehadi's U'tanse to tell me what I need so that I can save Rikna U'tanse lives. Are you telling me that *you*," he pointed at Aarison's chest, "can't read the Graddik Name's thoughts about whether to deal with Kakil?"

The man glared at him. "I'll get you a report, for what good it will do. Elehadi wants them all dead."

"Elehadi will stick to his word. If they die, it'll be because you and I don't work together. I've got to meet with the *ralak* at sunset. I'll be back after that for whatever you can provide for me."

Aarison snorted, turned and left.

Samson stared at the plate. He'd lost his appetite. First, Bruce started avoiding him, and now his second-in-command was showing his colors. When this was all over, he might not be welcome at Kakil Home any more. He might not be welcome at any Home.

Reconsidering the pastries, he finished them off and prepared to go to his meeting.

Running footsteps in the hallway stopped him.

"Hey, Samson."

"George." He was surprised to see a smiling face. "What are you doing here?"

He was panting. "I just heard you were here. Nobody tells me anything."

Samson put his hand on George's shoulder. "I'd love to stay and talk, but my schedule is tight. I may be back later. See you then?"

George's face fell, "Uh, okay. I understand. I just wanted to share some ideas."

Samson nodded, then slipped his breather back on. "Later." He went out the airlock, his friend already slipping out of his thoughts.

Joshua was intrigued by the visit, but as usual, the tenner's thoughts were blocked. His *sight* gave him little more, except he was puzzled to see George pull out a piece of paper and write something down, taking care to phrase something. But without his father's help, he'd never know what was written.

When George started jogging back into the corridors, clutching the paper in his hand, Joshua decided to follow him for a little bit. Samson's schedule was already fixed and he could find him easily, now that he'd gotten so familiar with the giant.

Kakil Home was heavily branched, leading from the main entrance, off into several work and living zones, with the living areas off to the left, conveniently closer to the bath next to the river.

George stopped and talked to someone, then took another branch. Without a telepathic connection, he couldn't hear what was said, but it looked like George was getting directions.

When he reached his destination, Omelia greeted him, and Joshua picked up the conversation from her.

"Hello, I'm George, a friend of Samson."

She nodded. "Yes, I know you. You were with him at the bath a number of times."

He looked uncomfortable. "Sorry, I just need you to pass this over to him. I think he might be back soon, but I'm so disconnected from everything that I'm afraid I'll miss him."

She looked at the paper, not reading it. "Okay, I'll make sure he gets it. Is there anything else?"

He shook his head. "No, that should be it. Oh, tell him that I'm confident he'll pull it all off."

She smiled. "I wish there were others that recognized all the effort he's putting into this."

He nodded, and left.

Frustrated, Joshua waited for a moment, but she didn't attempt to read the letter.

He shook himself in the water, leaving Kakil. It was time to for his nursery duty, and he was letting himself get too wrinkled in the water.

Explore Freedom

Sally shook her head. "I thought Jinger would have made some friends by now."

Debbie listened to her worries, sitting with Joshua and her at the table next to the storage shelves, away from little ears.

Debbie nodded. "Over the years, I've seen a lot of the Festival girls arrive. I was one of them myself." She looked over at the children playing in the next room, monitored by Comfort. "Sometimes it takes months before a girl, even ones more mature than Jinger, can get her feet under her when she's abruptly dropped into a new place."

Joshua said, "Sylvia used to cry in the nursery when she didn't think anyone was watching. But she's fine now."

Sally spread her hands. "But Jinger was a special case, even back at Rikna. She had three friends: Harmony, Mary, and Fancy. Those four went everywhere together, and they didn't really make friends outside the group."

Debbie asked, "Do you think she's still communicating with them?"

Sally shrugged, "Maybe. She doesn't talk to me much. She was fairly cheerful during the trip, when she thought it was just a game, but now that it looks permanent, she stays to herself."

Joshua asked, "Do cuties her age know *ineda*? Is it taught that young over there?"

Sally shook her head. "Not really. The teachers mentioned it. I learned it on my own."

Debbie asked, "Why?"

She hesitated, looking down at the floor. "Well, I was paying a lot of attention to some of the older boys and my friends were making fun of me. Kristin was a Festival-girl exchange from Sanassan and went out of her way to make friends with some of us younger ones. She knew *ineda* and offered to train me, so I could avoid getting picked on."

Joshua said, "Well, she did a good job. I rarely get even a hint of your emotions via telepathy, and none of your coherent thoughts."

Debbie nodded. "We were all impressed. Joshua, Ash, and Veronica have all been exposed to *ineda* and encouraged to learn it since they first learned to talk. We are less optimistic about the little ones you brought, but that can be fixed. There's no talent to *ineda*—it's all training. Even tenners can learn it well."

"Jinger might be your worst problem then. If she won't listen to us, she'll not likely be interested in training."

Debbie patted her hand. "Don't worry. We have a lot of time. You've only been here a few days, less than a week. And this isn't your problem alone. There are plenty of people to help you."

Debbie caught Joshua's eye. "Don't let Sally get too stressed out."

He laughed, "If she lets me know! She didn't even open up about her worries to me."

Sally laughed. "I'll do better. It's just that their mothers are gone, and they need someone familiar."

Joshua pointed off to the other room, where Comfort was seated in a circle with most of the cuties, "Karli and Kurtis are getting along well with the others. And once Ash shared his drawing supplies with Weelie, she's acting like he's her friend for life."

Sally nodded, but still tapped her fingers nervously on the table.

Debbie said, "And don't worry about your own training. I've passed the word around and there are five women ready and willing to help mentor you through your women's training. You won't have any problems there."

She folded her hands and smiled. "That's good. I'd only started into cellular healing and barely had an introduction into … reproductive biology before this all happened." She avoided looking in Joshua's direction.

Debbie smiled. "I'll send them by, one by one, to make their introductions themselves. Sylvia and Comfort you already know. You'll work it out among yourselves who will be your primary mentor. Is that okay?"

She nodded.

Debbie stood up. "I've got to get back to my other chores. It was nice having this chance to talk."

After she'd left, Joshua said, "Sorry I didn't realize you were stressing out. I've been off in other people's heads most of the time lately. Normally, I'm on nursery duty half the day."

Sally waved her hand. "No matter. It's not stress, exactly. I'm just worried about Jinger."

He looked at the next room and said, "You know, when I get the chance, I take a break. Maybe you should do that too."

She looked confused. "I don't know...."

He stood and pulled her to her feet. "Come on, while Comfort has them all enthralled in that game."

"Where are we going?"

He held his finger to his lips and led her over to the exit door and out into the corridor. When the latch behind them clicked into place, he said, "One of the things about living as a free U'tanse is that when you want to go outside, you can."

"What?"

"Come on, it's just a little swim."

She hesitated, stopping in her tracks, "Ah. What we said before. I'm not trained...."

He suddenly caught her meaning and felt a flush on his face. "Hey, there's nothing sexual about this. I'm not inviting you to a bath with me. But we have to swim to get to the place I want to show you."

She flushed, too. "Okay."

They started down the spiral. He asked, "You do know how to swim, don't you?"

"Of course. They taught us as babies." She followed, duplicating his habit of putting his hand on the inside curve. "And you have a nice bath here, too. Comfort showed me this small one on the third level, where no one ever goes."

He almost tripped, his mind racing. "We're going down to sea level. The only way out of the Base is underwater."

"Really? The only way?"

He nodded. "I suppose there are air vents, but I've been told they're hidden and too small for humans—and certainly too small for Delense or Cerik to traverse. The Delense wanted a place that could be defended, even if the Cerik found it."

She sighed. "Everything I know appears to be wrong. I was taught Delense were a quiet, subservient race that only made one attempt at rebellion, and it was their last."

He shrugged. "They might have been. With no real history, it's hard to know. Still, the Base is a solid piece of evidence that they were planning something. Building this place had to have taken a long time. They needed to invent whole new tunneling machines. They invented other things as well."

"What?"

They walked out onto the dock level. He gestured toward the submarine. "It's Delense design, with many U'tanse modifications. The Cerik never wanted or needed a water craft, so this was done in secret, for the Delense only."

"And we can take this?"

He laughed, almost choking. "Oh, no! If Robert ever thought I'd try something like that, he'd lock me away somewhere. This is Robert's baby. He inherited it from Aaron, the man who discovered the place. Maybe someday I'll get a chance to try it out, but Robert will be watching my every move, you can bet!"

He gestured toward the far wall, where the granite met the water. "Down below there is the opening to the outside. Without the submarine, we swim."

He led Sally to the storeroom and turned on the light. "We've got to find you an air-suit. Oh, I know." He dug around on the shelf and pulled out some leathers. "These were mine." He looked at her. "I assume you'd rather use a suit?"

She shuddered, "I had to wash my clothes for quite a while to get the airburn ointment out of the fabric. If you think it will fit...."

She looked at the leathers with a critical eye.

He hesitated, "You're smaller than I am, a little bit. And I was using these recently." He smiled. "I got new ones for the rescue mission."

"Oh, these'll fit. I was just looking at this seam."

"I meant to fix that. I've got a sewing kit here." He rummaged and came up with pouch.

She held out her hand for it.

He watched her work. She was better at sewing than he was. He dug around to find a tow-bag.

"What's that?"

"We can't swim in our leathers. I'll tow our suits in this."

She hesitated, "Okay. I guess I'd better try this out."

He chuckled, "Yeah. Better find out before we arrive on the shore."

She fingered the belt on her tunic, and then took a deep breath. "Don't get all funny."

He didn't quite know what she meant, but as she started undressing, he felt some tingles. As she shucked it off, he knew exactly what she meant.

Would she say something if he turned his back? He didn't know what to do. He clamped his teeth in his mouth and tried to stay calm.

She slipped into the old ragged leathers and struggled with the fasteners. It was tight around her hips and chest, but she made it fit.

"Can you breathe?" he asked, finally.

She laughed, "It's not that bad." She asked more seriously. "Are you okay? It's you who seems to have trouble breathing."

"I'm fine." He took his new leathers and packed them tightly into the bag. She peeled down and rolled them up for him to add to the bag. It was a struggle to pay attention to the job. But he packed them down, added two breathers, and squeezed the air out of the bag.

"Is it okay to take someone's breather like this?"

He concentrated on the bag, putting his weight on it as he sealed it. "No problem. There aren't enough for everybody. We have to borrow."

He glanced back at her, and then looked away. "I'll get undressed. You can go ahead and get in the water if you want. There's a ladder."

She nodded and hurried out. He undressed and stuffed his clothes on the shelf next to hers. He carried the bag out and jumped into the water.

Even with the dock lighting all the way up, the water there was dark. The bag had enough air that it was handy to grab for flotation.

Sally had the same idea. Her hair was slicked back and water drops glistened on her face. She had an excited smile on her face. "I saw the opening under the water."

"Take a deep breath. You'll have to swim through the tunnel, and once you're on the outside, it's unfiltered air."

She nodded. "I was terrified before the hike with the children. I'd never breathed unfiltered air before then and I was certain it would burn and sear my lungs. But it didn't hurt."

"Did you have any problem healing?"

"No. Not at all. One of the ladies offered to help, but I wanted to do it myself, for the practice. It took a little while, but I'm more confident now."

They sculled across the distance to the far wall as they talked.

"Good. We'll have breathers once we reach shore, but it's a longer swim than you're used to in the baths, and the sea has waves. If you have any trouble, grab onto the bag."

"Got it." She smiled and then began taking deep breaths.

He did the same and when she ducked under the water, he followed, struggling to drag the bag behind him. It was a reach to grab the cornerstone at the top of the tunnel while holding onto the bag's tow line, but he'd done it many times before. Once he had a grip on the stone, he pulled the bag underwater and pushed it ahead of him through the tunnel. A flash of kicking legs ahead of him told him she was having no trouble.

By the end of the tunnel, his lungs were heaving, demanding more air. He pushed the bag free and surfaced.

Sally was coughing and sneezing, and then the next wave pushed her under.

Mountain Climb

Joshua grabbed the tow line and swam to her position. Sally's arm flashed in the sun as she snatched at the bag. She gripped it tight and she struggled to keep from being dunked with each crest. As close as they were to the tall face of the cliff, the splash from the rocks kept catching her off-guard.

He kicked, pushing the bag ahead of him, dragging her along. He put more force into his kick, trying to push them away from the rock.

She grabbed at his arm. Once she focused on his face, and matched her breathing to his, she got into the rhythm of matching the waves.

"You okay?" he asked.

"Just caught me off-guard." She coughed again.

He put his arm around her and positioned her to face the shore. "See where the trees are tallest?"

She nodded.

"That's where we come ashore. If we get separated, meet me there."

She looked back over her shoulder at the massive granite cliff that stretched hundreds of feet in both directions and seemed to reach all the way up to the sky. "Where is the tunnel?"

"Don't worry about that now. I can find it. Concentrate on the shore for now."

He let her get used to the rise and fall of the water. "Ready?"

She nodded.

He took the tow line and swam ahead. She followed, holding onto the bag and kicking. With them both working at it, the swim to the beach was easier than he was used to.

When the sand showed up, he stood and helped her walk ashore.

She brushed strings of her hair out of her eye and smiled, "You're not used to swimming with girls, are you?"

He flushed. "No. Nobody my age." He wished she wouldn't look at him, but he couldn't look away from her. His body wasn't under his control and there wasn't any way to hide it.

"Come on, let's get ashore." They pulled the bag up under a tree near the creek. "I recommend you wash the sand off your feet before getting into your leathers."

She nodded, putting on her breather and pulling out the leathers. "How dry should I be?"

He kept his eyes on his own gear. "Your call. They *do* chafe after a while."

Sally held the leathers to her. "I'll dry out a little then. Thanks for not being a jerk."

He sat on a rock, his leathers draped across his lap. "I didn't mean for this to be so awkward. I mean, I've looked at girls with my *sight* before. I didn't know it'd be so different in person."

She smiled, "Don't worry about it. I'll let you know if you get too unpleasant."

He just nodded and shook his hair, and put on his breather.

She shifted, finding a place to sit, keeping herself reasonably covered. "Are you sure there are no Cerik around here?"

"There haven't been any in the area in over ten years. One of the things my father does is scan the area on a regular basis. We need to be alert, though. There could always be Rikna survivors who've gone nomadic."

"Other than me, you mean."

He chuckled, "Yeah." He got to his feet and walked across the rocks to rinse his feet free of the sand before stepping into his leathers. He kept his attention on the surf as Sally followed him and got dressed herself.

Reasonably confident his grin was concealed behind his breather, he admired her curves, even confined in a suit designed for a guy. The tunics everyone wore indoors were rather shapeless.

"Where to now?" she asked.

He pointed. "There's a path that leads up to the top of the mountain. There's a great view, if you're up for it."

"I wouldn't miss it."

He rolled the bag up tightly and hooked it to his belt. "This way."

The mountain was a dome of granite with a corner sliced off by the sea, its lower shoulders covered in trees and eroded gullies. As they walked, Joshua pointed to a huge slab of granite that must have split off the dome in ages past and slid part way down the slope.

She paused, "Can you see them?"

"What?" He stared at the cluttered scenery downslope from them.

She moved closer and pointed. "There's a family of *chitchits*, see?"

"No." He looked for any sign, but she just seemed exasperated that he couldn't see them.

"See the glint off their hides—right there next to the shadow of that boulder."

He saw something, but he'd hardly be able to identify them as *chitchits*, let alone something living. And then, they moved as a group.

He shook his head. "I'd never have noticed them. Sometimes one gets close enough that I can hear it moving in the rocks, but I didn't know they flocked like that."

She nodded. "One of my jobs was caring for some of the ones we had penned up. The Cerik like them, and we sold them to other clans."

She looked around. The higher they got, the more she could see. "I've never seen this much of the world at one time, ever. Daddy took me outside once, to see the *sendt* herds, but it was just for a few minutes, and you saw that pasture—ringed with rock walls. It's nothing like this."

He gestured in the other direction. "Come over this way." He led her to the edge of the cliff, where they could see across the bay, off to the lands beyond.

She gripped his arm, partly out of fright at being close to the edge. "I would love to be able to share this with my friends."

He sighed. "Not our lot in life, I guess. I get to roam the planet, visiting the thoughts of people far from here, but it's always one-way. They never sense me, if I'm doing my job right."

"Your job? Not just casual spying?"

He nodded. "Oh, I started out casually, but lately I've got a schedule and everything. If I weren't here, I'd be checking up on people."

"Like who?"

"Well, Samson, for one."

She looked shocked. "You mean the giant? The one who stood with the Cerik and ordered us to bleed?"

"Yes, I was watching through his thoughts when that happened."

"Well, I was in the last row. I was terrified when I had to cut myself like that. I screamed my lungs out when he ordered us to shout louder. He's a monster."

"I have mixed feelings. He's trying very hard to find places for everyone in Rikna. But it's just an impossible situation. Elehadi is the real monster here."

She grunted. With her face hidden behind her breather and nothing leaking from her *ineda*, he couldn't read her.

He pointed, "The peak isn't far. How are you holding up?"

"I'm not used to walking up a grade like this. My legs are hurting."

"Want to stop?"

She shook her head. "I want to get to the top."

The dirt underfoot had dwindled to bare granite.

They were soon walking on a nearly flat surface, with only a few potholes where rain water had collected with nowhere to run off. Green and brown scum grew in the water that remained.

"I feel very exposed here," she said, almost whispering. "What do we do if a boat flies by?"

"I had that very same thought the first time I came up here. There are split boulders over in that direction," he pointed, "but I wonder if it might be safest just to drop to the ground and hold our arms and legs in odd positions. From a distance, we might not look like anything other than an dark shadow, or a crack in the rocks."

She laughed, "Hey, you try that. I'll hide in the rocks myself."

A minute later, he pointed at an irregularity on the granite slab underfoot. "As near as I can tell, that little bump is the peak of the mountain."

She dashed over and stood there. "Hmm. Doesn't feel any taller."

"It's not really the kind of mountain that has a peak."

She turned in different directions. "Which way is the ocean?"

He pointed. "That's roughly the way we came."

"What's on the backside of the mountain?" She turned to face that way.

"It goes downhill a ways, and then joins the mountain range. Rikna is that way. I don't think this mountain is the same kind as those in the ridge. They're much more broken and jagged."

She nodded, "I'd like to see it, but maybe some other day. I don't think my legs could handle much more. Is it easier going down? I hope."

"It's faster, at least. You can count on your legs hurting for the next day or so. We'd better head back. Someone will wonder where we've been."

They turned back and walked toward the bay. The rock dropped away as the slope got steeper, and they could see more of the water and the distant mountains beyond.

She pointed, "What's that?"

"What?" He looked. It was far too distant for it to be more animals, but there was a flash.

"That's lightning. Lightning in a clear sky. How strange."

And then Joshua saw it. Distant wisps of dust.

"That's a quake. It's not a Large Moon, but I know the signs. Get down on the rock." They both sat down and seconds later, the ground shook.

Sally whispered, "That's a big one."

"Yeah. It must have started near those mountains."

She gave a nervous laugh, "I've never seen a quake. It's not quite as scary when you're out in the clear."

He didn't say anything, staring off at the distance.

She asked, "What is it?"

He pointed at a distant, discolored line in the water. "I'm not sure. I think that's a tsunami—and it's heading our way!"

"Are we safe? I've heard of them, but we're pretty high up."

"Yes, we're safe, but the others .... Come on!"

Tsunami

Joshua started down the path at a nervous speed, the slope giving him long jumps.

"Wait!" called Sally. "Can't we call them? Warn them?"

He stumbled to a halt. He turned and yelled, "No! Don't break *ineda*, even for this."

She caught up with him. "How bad could it be? The tsunami?"

He shook his head. "The last one happened while I was still in the nursery. I don't remember. But people still mention it. The submarine was damaged—out of service for months. The tunnel to the Base doesn't close. It can't close."

The run down the mountainside was hazardous, and Sally spilled out on the rocks. He stopped and helped her up.

She brushed at the dirt. "I'll have bruises, but no cuts. The leather took the worst of it." There were visible scrape marks everywhere.

They slowed down for a little, but when they reached the lower overlook, the bay looked entirely different. The water level had dropped so low that the tunnel was visible. There were rocks that were no longer submerged dotting the area.

Sally looked at the sky, fearing that there could be a Cerik boat in the area.

Joshua shook his head. "We're lucky. No boats. But outside air is getting inside the Base. If they didn't know before, they do now. There are alarms for bad air."

She leaned up against him. "Do you mind if we take it slower. I may have sprained my ankle."

He looked away from the water and checked her. "Okay. I can help." He took the weight off her left leg and they hobbled down the path, checking on the progress of the disaster below.

The water was rising rapidly.

"Good thing I brought the bag with us. The mouth of the creek is flooded, see?" They paused so she could rest.

The water kept rising, knocking over trees, including the ones where they'd rested when they arrived on the beach.

"Will they worry about us?" she asked.

"Probably at first." He tossed pebbles over the edge, watching them bounce down the slope. Some of them reached the water. "But Cyclops will know where we are, and know we're not in danger."

She chuckled. "Your parents can always find you. Neither of mine had very good *sight*. Mom was good at cellular work, healing and stuff, but she could get lost in the corridors. I was better at it than Dad when we went to see the *sendt*. I could tell when one was hurt and he couldn't."

He shrugged. "That's always how it's been. I can sneak away for hikes like this, but they always find me, once they realize I'm gone." He looked down at her ankle. "Should we focus on your injuries?"

She smiled. "Already working on it. I can keep the swelling down, at least, until I have time to concentrate better."

Below, the waters began to recede, and downed trees and other unidentified rubble and brush filled the brown outflow from the creek.

"It's a dangerous world, isn't it?"

He didn't reply at first. He was worried about all the things that could have gone wrong. He just didn't want to say them out loud for fear it would make them real.

"It's no more dangerous than it's always been. Quakes have happened forever."

"Yes, but it's just a rumble and things fall off the shelf. It was safer in the tunnels."

"Not really," he said. "Dallah's Home collapsed one time. Many U'tanse died then. Just because a Home has lasted through thousands of quakes doesn't mean it'll last through the next one."

Sally pulled off her breather, and brushed her hair back. The sunlight and their exertion had left both of them sweaty. She was getting ready to put it back on, when she asked, "What's that?"

Her finger pointed at a large object moving slowly at the edge of the water, well beyond where the creek emptied out.

Joshua stood up. "Oh, no."

"What is it?"

"It's the tub. It's broken free of its mooring."

She put her hand above her eyes, to shade them. "I can't make it out."

"It's a water-boat."

"Like the submarine?"

"No. It's like an empty bowl floating in the wash water. Only it's long and narrow, with a motor to push it through the water."

She struggled to make out details. "It's larger than the submarine?"

"Yes. But it can't go underwater. It's kept at a concealed dock near the factory just up the coastline. The flood must have broken its chains. This is bad."

"Why?"

"It has no power. The boat—the regular flying boat—it needed power quickly when the invasion happened and they drained the tub's power to keep the boat flying."

He closed his eyes and reached out with his *sight*. "Nobody on board. It's adrift."

Sally reached out to hold his hand. "What would happen if a boat saw it?"

He just shook his head. "It would be bad. Any Cerik with any intelligence at all would know it was a threat. He'd search the area, and more than just a simple fly-over. Cerik would wander the hills and discover the dam, the entrance to the factory and the hidden docks. They might even discover the Base. Then it would be all over. They wouldn't stop until they destroyed it, and us."

"What can we do?"

"I don't know. It might be safest to sink it."

They watched helplessly as it drifted closer. It stayed close to shore, and when the bay lowered again, it ran aground.

"I wish I were down there," Joshua said.

"What would you do?"

He shrugged. "Tie a line to it. Something."

"It's too dangerous to swim in that. The water is still swirling with the strange tides."

He could see she was right. There were even rapids near where the submerged rocks had appeared.

Sally spun around, her grip on his hand tightening.

"What's wrong?" he said, but then he heard it too.

There was the distant buzz of a boat in the air.

"Can you see it?" he asked.

"No! Is there a place to hide?" They were on the edge of a bare cliff, one too steep to climb down from, and with hardly any vegetation close by.

Joshua looked around, and then saw the motion in the sky. The boat was behind them, coming down from a higher elevation on the mountain.

Sally tugged at his hand, but he held her still.

"It's okay. It's our boat. Patrick is flying."

She sagged, leaning against him. Weakly, she said, "I was so scared."

He looked at her face and saw tears. "Go ahead and put your breather back on."

She sniffed and nodded.

The boat was heading toward them. Joshua waited until she had her mask fixed, and then helped her toward the flatter spot a few paces away.

The boat kicked up loose dust as it landed. Patrick opened the hatch and yelled, "Get in."

They climbed in and Patrick was lifting off even before they got a grip on the railing.

"Did you see the tub?" asked Joshua.

Patrick nodded, eyes still ahead, paying attention to the viewing panel. "I barely got the boat aloft in time. Lucky I was at the factory when the hidden inlet started draining out. The flood destroyed the camouflaged hut where I was docked. I hid in the trees behind the mountain, scanning the area. I noticed you two—why in the world are you out here anyway? But then I saw the tub."

Joshua ignored the question. "Is there anything we can do to get the boat back under cover?"

Patrick shook his head. "The submarine could tow it, but I don't know where it is. I scanned the Base, and it's not at the dock. The last I time I saw it was yesterday, when Robert took me over to the factory."

Sally said, "It was at the Base two or three hours ago when we swam out."

Patrick looked their way and gave them a grin. Then he got serious again. "Okay, then it was either washed out or someone drove it out. Either way, it's out of communication with us."

Joshua asked, "Can we beam the tub some power? It wouldn't take much to drive it back into the inlet."

"No. The power system on the tub has always been something of a kludge. I can drain the tub's power cell with a beam, but to get power back into it takes a cable connected to a converter installed next to the engine."

"We can't tow it with the boat?"

Patrick shook his head. "The boat was never designed for that. The stability of flight is a Delense automated system. I'd never risk it. Not with our only boat."

They were flying low over the water, approaching the tub. Patrick's view screen showed an external view, and the ocean was full of floating debris.

When they got closer, he put the boat into a hover.

Joshua asked, "Could you hover like this and drop a power cable to the tub? Plug it in for a few minutes to give it enough power?"

Patrick frowned at the image below. "There's water sloshing on the deck. If it's wet down below, the converter might be shorted out. And I don't have the adapter or cable here on the boat. It'd take me an hour to get it and come back."

"Then drop me over the side. I'll climb into the tub and check it out. I'll wave you a thumbs-up if it's okay."

Patrick asked, "What if it's unusable?"

"It's not too far from shore. I can always swim. And we need to be ready to open the hull plugs if a Cerik boat heads in this direction. Better to sink it than have it found. Debbie told me Aaron salvaged it from underwater originally. We could recover it when it was safe."

Patrick frowned. "Not my first choice."

"I wouldn't do it unless you signaled me first."

"Do you know what to look for?"

Joshua smiled, "Yeah, when Robert took me to the factory for the first time, I crawled all over the tub and he showed me how it worked."

Sally said, "It sounds risky."

He looked at her and smiled, "It's riskier to do nothing." He turned to Patrick, "Where is this converter?"

"It's wired next to the motor. You can see the big round plug. If it's dry, it's usable. If it's under water, then we'll have to find another way."

Joshua nodded. "Give me a minute to get these leathers off and then get me close to the tub."

Patrick sighed. "If you get yourself hurt or killed, Debbie will have my head."

Joshua started undressing and chuckled. He was aware Sally was watching, a slight smile on her face, but speed was everything and he didn't have time to say anything else.

He rolled the leathers and stuffed it in his bag with his breather. He didn't bother to push out the air this time.

Patrick nodded and unsealed the hatch. They were only a few feet above the water and the downwash was throwing up heavy mist. Joshua gripped the bag and jumped.

Talespeaker

The water hit him hard and drove sea water up into his nose. The bag was ripped from his grasp. For a few heartbeats, he wasn't sure which way was up.

He broke the surface, but was in spraying mist so heavy he could barely catch his breath. The boat hovered overhead, drifting to the side. The buzz was so high-pitched, it was deafening. He ducked back under the water and swam to the center of the ring, directly underneath the boat. The downwash came from the sides and left a relative calm directly underneath.

The tow bag had been pushed that way as well, and he grabbed it, catching a couple of breaths before swimming toward the tub. Patrick must have located him, because he lifted higher, moving out of the way.

The metal sides of the tub were rocking in the surf. He swam next to it, circling the hull, looking for a way to get up. Near the rear, he found it, a metal ladder welded in place. As he grabbed it, the tossing of the waves lifted the hull and his arm with it, dragging him partly out of the water. It was a struggle, pulling the tow bag along with him.

But soon, he was over the side and collapsed on the decking, water sloshing all around him. The urgency of the moment decided him. He left his bag with the breather and his leathers tied to a railing and scrambled over to the access hatch near the pilot's station. He tried to predict which way the water would slosh in the erratic waves, but then just risked it, moving the latching lever and opening the hatch.

Some water, less than an inch deep at that moment, tried to come in with him, but he ducked inside and closed the hatch above him.

It was lightless inside. There was no need to close his eyes, it wouldn't have made a difference. He concentrated, using his *sight* as his father did, as if there was light all around him.

Water sloshed underfoot, several inches worth, but not high enough to cover any of the machinery. He located the power adapter. He checked it by touch, not trusting his *sight* for this. It was good and dry. Over near the rear of the boat were the two drainage hull plugs, securely fastened shut. Robert had made a strong point that he should never touch those. They were only for draining the water when the hull was pulled ashore.

But the situation was good. He pushed the overhead hatch back open, getting a mouthful of water. Climbing out and re-sealing the hatch, he waved thumbs-up to the boat overhead. The boat tilted slightly to one side and buzzed away into the distance.

Joshua rescued his tow bag and started suiting up.

. . .

Finding the ports to drain the water off the deck took little time, and other than worry about the groaning noise when the metal hull bumped up against an underwater rock, he had nothing to do.

Rather than worry about the tub stranding itself permanently on the rocks, he leaned against the side wall and closed his eyes.

His *sight* told him that the Base was a maze of confusion. Nearly the whole population was clustered on the second level, with a few walking around on the muddy dock level. The nursery was safe, but as the only place where unblocked minds were casting their thoughts broad and wide, it was like a red hotspot on a empty pan left on a hot stove.

Joshua could feel every one of their minds—panicked because of the quake and the nervous adults.

He should have been there, holding the little ones on his lap, telling stories about Quaky the Clumsy Troll falling over his own feet and shaking the mountain, just like his mother had told them to him.

But that was just one more thing he was powerless to affect. Until he was there in person, others would have to do the job.

He shifted his attention to his other job, monitoring the giant.

. . .

Samson sat in the boat, holding the piece of paper Omelia had given him. George was a good friend, even if he never quite understood the little tenner. That he was finally considering his suggestion just showed how hopeless his task to save the Rikna was. The paper was stained and wrinkled from two days in his pocket.

But Rikna Home was falling apart as he watched. Every visit, the feeling of fear and panic was growing. He had thirty workers sold and gone, with a half-dozen still in negotiation. There had been no large purchases, none more than four workers at a time. His next push was to try to sell the idea that here were trained *chitchit* farmers, and include some of the *chitchits* along with the sale. Certainly, Elehadi had no need for the animals and they were doomed to be either turned loose or die of suffocation with their handlers when the air filtration was turned off.

He clamped his eyes shut and tried to shake off the feel of the place. The quake fears had been the last straw. There had been a minor quake, but panic erupted from the cuties—far out of proportion to the severity of the shaking. It was just a sign of how bad things were for those who had no hope.

...

Joshua frowned. He detached and started probing the Rikna Home.

It was every bit as bad as Samson had been thinking. He zeroed in on the quake fears and found the three little girls holding each other and crying. He reached into their thoughts and found all four of them, Jinger included, fearful of the strange shaking walls.

He broke free, shocked that the events at the Base had so infected the girls at Rikna. It made it even more important that he spend some thought finding ways to break Jinger out of her isolation. No wonder she ignored what was happening around her. She was clinging to her old friends back at Rikna so firmly that they were more important, more real to her than Sally or the others in the nursery with her.

But even those at Rikna who were ignoring the quake fears had nothing to bring their spirits up. The clock was ticking down, and only a few had managed to escape to new Homes. They could feel Elehadi's claws coming to take their air away from them.

...

It was one day before the New Moon, one day earlier than he'd been ordered to return to the Perch. Samson knew it was a risk. He entered the area and rattled the taps on his shoes.

Elehadi ignored him for several minutes. Samson had either the choice of backing out of his presence and suffering the ridicule that would come, or wait out his Name's patience.

<U'tanse, why are you here?> The growling voice was low, unconcerned.

Samson had practiced his request. <I seek the wisdom of the Cerik ancients to help with my task.>

There was another delay as Elehadi considered the odd request. Then he said, <Continue.>

<Never before has a Home of the U'tanse been taken apart and sold. I am a warrior and the task strains my strength. I wish to hear the tales and gain the wisdom to finish the task you have given me.>

<So, you have heard of Tenthonad's Talespeaker?>

<In my ignorance, I have not.>

Elehadi shifted on his Perch. He shouted to the air, <Second, bring me my Talespeaker!>

Second was nowhere in sight, but if he wasn't in shouting range, then there was certain to be a *rettik* nearby who would race to pass the message. Samson had heard of speaking devices, and had wondered if Elehadi had such, but the idea had been George's, not his, and he hadn't considered all the ramifications.

The Name *pree'd*, filling the air with the rumble of his satisfaction. <Khok, the Name of the Tenthonad clan had the Talespeaker that Tenthonad, the original Name of that clan, used when he captured the U'tanse planet and brought your kind back to serve him so many generations ago. Khok had brought it with him to the Faces several times, bragging of his lineage.>

Second arrived, a huge beast of a Cerik, perhaps a match for Elehadi in strength, but dimmer of mind and lacking the ambition to be any threat to the Name.

<For your Name.> He bellowed out the greeting and held the device in his claw. There were loops on either end of the flat device, about the size of Samson's head, making it easy for a Cerik to handle.

Elehadi took it and set it down on the *hurru* beside him. He waved a claw, skipping through a babble of introductions until he found the one he wanted.

<You, U'tanse, this is the one which inspired Tenthonad to give your kind a place as our slaves.>

He sliced the air with his third claw and a disembodied voice began:

<*Great floods covered the land of Sessene after the great mountains to the north awoke from their long dan. Ghader struggled to find prey for his clan, as prey and Hunter alike were drowned or caught in the new swamps. He said to himself, I will stalk the nests of the Builders, for they have prospered in this flood.*>

Elehadi and the others were silent as the Tale of Ghader and the Builders completed, telling of the first of the Delense, the Builders, taking a slave position under the protection of Ghader.

Elehadi gestured again and the device went silent.

<At the first Face after I took my Name, I told of my plans to take Kakil into space and no longer have to trade with Tenthonad for energy for my boats. Khok challenged at my feast, ridiculing my lack of wisdom, claiming I could never learn the skills necessary to take energy from the sky.> He gave a low *ruff.*

Moving again on his Perch, excited by the memory, he continued. <I had seen the Talespeaker and I told Khok that, perhaps, I lacked the wisdom of the ancients. I said that if he gave me the Talespeaker, so that I could gain this wisdom, I would delay my plans for finding my energy from the sky and continue to trade with him. Such was the force of my argument, that he agreed to let me use the Talespeaker and return it to him at the next Face.>

The rumble of satisfaction from his chest was loud enough to rattle pebbles on the floor. <When Khok returned from the Face, his Second used the disgraceful trade of Tenthonad's prize as the reason for his challenge and Khok was no more.>

Elehadi waved his claws through the air. <With no Khok at the next face, the Talespeaker became mine.>

He growled at the U'tanse. <This is a prize of my victory, and you wish me to hand it to you? Perhaps you expect my Second to relieve you of the duty to return it?>

Samson took a slight step back at the force of the Name's threat.

He rattled his taps again. <I wish only to hear the wisdom of the ancients. I have no desire for Elehadi's prize. Should I hold it, I would take great care to preserve it undamaged and return it quickly.>

Out of the corner of his eye, Samson could see Second watching him, wiggling his lower jaw from side to side in ridicule. Samson knew his place, and if a little Cerik laughter was all he had to suffer, it was a price he was willing to pay.

Elehadi gestured with his claw, <Take it, and learn wisdom. I will tell you the day to return it.>

Samson moved cautiously forward, well within the reach of the large, sharp claws. He took the Talespeaker in both hands and held it carefully.

So close, the blood-scented breath of his Name washed over him, Elehadi said softly, <Begin now the preparations to remove the power cell of the Rikna Home. I will tell you within a few days when my patience has come to an end and you will give the order to shut it down.>

Samson backed away, bowing low. <For your Name.>

Tow Back

Joshua was shaking from the shared fear that Samson had felt. Sally's voice startled him.

"Joshua! Are you there?"

He got to his feet, scanning the sky.

But she was at water-level, standing in the open hatchway of the submarine.

He felt a wave of relief at seeing the machine.

Sally was holding a line. "Can you catch this?"

He reached out and she tossed it. The first try failed. She pulled it back, took a smaller loop of the braided chain and tried again. He snagged it.

"Good throw!" he yelled, dragging it behind him as he walked to the front of the tub. There was an eyelet welded in place there. He tied the line as well as he could.

The submarine moved a couple of lengths away and then Robert climbed out of the hatch. He waved, then took the line and crawled across the outer hull of the craft to tie off his end of the line at the rear.

Sally talked to Robert once he re-entered the hatch. Joshua could only see their gestures. Robert shrugged and Sally nodded, taking off her breather. Robert wrapped it for her in a little bag, and then she climbed out, slipping down into the water and swimming across to the tub.

Joshua helped her up. She winced when she got her feet under her, taking the weight off her sprain.

Once she put her breather back on, her leathers drenched and squishy on the deck, she said, "Patrick saw the submarine surface while we were on the way back to the factory. He dropped me off and we decided to tow you back."

"Good. I was a bit worried about that idea of dangling a charging cable from the boat."

"Wasn't that your idea?"

"Yes. So? I still thought it was crazy."

The tub shook as the submarine took up the slack and they began moving through the water.

Joshua stared off at the shoreline. The colors were turning deeper as the sun approached the horizon. They had been out a lot longer than he had planned.

She was looking at him. "Problem?"

"The sun will be down shortly and you're soaked. It'll get cold pretty soon. Do you want to try to dry out your leathers while you still have the chance?"

He could see the smile even beneath the breather. "I've already had two guys make knowing grins at me when they found out we swam ashore together. Since people back at the Base are probably watching this rescue of the tub right now with their *sight*, I'd rather not give anyone else the idea that we came out here to get naked together. I'll suffer the wet."

"Oh. I didn't think of that. I'll explain it all when we get back."

She rolled her eyes. "Yes, sure—and you'll drop your *ineda* to prove you aren't lying?"

He frowned. "Sorry."

She chuckled. "Don't worry. I have more to worry about than what people think."

He nodded. "That reminds me. The children were frightened by the quake, and Jinger fed that fear back to her friends in Rikna. They felt the quake, but it was mild there. They didn't understand why those girls were so bothered by it."

Sally sighed. "We'll have to do something. If she doesn't make new friends here, it'll be bad for her. I'll ask Comfort for ideas. She seems to have a good connection with the kids."

She limped over to the railing and took a look at the waves. "The tsumani is all over isn't it?"

"I guess. There'll still be trees and things in the water for a while."

She pointed. "What's that?"

He stared, then used his clairvoyance. He shook his head with a sad laugh. "That's what's left of the hut that they used to hide the boat. They'll have to make a new one, I guess."

She wrapped her arms around herself. "It *is* getting chilly." She looked at him, "Too late to do anything about it, so don't get your hopes up."

He waved over to the steps that led up to the piloting station. "Come on, let's get out of the wind, at least." She didn't object to his help walking across the shifting deck, or the idea of cuddling together on the steps, just to stay warm.

. . .

The arrival at the factory dock was totally in the dark, with no moon. Joshua sat at the piloting station, steering the powerless tub more by *sight* than eyesight as they moved in under the overhanging cliff. There was a crunch as the hull scraped up against the dock and three men were waiting to grab lines and secure the tub in place.

They transferred over to the submarine and left the tub to the factory workers. The homecoming at the Base dock was met with cheers, but those were for the safe return of the submarine, not for them.

Robert had given his part of the tale to Sally and Joshua on the ride back.

Debbie had been struggling to find the two missing youngsters with her *sight* when, in a flash, she sensed the coming tsunami.

"She yelled out the order to get the submarine into deep water immediately, and I know that voice of hers. I didn't even ask the reason. But that ride out into the bay happened just as the water was leaving and it was frightening. All my memorized travel lanes through the rocks were all off and I had a scrape or two before I got to deeper water. I just decided to hide it out there for a while. When the ocean decides to change the rules on you, it's better to be far from shore."

They rotated the mechanical latch and opened the hatch.

Debbie was waiting at the dock, arms crossed. She waited until both of them got to the deck before she said anything.

"We found your clothes in the storage room and sent them to the laundry. Everything on this level has to be washed. Joshua, go to your room and get dressed in grubs, you'll be working here washing down all the rooms, and once you're done there, report to the laundry. We've got a week's worth of extra work there."

She turned to Sally. "I've put replacement clothes for you in the room next to the nursery. You're needed there."

Joshua glanced down at Sally's ankle, preparing to let his mother know that she needed help, but Sally gave him a solemn, single shake of her head. Trying not to show her limp, she headed for the spiral.

"Mom...."

She said, firmly, "You have work to do. Go get changed."

He hesitated a second, then walked away, veering at the last minute over to where Cyclops was talking with Terry, the electrician, about wet cables.

Debbie shouldn't have acted so angry. He'd expected to be in trouble for taking Sally for a hike outside—he'd always gotten a lecture when he escaped. But this was wrong. He'd done the right thing, showing Sally what it was to be a free U'tanse, giving her a stronger motive to protect her thoughts and protect the Base.

And they'd helped recover the tub, and that was important. Didn't she know that?

Sally needed help getting healed, not a scolding.

"Joshua, do you have something to say?" Cyclops asked.

"Samson has gotten an extension of the deadline." He gave a summary of the meeting with Elehadi.

Cyclops rubbed his forehead. He sighed, "A few more days. Well, any extension is welcome. And you say he has a Talespeaker?"

"Yes. He'll have to give it back soon, but the idea is to get some idea on how to sell more U'tanse."

"Advice from the Cerik." He shook his head. "You'll need to follow that as well. The more Cerik history we can document, the better."

"Debbie told me to mop floors and do laundry."

His father nodded. "If you don't know how to mop and monitor at the same time, then this is a good time to learn. We all have to double up our work for now."

Joshua sighed. "I know." He headed for the spiral.

Mop Up

There was more work than mopping. The water had risen to ceiling height on the first level. Every storage container, every drawer, and every closet was inundated with seawater. A good number of the containers that had sealed lids floated out with the receding flood, but their recovery wasn't his job.

The floors were strewn with dislodged supplies, grit, shells, and rubbery plants that he'd never seen before. When he opened one drawer, he found a large *jenna*. He walked the fish, holding it by the tail, out to the water.

"Hey, Hoop, do we salvage these?"

He was a muscular worker who Joshua had never seen anywhere but the docks, unloading shipments brought by the submarine. But today Hoop seemed to be in charge of the cleanup.

He shook his head. "Nice size, but no. It could as easily have been killed by our chemicals as by being washed up in the flood. We can't trust any of these for food. But don't toss it into the water. There's a crate over there that I'm going to dispose of far out into the bay. We don't want the water inside the Base to be full of rotting fish."

He looked up at the high-water mark. "I'd thought we'd never have a flood this bad."

"Why?" Joshua moved over to the crate and tossed the fish in with all the other sea life that had been stranded.

Hoop sighed, "I thought the air pressure inside the Base would keep the water from rising so much. But this tide was bigger than most. It compressed the air. The pressure inside popped the safety valves in the air intakes. It'll be days before the air is totally clean again."

Joshua went back to the room he was cleaning. Everything salvageable was stacked out on the dock. The containers were rinsed with fresh water, and only then could he start with the mopping. Above the noise of dozens of other workers doing the same task in other places was the whistle of the air system working at peak velocity, trying to purge the contaminated air. The gardens were their first priority. People could heal from air burns. The crops had their own sensitivity to the air, and Debbie was making plans for what to do if they had extensive crop failure.

But that wasn't his problem. He mopped, and slipped back into Samson's thoughts.

. . .

George hovered over the Talespeaker. "There appears to be an index of the tales when you move your hand over this side."

Samson watched. "So you can listen to them?"

"Oh yes! I'll start now, and transcribe them all. Do you know what this means?"

"What?"

George was wide-eyed and breathing hard. "It means that at one time, the Cerik must have had a *tetka* of storytellers. This is their oral history, and since they don't have a written language, their whole culture has to be told from one person to the next. I've never heard of them, but they have to exist."

Samson nodded, "Sure. But it's not a *tetka* exactly. The warriors who guard the breeding pits tell the stories to the cubs. By the time the male cubs get big enough to escape the pit, they've heard a lot of the tales. At least that's what I've been told."

"So adults don't listen to the tales?"

"Obviously some do, but none of the warriors I usually work with bother with it."

George nodded. "The Book tells of Tenthonad, who captured Mother and Father, regularly listening to the tales. So this is the very device he used?"

Samson nodded, "And it's my life if anything happens to it. Not a scratch, understand?"

George touched it gently. "I wouldn't dare."

"So, you'll listen to them all?"

"That's the idea."

Samson lowered his voice, "If you hear anything to help me place more of the Rikna U'tanse in other Homes, contact me immediately."

George nodded, "I understand."

He waved his hand.

<*A Hunter and a Builder met in the forest as cubs and resolved to treat each other as brothers. For a season, they worked together, the Builder helped to trap Runners with his clever snares. The Hunter killed a Treeclimber pack that was preying on the Builder as he worked on the river. One day while they sat together at meat, they resolved to exchange their food. The Builder drank blood and chewed at flesh with his dull flat teeth. The Hunter labored to chew and swallow tree bark. For three days they struggled to eat each other's food, until they became weak. We must go back to our natural ways, said the Builder. The Hunter agreed, Yes, we must. And he killed and ate the Builder.*>

Joshua heard the echo of the Cerik words, and the meaning from Samson's thoughts. He understood a word or two, but what was most interesting was Samson's reaction to the tale, agreeing with the sentiment as the Cerik ate his friend.

He could also see George's face as he winced at the end of the tale. George and Samson were two friends, too, and their view of the world had to be so different.

George said, "I'll review the index and start transcribing. This will be so valuable."

"Let's hope it saves some lives."

. . .

Cleaning and mopping progressed to restocking the shelves and an inventory of the damage. Joshua was sent off to laundry duty, and the endless task of rinse and soap and beating the cloth on the ruffleboard gave him plenty of opportunity to check out the Rikna Home.

People were checking each news of a sale with anticipation, hope, and despair. Even the people who were told to report to the main entrance with their bag of belongings and wait for a transport boat to arrive had to face friends and family who were being left behind to die. They didn't even have the option to refuse. A leatherworker who tried to stay with his family was met by the elders and convinced that missing his boat could trigger the anger of Elehadi and cause the instant slaughter of them all.

After a dreamless night, collapsed from exhaustion, Joshua was put on meal service, wheeling carts around the Base. He took the opportunity to update Cyclops on his spying, and then arrived at the nursery with trays of sweet-meal and a few pastries for the cuties and workers.

Sally smiled, but he could see she was exhausted.

"I hope you got some sleep," she said, "because I didn't."

He chose the best of the pastries and handed it to her. "Quake nerves?"

She shrugged, picking the pastry apart layer by layer and enjoying each piece. "It was different things. Everyone is a little nervous, probably from the quake, maybe from ... other things." She looked around, for watching eyes.

She whispered, "Jinger is having real trouble. I think it's from her friends. But she's not the only one. Your sister is having nightmares again. She won't talk about them to me, but Ash said something about knives."

"I'll see if she will talk to me."

Sally nodded. "She's worried about you, too."

The more Sally talked, the more depressed she seemed. Joshua asked, "How are you doing? Are you healed?"

She shrugged it off. "Oh, the scrapes and such are nothing. I'm just worried about my family." She lowered her voice, "Isn't today the New Moon? It's so hard to read what's going on back at Rikna."

He whispered back. "The deadline was extended. I'll tell you more when we can get a moment alone."

She smiled and it twisted into a grin. "If they *let* us alone again. I've been asked a few leading questions about what we were up to outside."

He sighed, "Speaking of which, I can't stay here any longer. I have a heavy work schedule."

She looked at his red hands. "What happened? Is that a skin burn?"

He laughed. "No, that's from too much soapy water. It leaches all the oils out of the skin and causes cracks. It's an easy heal. I just haven't had time to work on it."

She nodded as she went back to the others. "Don't forget Veronica."

He located his sister. "How are you doing, kid?"

She gave him a hug. "Quaky fell down and threw a tantrum." She grinned, then it gave way to a frown. "Are you okay? No burns?"

"No, I'm fine, really. Mom just has me on a heavy work schedule."

She leaned closer, "Were you kissing Sally?"

He gave her a squeeze. "Not yet. I'll let you know."

She punched him. "Be careful. I'm worried about her, too."

He was curious, but she wouldn't say anything more. And it was time to leave. Today would be very busy.

Distance

After two days working on his feet, it was luxury to sit in the maproom and report.

Joshua said, "George is working long hours, and it appears he has a locked room. I can't get much detail, but I see him playing a Cerik tale and writing it down as it happens. His *ineda* is solid, so I don't get any information about the tales. Every now and then, he'll pull out a second paper and write slowly, then put it away before he starts the next tale. It's puzzling, but with no telepathy and with no ability to hear what's being said or what's being written, that's all I know."

Cyclops asked, "Can you tell me where this locked room is? When I get a spare moment, I'll take a peek myself and see if I can read anything."

Joshua told him the location, deep in the Kakil Home, near the machine shop.

"Samson is having a little luck with his sale of small-animal specialists. They won't be picked up for a few days, because he has arranged to sell all of them at the same time, with the boats to pick them up arriving on a schedule so only one outside clan is in Rikna territory at any one time."

"This is the sale where he's including animals along with their handlers?"

"Correct. With the main supplier of *chitchits* going off the market, it's an opportunity for other clans to get into that business."

Cyclops nodded, frowning. "I suppose this is a good thing. Perhaps I'm just getting too old. I can remember when skilled U'tanse were always in demand—not products that need added incentives."

When Joshua said nothing, he asked, "Is there anything more?"

"Just more depression at the Rikna Home, some of which is bleeding back into our nursery. You already know that."

Cyclops nodded. "One thing."

"Yes?"

"You need to talk to your mother. She's upset and she won't come to you."

Joshua blinked. "Okay. I didn't realize." Usually when he was in trouble, it came and went away in a few hours, once they gave him his penalty chore.

Cyclops waved him away.

. . .

Joshua located his mother in the garden and headed in that direction, using the walking time to check on all the people he was monitoring.

He was surprised to see George walking the corridors as well. He paused in the spiral and watched what was happening in Kakil.

George was in the residential area, and located Omelia's cell.

Joshua tapped into her thoughts.

"Hello, George, what brings you here?"

She instinctively checked on Samson, but he was away at a meeting with *ralak*.

George pulled out a piece of paper. "Samson wanted me to search for information in the Cerik tales. I found something he might need. I suspect you could get that information to him quicker than I could."

She reached for the document. She started reading the text, then nodded to George. "Thank you, I'll get it to him as quickly as I can."

He turned and walked away.

She checked on Samson, and realized she'd have to wait a little bit. He was in some kind of ritualistic game with the *ralak*, where he had to convince the messengers that he was worthy enough for them to talk to him. Apparently, he had to do this every time. She decided to wait a little longer before attracting his attention.

. . .

He'd never really been afraid of his mother, but Joshua knew from long experience that Debbie hated being interrupted when she was in the middle of a demanding task. So, when he walked into the garden and saw her examining the leaves on palace bushes, he waited a moment. She appeared to be checking for dead ones, plucking the lengthy succulent strands and adding them to a mulch bag. He knew what had happened. Even though the palace bushes were native to Ko, they'd been selectively bred for many generations to prefer the filtered air inside the Base. He looked at the bush closest to him and saw the discoloration on nearly a third of the leaves. He got a bag for himself and started culling the leaves that needed it. If they were pounded to paste quickly enough, they'd still be good to feed the creepers. In turn, the creepers were scraped from the paste bin and when ground with the hard bits washed away, made a tasty protein bar.

Debbie saw him work and only after he'd been working beside her for several minutes she said, "Sally is new here."

He kept working. He nodded. He knew this.

She sighed, "She was also pulled out of her life there at Rikna before she'd completed her woman's training."

"I know." It was easier to keep hunting for discolored leaves than it was to meet her eyes.

She ripped a leaf from her bush with unnecessary roughness. "I never thought you'd take her swimming."

"We weren't doing anything… together, like that. It was just a swim across the bay, so we could hike up the mountain." He sighed, "I wanted to show her the view from up there."

"And you never touched her? Never felt the urge to do more?"

He remembered vividly the touch of her skin when he helped her in the water and the strong urges that did things to his body until they had finally dressed on shore. "Nothing happened."

Debbie plucked a leaf. "I know you didn't have sex. There are changes that happen in a woman's body, and I didn't see them when I scanned her. But the risk was too great to take."

He grumbled, "I don't know why you're so upset! She even reminded me she wasn't trained before we started. I would never have tried anything," his voice lowered into a sigh, "even if I knew how."

She stopped what she was doing, and he saw she had her eyes closed for a moment. Then she said, "It's my fault. You grew up alone, with no one your age. Everyone else grew up in a Home with all this kind of thing going on all the time to the new adults just a year or more older than you were. You never saw how normal guys turn into idiots around girls."

She looked him in the eyes, "If you go swimming with a girl, part of your brain turns off. You can count on it. When you touch a girl, part of her brain turns off, too. Two intelligent and responsible young people will turn into instinct-driven animals if they're alone and the conditions are right.

"If you had grown up in a Home, you'd know all this stuff. You'd have seen it happen. You'd have some warning that you'd need to keep a certain distance."

She ripped out some more leaves. "It's so much worse that Sally isn't trained. Mistakes can happen. We're programmed to make mistakes. If we all waited until the wise and responsible time to have children, then we'd all grow old and alone."

She put her hand on his shoulder. "We waited too long to have you and Veronica. The conditions weren't right. We thought we had to be responsible, and I was a particularly stubborn girl, wanting to find my own way in the world. I'm sorry. Maybe it would be better if you had grown up with an older brother and sister."

"Sally's condition is dangerous. She's physically mature enough to conceive a child, a *random*, but she lacks the training necessary to make a U'tanse. In Rikna, she was getting that training and protected by her friends and things like fear of gossip from getting too close to some guy in the baths. The right time was coming for her, when she was trained and the women of her Home permitted her to have a child.

"But then we disrupted all that when we rescued her. She has no girl friends at her side to protect her and no women's council to guide her steps. We're starting, but we weren't ready for her. We thought we had years yet to get ready for Veronica."

Joshua kept his mouth shut, listening. Sally had said Comfort had taken her to the third-level bath. Was that part of this? To keep her safe from guys until she was ready.

He wasn't really sure of this idea that guys turned into mindless beasts around girls. He didn't feel mindless around Sally. But it worried his mother.

"Running all these other errands won't keep me out of the nursery, you know. I'm needed there. Veronica needs me, and Sally needs to talk to me about Jinger's problems."

Debbie brushed through the leaves and then moved over to the next bush. "I'm not trying to keep you two apart. I just need you to respect a certain... distance from her."

Joshua didn't know what to say. He had no intention of staying away from Sally.

"I understand."

She nodded. "Okay, I'm sure you have other tasks. You don't need to help me with the trimming. I'll be at this all day."

He suddenly remembered Samson and the note from George. "Yes. I guess I do."

She smiled, "But I'm glad we talked."

He nodded. "Me, too."

Rule of Dalna

Samson struggled to pay attention to the *ralak*-to-Sanassan. The message from George, as relayed by Omelia, was taking him a moment to digest.

It was a welcome excuse to double the U'tanse sent off to new Homes, but would Elehadi approve? He stretched out his *sight* in an effort to locate the Name, but he wasn't at the Perch. On a hunch, he checked the private hunting meadow where Elehadi and Stakka spent their secret meetings, and there they were, deep in conversation. There was no chance he'd be able to get the Name's approval in time to inform the *ralak*.

He listened again to the messenger, detailing the negotiation with the clan to the north about taking on more of the herders.

But maybe, Samson said to himself, *I've already received Elehadi's approval.* He toyed with the idea. Elehadi had approved the idea of looking to the wisdom of the ancients for ways to sell more Rikna U'tanse. The Tale of Dalna and Builder was from the Talespeaker of Tenthonad. It had to be Cerik wisdom, straight from the ancients.

I could be punished for overreaching. But I could also be punished for failing at my task.

Samson gestured with his gauntlet, interrupting the *ralak*. He spoke, <Sales of the U'tanse will be conducted as the sale of Dalna.>

The *ralak* raised his shoulders, <What is this?>

<You know the tale. Goladen conquered the clan of Huuk in the old times. The lesser name Dalna, of the herder dance, was being sold as a slave to Ruthenah, and risked his eyes to demand that a Builder accompany him.

161

Goladen and the Name of Ruthenah agreed that a slave of lesser or no value could be considered part of the sale of the more-valued slave.>

When Samson saw that the *ralak* had actually heard the tale before, he continued, more confidently. <Elehadi has approved that sales of the Rikna U'tanse can be treated the same. A U'tanse sold may take another with him to his new master.>

The *ralak* grumbled, <A change in terms might turn Sanassan's head away.>

Samson pushed, <It is also giving them two U'tanse for the price of one. These are the terms.>

There was more argument, but the *ralak* never challenged Samson's authority to establish the new rule. It would likely take another day to get the message out to all the clans, but if it saved more lives, he was happy to take the risk.

Joshua ran up the spiral to get the news to Cyclops. But by the time he'd reached the maproom, the telepathic gossip had already started to spread across the planet. Samson's estimate of a day to notify the other clans was pessimistic. As long as he kept his mind open, anything Samson thought was likely to be passed on quickly.

...

Joshua's new job schedule didn't evaporate after he talked to Debbie. He was still on duty to deliver food, work laundry shifts, and attend map-room meetings. He arranged to spend time in the nursery during afternoon meals.

Sally appeared happier. She, Veronica and Ash joined him as they ate.

"Hey, Very, how are you getting along with your new friends?"

She looked over at where the others were sitting, "Oh, they're okay. I like Sally."

Sally mumbled, "Thanks."

"Weelie is okay, as long as she and Ash stop talking on and on and on about colors, and drawing, and stuff."

Ash shrugged, "Sorry, it's just you were never interested."

Very dismissed the others. "And I like Bruce and Green. I like all the babies."

162

Ash said, "It's made the maze more fun. It was getting so I could always guess where Very was going to hide. These new cuties—I never know what to expect from them."

Veronica leaned close and whispered, "Did Debbie get mad at you for kissing Sally?"

He frowned, "What are you talking about? I ... I didn't kiss her."

Sally was watching, and smiled.

His sister said, "Ash said he saw you and Mom arguing in the garden."

He looked at Ash, "Did you sneak out again?"

Ash looked innocent, "No! Honest I didn't. I just sort of *saw* you. Your were frowning and picking leaves. You looked like you were in trouble."

Joshua sighed. "Ash, you have to keep anything you see like that a secret. Don't even tell Very."

His sister griped, "That's no fun—secrets all the time!"

Ash nodded, solemnly. "That might be hard. Very is ... Very."

When it was time to collect the dishes, Sally helped him. When they had a moment alone in the corridor outside the nursery, Joshua shook his head.

"If Ash is getting a handle on his clairvoyance, then it won't do any good to hide the lock settings behind my hand, he'll just *see* them. That might have been how he escaped the first time."

Sally nodded, "Half the cuties in here are too old to be kept restrained in a few rooms like this. Back Home, they'd be roaming the halls and getting into trouble."

"Both Ash and Veronica are close to being let loose. I was, by their age. It's all about their *ineda*. I don't know how experienced the others are."

"We need to give them better training—mentors who come in on a regular basis."

He agreed. "Yes, and how about you? Are you getting your training as they promised?"

She nodded. "It's going slow, but we're working on it. By the way, did your mother get mad at you?"

He nodded. "Just as Ash described. We had a talk. I'm supposed to keep my distance."

She sneered. "Like this? Or just when we're naked?"

He shook his head. "I'm not supposed to think about things like that. But anyway, I insisted I'd still be coming by the nursery. This has been my job so long I can't give up taking care of the little ones.

"And, by the way, how about Jinger? Is she doing better?"

"Not really. In her mind, she's still back at Rikna, and barely pays attention to what's going on here."

He sighed, "I was hoping that with Samson's new rule, things would get better."

Sally smiled, "For some of us. My parents are starting to have some hope. If Dad gets an offer, he'll take Mom along. And there is already some interest in Jack on his own. With luck, my family might just make it out.

"But for some of the others, the new rule is just making it harder. What if a man gets an offer and he has to choose between his wife and his children? He can only bring one other."

Joshua nodded, "Yeah, that's a tough call."

Sally looked off at the wall. "You know, I've had a thought."

"What's that?"

"Jinger. You know she has a little experience with *chitchits*? The little ones sometimes wander over to the animal pens and play with the gentler ones. What do you think about the idea of going back to the mountain and catching a *chitchit* for Jinger to take care of? That would force her attention back to this place."

Joshua thought about it. "How do you catch a *chitchit*?"

She waved her hand, "Oh, it's simple. I can make a trap. I've done it before. And we know where they live."

He looked at her sternly, "We can't swim."

She grinned, "I know. How hard is it to use the submarine?"

"I'll ask. I like the idea. I'll just have to see if they'll permit it."

...

Cyclops was updating some of the monitors when Joshua entered the maproom and found a chair.

"Samson shook up a lot of people by changing the rules of the sales. The rule of Dalna hadn't been used in a long time. Some of the Cerik had forgotten the times when Cerik enslaved other Cerik, and the whole idea of applying a rule meant for Cerik to a U'tanse was disturbing.

"And Joshua reported that Samson took this step without prior approval from Elehadi, and it certainly took the Name by surprise. He and his telepath were on their way back from the private hunting ground when Stakka yelled at him, they turned around and went back to confer privately. After thirty minutes or so, they appeared again and when questioned at the Perch, Elehadi shrugged off Samson's action as if it was of no importance. Samson had asked for the wisdom of the ancients and he had permitted it."

Hugo said, "This can't be popular. Cerik has effectively enslaved the workers of Runa and Rikna, and now, he's saying that Cerik slaves and U'tanse slaves are the same in his mind."

Patrick asked, "Is that a good thing, or bad, for us?"

Cyclops said, "Short term, it'll depend on whether more lives are saved or not. Long term, it's beyond me. I suspect it's beyond Elehadi as well. He's either the smartest Cerik in many generations, or he's just been lucky. I wish I could penetrate those private conferences between those two. If there is a long term plan, Elehadi and Stakka have to discuss it then."

Debbie said, "The Name of Lakka and his Second are discussing whether to increase their order of small animal experts from Rikna. That Name is actually aware that U'tanse females are skilled at certain tasks. The rule of Dalna makes this a bargain for them."

Others around the circle reported what their targets were thinking. Distant clans were more favorable to the change than those within range of Elehadi's calculating eyes.

Then it was Joshua's turn.

"Samson feels trapped. He expects to be killed by Elehadi for failing in his task. That's the reason he made the Dalna decision—he didn't have anything to lose.

"I've also been checking out the response among the Rikna U'tanse. It's a very mixed blessing. Some families are seeing hope that they can survive, and that makes it even harder to bear for others who see no hope."

As the person to his right began to report, Joshua sensed tension from the distant giant, and ducked out into the hall. People looked at him as he exited, but no one said anything.

Planning the Shutdown

Samson was arriving back at Rikna, looking out the pilot's viewport as they flew into the area. The pilot was arguing with his other passenger, a different pilot being landed at the crash site where Rikna's Name had landed.

<I told him that I won't be able to fly a damaged boat. Doesn't Elehadi have enough boats as it is? So he had two of them damaged in the crash, he gained seven when he took Rikna's eyes.>

The pilot who was handling the landing asked, <What's wrong with the boat?>

<How should I know? The Delense voice just says it's unable to take off. Who am I to argue with the dead?>

<But the Name says try again.>

He grumbled, <So I try again. But come back for me shortly when this junk fails to respond.>

Samson looked over at the three damaged boats. One had its hull ripped open on the side. Another had its hatchway dangling by a scrap of metal, and the third, probably the one the Name rode in on, had the whole front end of the ship crumpled by repeated impacts. None of them looked usable to him, but he was hardly an expert. No one was asking his opinion, so he didn't bother to speak.

But it reminded him that he had another, very difficult task to complete.

After dropping off the spare pilot among the wrecked boats, Samson was landed at Rikna Home.

Samson walked out without a word to the pilot. They'd had their snarls before and had reached a silent truce. Neither was happy with his assigned task, but they were both in service to the Name and had to push on.

Dario met Samson at the entrance. This time Samson ignored the refreshments on the table that had become his local workplace.

Samson handed Dario a list of the current sales. Over time, perhaps a third of the Home's workers had been given their travel orders. With the new offers, the number would climb, approaching half the Rikna population.

"Your name is on the list."

Dario blinked, "I am surprised."

"Carpentry is always needed. Do you have your companion chosen?"

Words stalled on the man's face. Then he said quietly, "I have yet to choose."

Samson nodded. He could imagine it was a hard task. "You have until your transfer, scheduled late tomorrow. However, right now, I have a task of my own."

"Yes?"

Samson asked, "You understand that the Home is to be shut down, no matter how many are left?"

Dario nodded stiffly.

"I have been ordered by the Name to plan the shutdown process. Some day soon, Elehadi will give the word and I must take action at that time. Understand?"

Again Dario nodded.

"Then, today, I want you to show me the air filtration machinery and the power system that runs this Home."

Dario's eyes widened. He hesitated, then with teeth gritted tightly, he said, "Follow me."

Joshua could feel Dario's silent scream, having to walk step by step to the machinery, forced to assist the process which would kill the people he was determined to save.

There were numerous cells which branched off the corridor they walked. Every person they passed had stopped what they were doing to watch as Samson the giant passed by, head bowed low to fit the passage.

Every step through Rikna seemed to be like through mud. The fear and depression in the place even made breathing hard. Joshua wondered if the tenners had it any easier.

There was a crossway in the corridor. One way went to an interior landing dock where Rikna's products, like cages of *chitchits* could be easily loaded for shipment. It was open to the sky, a lone portal to the outside with an airlock to the rooms around it. In the opposite direction, the corridor soon opened up into the gardens. Branching off to the left was a room that droned from spinning machinery.

Dario pointed. "The air filtration is behind those doors. Air is taken in from the main corridor and processed. The clean air is vented into the gardens. There are four other branches from the gardens and air follows those corridors throughout the whole burrow—all except some of the animal pen areas. Those we circulate with outside air."

He worked the code on a lock and opened up a smaller room. Cables ran from a cylindrical machine into small channels dug into the clay of the walls. Dario put his hand on the cylinder. "This end is the power storage cell. It's just like the ones used in the boats, only this one drives a rotating converter that generates electricity that is used for the air filtration, the lights, and all the other machinery in the Home."

Samson looked over the setup. The power cell was designed to be replaced on a regular basis. He asked, "You land a boat in the outdoor dock, and wheel the power cells in and out?"

Dario nodded.

Samson asked, "How do you keep the lights on during the transfer?"

Dario pointed at glass tanks lining the wall. "Those are chemical storage batteries. They can keep the lights running for several hours, certainly long enough to install the replacement power cell."

Samson put his hand on the power cell and Dario winced. There was a control pad near his hand, a simplified version of the type used everywhere. Hesitantly, Samson tapped the circular pad. Dario was struggling to keep himself from jumping to grab his hand away.

A curved band appeared on the white enamel. The power cell was just less than two-thirds full.

Samson dismissed the reading. "How long does a charged power cell last?"

Dario said, "Over two months. The ... former Name of Rikna had purchased a second cell so that we could always have one on hand, but it was out for charging during the Face. I'm sure it's gone forever."

Samson asked, "How long do you estimate the air would last before you have to open the outside doors?"

Dario wouldn't meet his eyes. "That depends on how many people are left. A couple of days perhaps. I really don't know."

Samson looked around, his eyes lighting on a cart with a curved cradle mounted on its top. He nodded. All it would take would be two men to shut the place down and remove the power cell. In a pinch he could do it himself.

That might be better. How can I order men to kill their friends and family?

Joshua wondered how Samson could quietly contemplate doing the task himself. The man had a fatalistic streak that he could not understand.

. . .

Joshua reported what he had learned. Most of the people had left, but Cyclops, Hugo and Lincy were still at work.

Hugo said, "Half the engineers on the planet could cobble together a generator to burn vegetation to keep electricity running. I just don't know if it would be enough."

Cyclops shook his head. "Even if Elehadi tolerated it, most of the skilled engineers have already been shipped out. They could extend the time to die, but not by much. I don't believe Rikna has a large store of filtration chemicals either. Certainly they haven't been buying the stuff we make.

"Politically, Elehadi can't let them live. If he left them to survive on their own, then they would be free U'tanse. If he makes them work for him, then he is responsible for their survival."

Hugo nodded sadly, "And he can't change his mind about shutting the place down. It would make him appear weak."

Cyclops noticed Joshua fidgeting in his chair. "Is there anything else?"

Joshua gave a weak smile. "Nothing concerning Rikna."

"What is it?"

"You know we've been having trouble getting Jinger to break her ties to her friends back there. Sally suggested we capture a *chitchit* and give it to Jinger to care for. We saw a group of them on the mountain."

Hugo smiled, "So that's what you two were doing out there." He got a thoughtful look. "Can *chitchits* live in filtered air? Is it something we can breed for meat?"

Cyclops shook his head. "Not for meat. But I know several Homes that breed them indoors. They bleed freely in filtered air, but if they aren't injured, then they do okay. But I'd hesitate to start a breeding operation here."

Joshua said, "We're just looking for one, something a little girl can focus her attention on."

Cyclops sighed. "How long would it take to catch one?"

Joshua shrugged. "We ride the submarine out, deploy the trap and hope. Sally seemed to think she could capture one quickly."

Cyclops waved a hand. "I can't authorize a special trip, but check with Robert and hitch a ride to and from the factory. You'll have to work with his schedule. And don't do anything to upset your mother."

Chitchit Hunt

Sally griped, "This would be a lot easier if we could use telepathy to make sure everyone is in place."

Joshua and Bernard took their fishing nets and moved where she directed, having to signal each other waving their hands. The *chitchits* could see them and retreated back into a dark corner in the rocks.

Joshua could see them as well, but he hesitated to move closer. Sally warned him that they could bite if panicked. She'd been frustrated that they had to catch the submarine early in the day, which gave her no time to find the materials and build her trap. Nets were at hand, but that required getting close enough to toss the net.

Sally moved to the ledge above the huddling creatures and waved everyone in closer. Bernard grinned at him. He'd jumped at the chance to join the hunting party. From what he said, the factory was still recovering from the flood. It had deeper levels than the base and there had been a struggle to get the secure doors closed to stop the incoming waters. They had to pump out the lowest levels and wash out the contaminating salt deposits.

When the Delense had abandoned the factory, they had left it well-sealed, but over the years the U'tanse had discovered the deeper levels and put them to active use. Luckily, the doors still worked as water-tight barriers, once they got them closed.

It was just a fluke of the work-schedule that no one had been trapped down there that day.

Bernard said, in a level voice pitched to keep from spooking the *chitchits*, "Spread your net to block the gap between those two rocks."

Joshua saw the gap he meant, and started shaking the net out wider.

He was barely in place, when Sally yelled, "Hey! Hey! Hey!" She jumped down from the higher point and the animals started running, screaming their chit-chit noises. Bernard had blocked one passage, and Joshua the other, but the animals could climb and they did. There were nearly a dozen of the beasts moving in all directions.

Joshua concentrated on the three that were closest to him and tossed his net. For an instant, he had them, but then first one wiggled its way free, and then a second. Joshua jumped down on the net, trying to close off all exits.

An instant later, another net came down on top of him. Sally had them both.

Joshua wrapped the net around the struggling beast, keeping his fingers clear of the sharp beak. Sally was down there with him, helping him get free of her net, and then taking the prize in her arms.

Bernard was beaming at his own capture. "You only need one of these, right?"

Sally laughed. "Sure."

Sally wrapped the legs in twine, and they folded up the nets.

Joshua said, "We need to hurry. The submarine is due to head back in a few minutes."

Bernard held his beast. It squeaked. "What do you feed these things?"

Sally said, "Anything. They eat creepers and roots out here, but back at Home, we fed them scraps left over from the meals. Once she gets used to you, she'll sit by your table and hope for anything that falls to the floor."

Bernard beamed at his beast. "It's a she?"

Sally nodded. "Both of them are. The males have a white ridge along the spine."

Joshua held their little bundle on the ride back to the Base. He stared at the formidable looking mouth, even though the ridges on the beak like teeth were too small to do much damage to something as big as he was. It … she stared at him, and he stared back.

There was some kind of a mind there. He could see himself as an enormous beast hovering over her. The background was just a maze of nightmare shapes.

Hesitantly, he stroked the leathery hide. There were ridges in the skin that protruded when he touched them, but then they receded when the animal calmed down. What they were for, Joshua had no clue.

"Do we name it?" he asked.

Sally said, "Let's leave that up to Jinger."

"Right." Joshua nodded, thinking that he just might like to catch another for himself some day.

Sally scooted close by his side and stroked the animal's hide as well.

He said, "You know, you really didn't need to throw your net over me. I had it."

She smiled, "I know."

...

Jinger sat alone against the wall, not far from the entrance to the nursery. The place was generally secluded, far from where everyone played. She tolerated the smell of over-ripe diapers and brown-buckets in their containers awaiting pickup for cleaning. It was the quietest place among the nursery rooms.

Joshua wheeled in the meal cart and an additional metal box. He didn't do more than nod at Jinger as he entered, but he set the box near her and began the process of parceling out the food as all the cuties began clustering about. Sally entered a moment later.

With nearly everyone else working on their plates, he looked over at Jinger, still sitting against the wall, but focussing on the box near her. It made scratching noises.

Sally called, "Jinger, bring the box over here."

Jinger jerked. She hesitated, but then without a word, picked up the large box and walked it over to the food cart.

The other cuties were curious. Joshua handed Jinger her food. Sally said, "Jinger, you're the only one who knows how to feed and care for it, so it's your responsibility."

Jinger took her plate and then opened the lid on the box. There was a net over the top and a frantic little face looking up. She broke off a piece of her fish and stuffed it through the netting.

The others crowded around. "What is it?"

Jinger hesitated, unsettled by the attention, but the little beast was demanding more. "It's a *chitchit*." She reached for her plate, but Ash pushed a portion of his into the net like she had. Jinger slapped his hand. "Don't overfeed her."

Sally smiled at Joshua. This was the most she'd interacted with anyone since the day she woke up in the nursery.

. . .

Hugo looked up as he entered the maproom and hurriedly turned his paper face down on the table. Joshua looked surprised.

Hugo frowned, "Hey, kid, just because you have secrets doesn't mean you're the only one."

Joshua didn't think much about it at the time, reporting Samson's rather boring activities for the day, and then moving on to his other chores.

It was later, as he was washing dishes that he wondered, *What does Hugo think I'm keeping secret?*

He'd been working long hours for many days now. Any spying he was doing was all being reported to Cyclops and then went straight into the log books. He was too busy, and too tired to do any spying on his own. It had been ages since he checked out the girls in the distant Homes.

And now that Sally was here, he didn't feel the need.

He wondered, just casually, when it was that she took a break from the nursery and visited the bath. Not that he'd do anything about it. If she wanted him to swim with her, she'd ask—once she was fully trained in all the women's things.

And how was that coming? It wasn't something she tended to talk about, not unless he asked. And it would be embarrassing to ask.

Was that what Hugo was saying? Did he think that he and Sally were sneaking off together? With everyone using *ineda*, it was possible that could happen. He used his *sight*, but it was nearly always directed outward, monitoring Samson or the other Homes.

Cyclops and Debbie could find him. He'd experienced that many times. Were they checking in on him now, making sure he wasn't bothering Sally?

There was no way to know.

Almost with no effort, he looked back at the nursery, checking to see what she was up to. She wasn't there.

No, I'm not going to check the third-level bath.

But as he scanned the corridors, he saw her, walking into his private cell.

She looked around, just checking to see if he were there, and then hurried back out, running toward the spiral.

Joshua quickly dried his hands and chased her down, catching her in the spiral.

"What's up?" he asked.

She looked worried. "Oh, it's silly, but I can't find the *chitchit.*"

He waited. It didn't seem to be a big thing to worry about. Even if it escaped its cage, it'd be restricted to the nursery area.

"I'm sure we'll find it," he said.

She looked guilty. "It's just, the cuties had it out of the box, playing with it when we wheeled out the bedding laundry. It was after that when Jinger started throwing a fit, and we couldn't find it."

He nodded, "So it could be out in the corridors somewhere. How long has it been gone?"

"Nearly an hour. I tried to find it myself, but the place is so big, I get lost."

"Okay. Hang on a minute."

He closed his eyes, trying to remember the little mind he'd contacted before. He reached out, feeling the area, floor by floor, starting at the nursery.

He caught a whiff of thought. "It senses water."

"They can swim."

"Second level." They started up the spiral.

He could feel it now. It was frightened of all the beasts, hiding in the shadows. If it could find water, it could escape.

"This way!" he started running. He was close, he could feel his footsteps through the animal's skin.

Sally yelled, "There it goes!"

It was a chase, but Sally had experience, edging it into a corner, talking to it gently. The walls were too steep to climb, and with a snatch, she had the squirming beastie.

She wrapped its head with the cloth of her sleeve.

"Does that calm them?" he asked.

"No, not really. I was just worried, you know."

"No, what were you worried about?"

Her face was wrinkled with distress. "I mean, we have *ineda*, and the cuties are confined to the nursery, but what if someone was reading Bella's mind while she was running around inside the Base. Couldn't they see all the stuff here? I was panicked that she'd make it down to the dock level."

"It's not that bad. I don't think you have to worry. I was looking through her eyes—it's 'Bella', huh?—and although she sees stuff, I'm reading her thoughts, which is like what her mind sees, not what's before her eyes. It's all crazy shapes and strange colors, not doors and corridors."

Sally sighed, relieved. She pulled Bella's head free and stroked her skin. "That's okay then. I've never tried listening to the thoughts of a *chitchit*. At least until she was already missing. Thanks for finding her for me."

She headed back to the spiral. When she vanished around the corner, he returned to the dishes, with some things to think about.

Old and New

It was rare that Joshua had a morning free. Comfort had arranged a birthday party for Olive and volunteered to bring the morning meal up from the kitchen. He was also invited to the party, but the chance to sleep late was too appealing.

Of course, when the corridors started whispering with the morning activity and passing footsteps, he woke up at his usual time anyway. He stared at the ceiling, puzzling out the brush marks etched into the granite by the ancient Delense tongue machines. There was dust up there, somehow clinging to the ridges. Maybe in a few days he'd find time to clean it.

But right now, the bed was too appealing. He stretched and relaxed.

Unfortunately, his brain churned away with familiar chores.

Samson had managed a night at home with Omelia, his lone island of humanity. Joshua just touched his sad dreams and left him alone.

He wondered about Jinger. She was up, playing with Bella, the *chitchit*. A stray thought nagged at him, and he pushed his concentration over to the Rikna Home and tracked down Jinger's friends.

Harmony, Mary, and Fancy were bundled in adjacent beds in the girl cuties cells. He lightly touched their dreams and found Bella in all of them.

Was that a good thing? Maybe. Since the rescue, the Rikna girls' fear and depression, even across that distance, had kept Jinger a constant recluse. Now her affection for the rock beast was easing their dreams.

Joshua broke away and checked other minds there in Rikna. There were no other dreams of *chitchits*. The place was falling apart as a Home.

A few lucky ones—people being sold and their selected companions—were preparing to leave, selecting what few personal items they could take along. But these people were isolated. Goodbyes between friends and relatives were strained.

He found a room with a number of older people sitting around a table, chatting.

"I wouldn't have it any other way," Natalie said. "Jess can only take one. He and Seren had a long talk and it all comes down to numbers. Seren is carrying my granddaughter. There's no way I'd allow Jess to take me instead. They have a future and I don't. That's the simple truth."

Franklin, across the table, moved a pebble from one square tile to the next with his left hand. "I know all that. I don't blame the kids for getting out if they can, but it sours my stomach to be automatically the old geezer who's left behind to die. I'm so mad I want to punch someone."

Hal, beside him said, "Wanna give the Name a good right cross?"

Franklin held up the stump of his right arm, the hand taken long ago in a timber collapse. "Ha. Ha. Good one. Maybe I'll punch you."

Lila sniffed, her eyes tearing up. "We don't need to fight each other. We're old. It's okay we're going to die. I'm just torn up about my Mary and Sybil. Even if their father is chosen, he can't take his wife and both children. I'm... happy to stay behind with whoever is left."

Natalie took Lila's hand. "We're all here for each other."

. . .

Joshua started his midday meal deliveries early and ended the loop at Lemm's cell.

The tall, thin man was stretched out on his bed, a scroll book in his hand.

"Hello, Lemm. I've got sadapple pudding and *jenna* with pepper sauce for you today."

The old watery eyes looked at him for an instant before recognizing him. "Ah, Joshua. It's good to see you."

Joshua moved the plates over to the side table and helped the man move into a sitting position. He glanced at the book. It was an factory logbook. Lemm had been one of the first men to bring the factory back to work after being idle since it was deserted by the Delense.

"Checking the logs?"

Lemm tasted the fish, then took another bite. After chewing a little, he said, "They won't tell me anything. Someone said there was a flood, but I thought it was a chemical spill." He grinned, "But I know where they keep the logs. I'll figure it out."

Joshua was surprised. The book shelves were on this level, but Lemm could barely walk. It had to be frustrating to be out of the daily churn of the factory work. He was deteriorating fast. Debbie had told him that was the way it often happened. Getting old could only be held off for a while, by healing the aging tissues and keeping the muscles working. Eventually, things started going bad too fast to keep up with.

Joshua sat on his food cart. "Oh, there was both. We had a tsunami from that last big quake." He told the man the tale from his viewpoint on the mountainside.

Lemm chuckled at the story, especially the bit about having a girl along. Then he started talking about the lower levels in the factory, and all the machines they discovered when they opened them up. Most of it was stories Joshua had heard before, but he gave the man all the attention he could.

By the time Lemm wound down and had to stretch out for a "little nap," Joshua had used up all the spare time he could afford. He promised Lemm he'd come by again soon.

He was surprised to find Debbie waiting for him out in the corridor.

She looked in to see Lemm already dozing off. She gestured and when they were a few paces distant, she said, "It was nice of you to visit him."

He just nodded. "Did you come to see him? I didn't mean to be in the way."

"No. It's all fine. I was looking for you. Could you get Sally and come to my workshop?"

...

"Is it about Bella's escape?" Sally asked.

Joshua shrugged. "She didn't say. She didn't look angry."

Debbie's workshop was next to the gardens. She had a table almost as large as in the maproom, but half of this one was covered in a grid work of wooden slats a hand high, many of them full of different types of dried leaves or ground bark. Probably Debbie knew what they all were, but all Joshua knew was that they changed every time he came by. She was always trying new plants to find out what they were good for.

This time there were chairs around the other end. Comfort was talking to Cyclops and Debbie was writing something in a ledger.

They looked up when Joshua and Sally arrived.

"There you are. Have a seat." Debbie gestured to two vacant chairs, next to where Comfort sat.

Cyclops folded his hands. Debbie was in charge of the meeting.

She held her pencil and asked, "Tell us about Ash. Comfort thinks he's becoming clairvoyant. What is your opinion?"

Joshua nodded. "I think so. Several times in the past few days, he's seen things out of visual range. He saw our visit in the garden when we were culling palace bushes. It may have been coming on for weeks. He's gotten very good at finding people in the maze."

Sally added her opinion on that. She'd had to hunt Ash down several times, and with his thoughts locked down and better *sight* than hers, he could beat her at chase-and-hide every time.

Debbie had a number of specific questions to try to nail down exactly what kind of clairvoyance he was displaying. Even among the people around her table, the differences were significant. Debbie could instantly comprehend miles worth of detail in a flash, but the flash wasn't under her control. Comfort had little of the same distance perception, but she had every woman's skill at controlling the cells in her own body and was also good at sensing and healing the injuries in someone close enough to touch. Sally was still in training, but had not experienced any *sight* other than within her own body.

Joshua hoped to have his father's skill some day, but it was just a wish. Nobody matched Cyclops. He could read text thousands of miles away.

But the controlled distant perception used by Joshua, Cyclops, Patrick and Robert were important skills necessary to the Base's long-term survival. If Ash was developing that talent, then he needed more specialized training.

Joshua said, "I suppose I could teach him some things."

Cyclops said, "Thanks for the offer, but you need more training yourself. We'll work out a rotating schedule as soon as Ash passes his *ineda* test and can be counted to keep his thoughts under control."

Debbie made some notes in her ledger and then asked, "And how is Veronica doing? I've had very little luck getting her to talk to me about her nightmares."

Comfort said, "For a little while, I wondered if she was developing *sight* as well, but..." she shook her head, "the things that are frightening her don't make any sense."

Joshua drummed his fingers on the table. "I tried tracking down her fears as well, and I guess I think she's just extra sensitive at picking up the fears spilling out of Rikna. There's a lot of stuff going on there that she just doesn't have any experience with. The nightmares those people are suffering make me shiver sometimes."

Sally nodded. "I check on my family back there, hiding my own thoughts, of course. They are hoping to make it out before the deadline, but the uncertainty is draining."

Debbie set her pencil down, "Sally, I hope you know that every one of us here knows what you're going through. We have all had to leave family behind—to play dead. If it gets to be too much, please come and talk to us."

Timidly, Joshua raised his hand. "I'm the odd one here. But they're right. Sometimes people sit around the meal table and talk about the old times. The Dallah people are especially good at that."

"Hush, Joshua," his mother said.

Sally smiled. "I'm dealing with it. I'm doing better than Jinger at least."

"How is she?"

Sally shifted in her chair. "Better. I think giving her the *chitchit* has really helped."

Comfort nodded. "I agree. She's still resistant to any attempt to make friends, but she's no longer curled up against the wall all day long. I've even seen her smile when she's feeding Bella."

Cyclops asked, "Bella?"

"That's the *chitchit*'s name."

Comfort smiled, "It got out, but Joshua and Sally recaptured it quickly."

Sally winced. "I'm really sorry about that."

Joshua recognized the slight tilt of his father's head. He didn't understand the apology.

"Sally was worried that the escaped animal might be a security risk, if someone could see through the *chitchit*'s eyes. I told her that it wasn't an issue, because animals couldn't understand what they were looking at. Was I wrong?"

Cyclops said, "You're right. I've tried sampling the thoughts of *sendt* when following Cerik. Simple animal dangers can get through, but they just don't comprehend machinery or any kind of manufactured item, actually. With no concepts in their brain for them, no common references, I couldn't recognize them either. I can't think there would have been any risk from your pet."

He got a thoughtful look on his face.

Debbie added some notes in her ledger. "I guess that's all for now—unless there are any other nursery problems we need to be alerted to?"

When everyone got to their feet, Cyclops asked, "Joshua, would you walk with me back to my cell?"

Joshua gave Sally an apologetic shrug and watched her leave with Comfort.

Cyclops never had any problems walking the corridors of the Base, so Joshua just kept at his side. His father would talk when he was ready.

They were walking up the spiral when he said, "Joshua, I would like you to be ready for a trip over to the factory an hour before dawn. I'd like you to show me where these *chitchits* have their den."

Meeting in the Meadow

Debbie was there to see them off. She appeared worried about her husband.

Cyclops said, "There's no problem."

He'd rarely seen his parents leave the Base, but Joshua knew they had. Cyclops had business at the factory on occasion, and Debbie went outside every few months with some of her helpers to scout the surrounding lands looking for new plants.

Robert looked like he was still dopey when he arrived. "Sorry. Not much sleep lately. You okay, Cyclops?"

"I'm fine. Let's go."

Cyclops entered carefully through the submarine's hatch and Joshua followed.

Robert cast off the lines and sealed the hatch behind him. "We'll stay on the surface as much as possible." He engaged the side engines and the submarine rotated to align with the tunnel. Water splashed over the viewing window.

Joshua had seen this view while swimming, but viewing the tunnel entrance through glass gave it an extra clarity. There was trash on the bottom of the underground docking area. Not everything had been cleaned up from the flood.

The submarine slid slowly through the tunnel. Joshua was interested in the circular creatures clinging to the rocks. He wondered what they ate down there.

Then he noticed his father gripping the seat so tightly the veins in his hands seemed ready to burst. There was a stiff look on his face.

Cyclops turned his blindfolded face his direction. "Don't worry about me. I'm just nervous about being underwater. I nearly drowned when I was young."

Joshua flashed back to his younger days when he was first out of the nursery and Debbie was teaching him to swim. His father had been there from time to time, but he always sat on the ledge and never came out into open water. He guessed there was a story there, but he'd learned to be patient. His father had never told him how he lost his eyes either, and he had asked many times.

They were out, and the submarine surfaced, the tinted light of very early dawn providing just enough light for Robert to steer by.

Once they unloaded at the factory dock, Joshua took the lead, heading past the new boat-landing pad, currently concealed by a dome constructed of tree branches.

They kept going, out beyond the factory work areas.

"There's a path here. It leads up to the mountain."

Cyclops nodded. "I'm familiar with it."

Joshua frowned. "Have you been up here before? I didn't know you hiked."

His father chuckled. "You didn't invent the world, Joshua. You aren't even the first guy to take a girl on a hike to the top of the mountain."

Did that mean Cyclops and Debbie went for a hike together? It was a disturbing thought.

They were half way to the place where the *chitchits* were captured, when Cyclops said, "No, take this branch to the right."

"That doesn't go up the mountain."

"I know. We'll go look at the animals later. I need to check on something up in the meadows."

This was an area Joshua hadn't explored before. They followed a ledge overlooking the creek until they reached a waterfall.

"Watch out," his father said. "The ground is mushy in places."

He was right. The creek was now on their level and formed several marshy pools. His father pointed to another branch of the trail that took them up slightly higher into a wide meadow. He waved at a ledge.

"Sit there for a bit while I walk a little farther. I'll be back for you. Stay put."

Joshua was puzzled. He was even a little concerned that his father would get tripped up by something and fall. He was blind, and even if his *sight* was excellent, sometimes eyesight was better at seeing shadows and things that could trip you up.

So he kept an eye on his father, at least for a while. Cyclops walked a path that was nearly hidden by waist-high vegetation until he vanished behind a boulder left deposited in the meadow by some avalanche.

Joshua fidgeted, sitting on the ledge. Then he stretched his *sight* and found his father standing alone in the far meadow, his arms stretched wide, silent, as if he were listening.

Okay. He was doing something unusual, which was typical for his father.

I'm supposed to wait here, so I'll wait.

But that didn't mean his mind couldn't wander.

. . .

Samson was off in more negotiations, this time standing in a boat, yelling over the shouter at some Cerik in another clan. There wasn't much to hold his attention, so Joshua moved on. George was in his private cell, still transcribing the tales of the Cerik. He couldn't hear them or see what George was writing, so that was boring, too.

Rikna Home wasn't a pleasant place to visit, but there were people he had connected with before, which made them easier to find and reconnect.

Lila was excited. She hurried through the corridor and found that same room where several of the older residents waited, playing their games and griping about their fate.

"Hal!"

The wrinkled-faced man looked up, giving her a quizzical smile. "Yes, what is it?"

Franklin frowned, "You're not going to interrupt the game again, are you?"

Lila straightened herself up as much as possible. "Yes, I am. Hal, come with me, I have to show you something."

Hal sighed. "Sorry buddy. But when Lila calls …."

Franklin growled and brushed the pebbles off the table with his left hand. Hal hurried to follow. "What is it? I'd just gotten Franklin to calm down."

"You've got to see this."

She led the way over to the cuties cells. There was a playroom just down the corridor from several of the sleeping areas. Lila paused as they entered.

Harmony, Fancy, and Mary were sitting side by side, holding hands. They stared at the wall, not paying attention to the adults who had entered. But strangely, they were humming.

Hal asked, "What's that noise?"

Lila smile, "Isn't it pretty?"

The girls hummed together as a group, pitching their composition up and down all together. Mary looked up at her grandmother and held out her hand, never stopping her part in the rhythm. Lila stepped over and sat beside her, and took her hand. Then she, too, began humming with the others. Lila smiled up at Hal and raised her other hand to him.

· · ·

Joshua shook his head. There was only so much of the strangeness and depression going on at Rikna that he could take at one time, even if the people there were finding ways to cope with the fear of coming death.

He turned his attention back to the meadow and located his father again.

Cyclops was still standing in the same spot, but it looked as if he was talking. He couldn't see anyone else.

Could someone be hiding in the bushes?

He reached out to sense if there was a mind. Cyclops was a blank, but even with a solid *ineda*, Joshua could sometimes feel the life itself, as if the cells had a force within them.

There were animals out there, he was sure. There were always creepers of some kind.

Quickly, he was sure that there was no person hiding in the bushes unless they were *ineda*-blocked as well. But there was something.

He could feel it, down below his father.

Was there a cave entrance?

He looked, and didn't understand what his *sight* was revealing.

Cyclops was standing above a large flat circular living thing. Joshua could feel the life from it.

His father was talking to it.

Joshua stretched his telepathy, reached down and made some kind of connection.

This was no animal. This was the mind of a person, although nothing like U'tanse or Cerik. He could feel echoes of Cerik speech. Cyclops and this being were talking in that language. That didn't help Joshua understand what they were saying, but it nailed down even harder the idea that this flat living pancake was a *person* with a mind on par with his own.

His father had come out here to have a private meeting with … something.

Joshua remembered what Hugo had said about not being the only person with secrets.

Unable to listen in on the conversation, and aware that Cyclops had left him here so that he could talk in private, Joshua disconnected and stopped trying to observe, but that didn't stop him from thinking about this new revelation.

Robert had lived part of his life with the Uuaa. Joshua had heard his tales of the climbing ones, who Robert claimed were intelligent even through they couldn't talk. They had come from some other planet just like the U'tanse. Were the flat people captives, too, or were they native to Ko, like the Cerik and the Delense?

Some part of him must have kept watch on his father, because he found himself standing up, just as his father walked into view from behind the boulder.

As he approached, Joshua asked, "What was that?"

Cyclops paused a step and then sat down on the ledge. "You saw?"

"Uh, yes. I saw you talking and could see who you were talking to, at first. What is it?"

"A Ba. Formally, they call themselves Ba-on-Ba-on-Ba, or Bababa. The Cerik pronounce them Dadada. They were captured from their home planet."

Joshua nodded. "Okay. I hadn't heard of them. Does everyone know they exist?"

"They're in the records. They arrived before the U'tanse, but their numbers have stayed small. A few have managed to escape and roam freely."

"They walk?"

Cyclops laughed. "They have legs, lots of them. But there's a couple of things you really have to know."

"Yes?"

"Free Ba are just as resolved to stay unknown from the Cerik as we are. Aaron, the first of the free U'tanse made an agreement with Ba. Only one U'tanse, and his successor, must know about their existence."

Joshua felt a warmth in his chest. Successor meant him. Aaron told Cyclops and Cyclops told him. He nodded. "A secret we can't even talk about at the Base."

"Exactly. And there's another thing. The free U'tanse owe the Ba. Aaron was on the verge of death when he was alone, with no breather. Ba brought him to the factory. The free U'tanse owe their existence to the free Ba. Someday, when we have the ability to leave this planet, we owe the Ba a ride home."

Joshua's breath caught. It was an idea beyond anything he'd considered before. Someday the U'tanse might travel to other worlds. Someday they might go home.

Cyclops let him think quietly for a moment and then stood up. "I guess we still have time to take a look at the *chitchits*."

Joshua stood up too. "What did you talk about?"

His father shook his head. "There are still secrets. Sometimes we just talk. Sometimes we trade favors."

He started back along the trail. Joshua followed.

Gray Alert

Robert caught them on the trail. He'd been running hard.

Cyclops asked, "What's wrong?"

"There's a gray flag at the Base. Nobody there knows how to work the semaphore."

"Go start the submarine. We'll be right behind you."

Robert nodded and took off down the slope.

Joshua gasped out, chasing his father, "What's a semaphore?"

"Flags. We can spell out words."

Joshua saved his breath. Now was not the time to try to understand. The gray flag was enough. It meant, "Some Home reports an emergency, monitors report to the maproom."

By the time they were moving across the bay, all they knew was that the gossip among U'tanse Homes was shut down. Cyclops and Joshua both searched their contacts. Runa and Kakil U'tanse weren't aware that a problem existed. Lakka and Sanassan elders had a tight *ineda*. Joshua was searching Rikna, but some of the people he expected to contact were either asleep or under *ineda*. They just didn't seem to be available.

...

Samson was in the air, just arriving at Rikna. He walked into the entrance, surprised to see Roger, Elizabeth, and Kathy, all holding their finger to their forehead. The expressions on the elders' faces led him to believe the worst, although he had no idea what that could be.

He held out his sheet of paper, "This is the list of deliveries." Roger took it, and passed a different paper back to him.

Samson went into *ineda* before looking down at this note.

Joshua hurriedly examined the scene with his *sight*, having lost contact with Samson's mind. Everyone was tense, but they still talked evenly, as if nothing was wrong. He could tell it was just an act. Something bad was happening.

...

Joshua and his father hurried up the spiral and entered the maproom.

"What's going on?" asked Cyclops. Nearly all the seats were taken.

Debbie said, "I was monitoring Graddik when the elders there hurried into a meeting and locked down their *ineda*. Others are seeing the same thing happening in other Homes."

Joshua said, "It's at Rikna, I think. The elders there just handed Samson a piece of paper, and they are all now under *ineda*."

Cyclops put his hand to his temple. "Samson is at the Rikna entrance?"

"Yes, where he usually meets the elders."

Everyone was silent while Cyclops tried to read the paper in Samson's pocket. He quoted, "'Attachment has broken out, mainly among the children and the elderly. We need to move everyone out that we can before it becomes public knowledge.'"

Attachment. It was the plague of the telepaths. Under the right conditions, minds became locked together. It was the death of identity, as people became part of a hive mind.

Joshua gasped. "I saw it. I think. I was monitoring Rikna earlier and saw Jinger's three friends sitting together humming with the same rhythm and tone. Mary's grandmother sat with them, holding hands, and started humming right along with them."

Comfort said, "I saw Jinger humming, this morning. I didn't think anything about it."

Debbie and Comfort got to their feet and hurried out. Joshua had the urge to follow, Sally, Veronica, and all the others were down there and in danger. But he resisted. He might be needed here.

Hugo said, "If this is really attachment, what can we do?"

Lincy looked up from her notes. "Historically, there have been several cases. Isolated individuals sometimes lose the will to live, essentially, and form a one-way attachment to anyone. In even rarer cases, small groups, like those three cuties, will bond together. In most cases, the Cerik kill them. Supposedly in the first generation, some sisters were cured with torture, the pain breaking the link. That's the only case I can think of."

Robert arrived after securing the submarine and was brought up to date.

Debbie came back, panting from the run. "Definitely, Jinger has attachment. We've dosed her with a sleeping potion. As far as I can tell, none of the others have been affected. Comfort is moving her to an isolated cell."

Joshua felt at a loss. Would they have to torture Jinger?

Robert asked, "If Rikna has attachment, are we still going to try the rescue?"

Joshua was surprised. This was the first time he'd heard that another rescue attempt was being planned.

Cyclops said, "Robert, go back to the factory and have Patrick load the boat with as many eggs as will fit, then prepare the submarine to carry as many people as possible. Get back here when you're done."

"Joshua, go talk to Sally. Ask her if she is willing to participate in a very dangerous rescue attempt. It may be impossible to try, with the extra guards in place, but we need to be ready in an instant if an opportunity opens up."

He stood. "Um, is it safe to bring them back here, with the attachment problem?"

Cyclops waved his hand. "We won't be bringing them here."

...

Sally was crying. "It's true. Jinger was just not really here. I tried to touch her mind, but it was if she was back at Rikna, sitting beside the others, all humming together. I shook her arm, but ... nothing."

Joshua looked at the others in the play room, Ash was drawing, the siblings were fighting, Veronica was looking his way.

"Are the others okay?"

Sally nodded. "All normal. They're worried. Debbie and Comfort came in and took Jinger away. They don't know what's going on."

She shook a little, looking around. She whispered, "I checked my family. My parents are gone—off to Sanassan. My brother is still waiting for confirmation of his sale. He's heard about the attachment and he's moved to the other side of the Home, as far away from the attached ones as he can. The whole place is dividing up like that. Sometimes a person will go check on what the attached group is doing, and then … they get attached themselves. It's like glue. I don't dare look at their minds anymore."

Joshua took her hand in his. She clutched at his.

"I've been told to ask you … v. If there were another rescue attempt, would you come?"

Her eyes were wide and fearful. She looked through the door at the cuties she was supposed to be caring for. "But the Cerik guards, and the attachment—it would be dangerous."

He nodded, "It's not certain we can do it. Preparations are underway, and if something changes—if there's any opportunity—we'd be ready to move."

"You are going along?"

He nodded. "Roger and Elizabeth know me, and I know the trail into the back of the Home."

She squeezed his hand. "Okay." She held her tongue between her teeth, then nodded to herself. "Okay, I'll go with you."

Veronica walked through the door. "I knew there was something going on between you two."

Joshua dropped Sally's hand. He said, "Oh, you're just being nosey."

His sister grinned, "Yes, I know. By the way," she frowned a little, like at an old memory, "do you know how to make burn ointment?"

He blinked, "No. Did you burn yourself?"

Veronica shook her head, "No, just a dream. Forget it."

Then she looked at Sally, "Did he say something to upset you?"

Sally put on her smile, "No, nothing like that. I'm just worried about some people I know."

. . .

Samson had retreated to his hut near the Kakil Perch. He took the paper out of his pocket and read it again.

Roger of the Rikna wanted him to hold off spreading the news, but that was a senseless hope. Something like attachment could not be hidden. It was probably already spreading around the world.

I am a *rettik* of the Name.

It is my duty to take this news to Elehadi instantly.

But he knew what would happen. There was only one thing that scared the Cerik—the hive mind on the planet of the Ferreer, the ones who could take over a Cerik's mind without a struggle and make them into just another one of them. When it became known that such a thing could happen with the U'tanse as well, there had been an outcry to destroy all of them.

But by then, the U'tanse had powerful protectors, clans such as the Tenthonad, which had become rich and influential due to the service of their technical experts.

Elehadi had no such high respect for the U'tanse. He would kill all of Rikna with no hesitation now that attachment had taken root there.

And that meant the Home would be *flicked*. No Cerik would slaughter an attached group with claw and talon. They had learned that lesson from the Ferreer. They had to be killed at a distance. A power cell could be coaxed to release all of its stored energy in one instant, vaporizing everything around it.

As far as he knew, no Name had *flicked* any foe since the days of planetary exploration. Perhaps the last one was during the conquest of the U'tanse.

That a power cell could be so used was a design defect, one placed there on purpose by the Delense in their plan to win their freedom from the Cerik.

Samson shook his head. The Cerik could not be defeated. That was a miscalculation on their part, and for that mistake, the Delense were exterminated to the last cub.

And for his failure to prevent this, he knew what would happen to him.

Samson. Omelia's thoughts reached him.

He reached back to the Kakil Home where she sat, worrying about him. He didn't attempt to speak to her. They were past words.

She understood.

An image formed in her mind, a visualization of what she could sense growing within her. A tiny bundle of cells, growing and seeking its own life. He could see five fingers on each hand.

He will be a giant, perhaps not as large as his father, but he will grow to be as noble and brave.

Be careful.

He took a deep breath and began to prepare himself.

He took his gauntlets and sharpened the edges. He took a polishing cloth and buffed the metal trim on his breather and cleaned the jawbone of the *haeka*. He repaired a burst stitch on his leather and made sure there was no dust showing.

Fitting the breather in place, he took deep breaths, and went outside, heading toward the Perch of Elehadi.

Cost of Failure

Joshua was caught standing in the corridor, unable to take his attention away from the events at the Perch. Someone said something as they passed by, but his heart was pounding as he watched.

Samson stood straight as he entered the presence of Elehadi.

He rattled the taps on his heels.

Fierce, irritated eyes turned to him. Elehadi expanded his chest and his right claw scraped against the metal-capped support beam of the *hurru*. <U'tanse.>

Samson took this as permission to speak. <I have been informed by the elders of Rikna Home that attachment has appeared in their ranks.>

Elehadi screamed and leapt. The sight of the massive Name in full leap had caused him to marvel in times past. Now, it caused him to freeze.

He never saw the claw strike him.

Joshua stumbled and collapsed to the floor.

What! Is he dead? Did Elehadi just kill him?

Breathing heavily, he waited a moment for his heartbeat to slow. That stroke didn't kill him. It hit Samson.

But did it kill him?

He reached back, hesitantly trying to find a mind he wasn't sure still existed.

He used his *sight* to focus on the Perch.

There was Elehadi, still standing over the body of the U'tanse warrior. He was face down, the breather split in pieces and a stream of blood trickling across the floor.

Elehadi's *'eeh* pounded through his veins and he roared with triumph. But then … there was a sound at his feet. He stepped back.

The U'tanse was still alive!

Joshua broke free of the Cerik's bloodlust and tried again to reach the mind of Samson.

It was a roar of pain, his eyesight was nothing but a swirl of red—no images could be resolved.

Samson's thoughts weakly formed. *He's taken my eyes.*

Habit kept him alive. Battle training over the years had given him the instincts to keep going. His healing skills were concentrated on stopping the bleeding. His eyes—slashed, destroyed, with only a scrap of retina to tell him of his loss. Eyesight was gone. *Sight* had to serve.

Elehadi was still standing over him. He knew the killing stroke of *ssitt* should have stopped him. It had killed every opponent he'd ever faced.

The Name must be wondering why he was still moving.

Joshua could hardly bear the pain. It nearly swamped all coherent thought.

He reached over to Elehadi's thoughts.

Memories of old tales—the monsters of the swamp that had existed since before Cerik formed clans and took slaves—there were beasts that could not be killed. There were even tales of the first U'tanse, who took killing strokes and yet stood.

He'd seen marvels of strength in this one, but nothing that hinted at such supernatural resilience. Should he strike again? Strike the dead?

But… what was his U'tanse doing?

At his feet, he was pulling himself up, shifting, not into an attack posture, but into the kneeling supplication pose of a *rettik*!

Elehadi shifted his position to where he could see the ruined face. The eyes were gone! Blood still dripped from wounds down to the bone. And yet, he knelt, as if the strike had been nothing more than the cuff given a student for an error.

His U'tanse rattled his feet.

<Speak!> Elehadi's response had been instinctive. But could he still speak?

Joshua forced himself back into the pain-wracked mind of Samson.

<For the Name!> Samson knew his voice was unsteady, but he had to continue. He breathed the raw air of Ko. His breather was destroyed, but perhaps it had shielded the blow just enough to enable him to survive just a little while longer.

<You have given me this task, to deal with the Rikna U'tanse. I have failed, but give me the chance to fix it.>

Elehadi hesitated, then asked, <How?>

Samson felt his throat choke up from blood, seeping through the remnants of his face, he forced a cough. <The power cell at Rikna Home. I am U'tanse. I can short it. Force it to *flick*.>

<You would do this blind?>

<Yes.>

Joshua felt his arm being tugged. He snapped back to the corridor in the Base.

Hugo was standing over him. "I've heard that Elehadi has killed Samson. Are you okay?"

Joshua shook free of his hand. "Let me go. It's not over yet."

He reached back to the scene. Elehadi waved his claw. <Go!>

Unsteadily, Samson rose to his feet and croaked out, <For the Name!>

He turned and walked, his shoulder almost clipping the entrance post, but heading toward the landing field where his boat waited.

Joshua reached up and gripped Hugo's tunic. "Samson is going to Rikna, to overload the power cell. Where is Cyclops?"

. . .

The word spread around the world. The sight of a killed U'tanse walking across the Perch's gathering yards—a *Rakladel* out of legend gone to destroy the U'tanse-Ferreers—was not a story to be kept quiet. Even before Samson stumbled into the boat, telepaths told telepaths, and telepaths told warriors. Warriors passed the word on shouters, and all across Rikna, Kakil warriors began running to the landing field to find a boat, any boat to take them away. No one wanted to be there when the demon arrived. No one wanted to be in range when the Rikna Home vaporized. *Flick* had grown in size with the telling of tales and no one was sure just how powerful it was.

Joshua burst into the nursery at a run, grabbing Sally's arm. She didn't say anything until they were in the corridor and the door was locked.

"The rescue is on. The Cerik guards are all deserting their posts. Samson is going to vaporize the Home. There might be just enough time to get in and out before it happens."

She snatched up her leathers and breather and they ran. The submarine wouldn't wait for them.

Hugo was holding the hatch open for them as they raced up. They were moving before he sealed it shut.

Terry watched Robert for a moment and then joined them. He held out his hand to Sally, "Nice to meet you."

Then he nodded to Hugo, "We've worked out an evacuation plan, but many things can go wrong. Sally and Joshua are the only ones who've been there in person, and clairvoyance can confuse distances and directions if you're not careful."

They felt the submarine speed up as they cleared the tunnel. Robert was running the engines at maximum.

Terry held out a sketch of the rear entrance and the *sendt* pastures. "We'll land here. Patrick will drop us off and then hide the boat behind the ridge. We can't risk losing the boat if Samson *flicks* the place before we're done. We'll collect the people free of attachment that have been gathering here, near the small animal pens. Then, we'll head back out the rear entrance and make our way over the ridge where we can all be picked up."

Sally nodded, "Um."

Hugo said, "Go ahead. You're here for because you know the layout of the Home."

She pointed at the sketch. "There's a landing pad right here, which is closer to where the people are waiting."

Hugo nodded, "You're right, but we think that Samson will try to land there himself. It's really close to where the power cell is kept."

She sighed, "You're right."

They went over the plan a couple of times. Sally described every corridor, and what to look for near the animal pens. "My brother is hiding there."

Hugo asked, "What about your parents?"

She sighed. "They were taken to Sanassan."

Hugo frowned and asked, "When? When were they taken?"

Her face went pale, "Yesterday, late yesterday. Why?"

Hugo breathed out. "Okay then. This morning, when the word came out about the attachment, there was a boat taking workers to Sanassan. I don't know the details, but the Rikna people were pushed out the hatch at high altitude. They probably weren't attached, but the Cerik flying the boat didn't want to take any chances."

She shook. "No. I know my parents made it all the way to Sanassan. But will they kill them anyway?"

Hugo shrugged. "It depends on how frightened their Name is. Other Rikna workers are at risk until this all calms down."

Joshua didn't say anything, but he thought of Jinger, still sleeping under the drug. What would they do with her if she never shook free of her attachment?

. . .

Samson had spent the time waiting in the boat attempting battle-ready healing. He'd tested his ability to *see* the controls enough to adjust the air to U'tanse friendly while he worked.

His pilot had attempted to escape, and was now arriving with two guards at his side to make sure he took his station. The guards were going with them into the range of a hive mind and a *flick*, but they could be sure the pilot did his job.

Samson was happy the pilot had made his run for safety. The rest time had allowed him to stop the bleeding and dampen some of the nerves that were telling him that he'd been severely injured.

He was also glad that his eyes were gone. He'd never have to look at his own face in a glass.

A tiny fraction of his mind was listening to Omelia wailing her grief. She knew he'd never come back.

The pilot growled at him. <I'll drop you off, but I won't come back.>

Samson said, <I knew you were a coward, but I don't expect you to be stupid.>

The boat lifted with a buzz.

. . .

Joshua yelled at Patrick, "Samson has just left Kakil!"

Their boat was already in the air, speeding along the mountain ridge.

He yelled back, "We'll have just a couple of minutes to drop you off. Be ready."

Sally and Joshua wedged themselves into a gap between the eggs.

The "eggs" were metal boxes, rounded and long, with room enough for two people to rest side by side in filtered air. Their shape was reminiscent of *jenna* eggs, although a fish large enough to lay those eggs could also be able to eat the boat whole.

No one knew how many people they could rescue, but if luck were with them, there would be too many to carry out with the boat. Survivors could wait in the eggs for another trip.

Joshua was glad to be holding Sally's hand. He didn't think of his own death very often, but riding in Samson's mind, he could hardly avoid it now. This rescue was risky in so many ways. If the hive mind didn't get them, the *flick* might. And there was always the chance that Cerik would see them, and Patrick would have to abandon all of them for the sake of preserving the Base.

How did Samson handle it? How could he stick to his duty, even as his own death approached?

Into the Maze

Joshua pulled Sally to her feet. The boat had never really landed, just hovered above the field while they stumbled out into the raging windstorm and blowing dust. The shadowed airlock embedded in the near dome was safety. They hurried toward it, across the field as the boat lifted away, taking the winds with it.

The boat's distant buzz was fading when from another direction, the noise of a second boat alerted them that Samson was approaching. They huddled in the rear entrance, alert to the possibility that Samson could land at the rear as well.

Hugo looked at Joshua and asked, "Can you tell where he's headed?"

Joshua hesitated, remembering the last time, then reached for Samson's mind.

The healing he'd done had helped considerably. The pain was a strong ache, no longer an overwhelming tide.

Samson yelled at the pilot. <Can't you see the landing platform?>

<Yes,> he screamed back, <but the Ferreer have piled it high with ... things. I can't land there.>

Samson stretched his *sight* to the landing platform he'd seen in the earlier trip. They had expected his arrival. Instead of the animal pens arranged neatly against the inner walls, now there were pens, tables, storage cabinets—anything that could be moved through the connecting corridors—piled high over the landing area, making it impossible to land a boat there.

The pilot pulled away, gaining altitude—anything to increase his distance from the mind-stealers.

<Land me!> Samson yelled, slamming his blade against the hull. There was no turning back.

The pilot sloped down, putting distance between himself and the cluster of brown domes.

Joshua whispered, "Samson's been dropped some distance from the main entrance—bad pilot. The attached have blocked the inner landing pad."

Terry said, "They're doing more than just humming then."

Sally looked dazed. Joshua whispered, "Sally? Are you okay?"

She blinked. "They know me. They're calling me."

"Resist it."

"I can. It's just—I know these people."

"Keep your *ineda* tight. Don't let them get into your mind."

Hugo looked directly into her eyes. "We're counting on you."

She nodded, her shoulder hunched. "I'm here to rescue my brother—and the others." She pointed off to the right. "There are a dozen people hiding from the attached over there. They've got the door barricaded. The attached are wandering around the whole place. The uncontaminated ones are afraid that if they are touched, the hive mind will take them over."

Terry asked, "Is that real?"

Hugh shrugged, "It could be. Healers say skin-to-skin touch improves their ability to control the cells. Keep your distance."

Joshua said, "We've got to hurry. Samson is moving slowly, but he's halfway to the entrance."

Hugo asked, "His boat?"

Joshua shook his head. "Long gone. Headed for Kakil as fast as he can fly."

Hugo said, "So, we have the air to ourselves."

Sally straightened up, her head turned to the corridors, "Another group—my brother's—they're hiding among the animal pens. This way." She started moving, taking the branch toward the pens.

Hugo said, "Let's split up. Where's the other group?"

Sally said, "Uh, the other corridor. Door marked 'Brass Works'. Elizabeth is there. Tell her you're with me."

Hugo turned back, "Okay, meet at the rear door, and hurry. This place will be vaporized soon." He gripped Joshua's shoulder. "She's going for her brother. Elizabeth has talked to you. For all she knows, I'd be a hiver lying to her."

Joshua followed, giving Sally one last look. She was already vanishing down the darkened corridor.

He checked on Samson.

...

It was a long walk over uneven ground, but Samson moved straight ahead.

Sight revealed different things than he was used to viewing through the lenses of his breather. The vegetation that grew where the pasture met the rocks at the base of the cliff was filled with life—small things he hadn't paid attention to before. A trio of *sendt* hopped through a gap, clearly escaping from something.

He had entered this Home so many times, he'd memorized the flat stones that generations of U'tanse had laid as an entrance walk. This was the last time he'd step this way and feel the panic and depression that lived inside.

We greet you, Samson. Come join us. You don't have to walk toward your death. We can fix your eyes. We can remove your pain.

He could feel the joined minds behind the words. There were still hints of individuality, like bumps on a clay ball, molded together of smaller ones. They had been men, women, and children, but they had become something larger.

But he could feel the others, too. The rest were panicked, trapped in the Home, an island of breathable air, trapped with friends who had become a predator, ready to eat their minds. And everyone knew what he was here for.

Some would try to escape, as senseless as that would be. Maybe they could even reach safety. He didn't care. He knew what he was here for. The others were Elehadi's problem.

He knew his duty. He would destroy this place.

...

Hugo snatched Joshua by the neck and pushed him up to the door. "Elizabeth! This is Joshua. Open the door."

A voice inside, male, yelled, "Go away!"

"Get Elizabeth! She can vouch for me. We're here to rescue you."

There was a whispering that he could hear in the distance—at least he thought he could hear it. It could have been something else.

Hugo looked worried. They were on a race—racing Samson, racing the *flick*. Delays weren't good.

"Who are you?" came the woman's voice behind the door.

"It's Joshua, Elizabeth. Sally and I came back. The Cerik guards all left, so we were able to sneak in. We don't have any time!"

"Lift your *ineda*!"

Joshua felt a spike of fear. He lived with constant *ineda*. It was like breathing. But like holding his breath, he could do it. He recalled the memory of Elizabeth and Sally bringing the babies and leading the cuties to the room where he was hiding.

"Okay. Open it," she said to someone.

"You can't keep it closed!" yelled Samson.

Joshua shook off the thought. The man was so close, and so important right now that it was hard to ignore his thoughts, but he had to stay focused on the task.

The door opened a crack and Elizabeth peered out. She nodded. "There are just a few of us here," she said as they began to file out. "There are more, hiding in the baths. Can you get them?"

The others, framed in the brighter light of the metal-casting workshop, looked his way with fear and suspicion. Eyes flickered to Elizabeth, looking to her for reassurance.

Hugo said, "All of you, follow me. There will be some running in the open air, but that can't be helped." Hesitantly, they started to follow.

Joshua said to Elizabeth, "I'll go check the baths, but time is running out."

She looked him in the eyes, and then sighed, "Don't let them trap you. They take over everyone they can touch."

He could feel her worry that she was sending him to his death, or worse.

He nodded to Hugo, "I'll meet you over the ridge. Go!"

Before he could second-guess himself, he headed into the dark corridor, deeper into the Home, in the direction of those whispers.

. . .

Samson held a large flat stone, ripped from the ground, and used its edge as an ax, attacking the thick wood of the entrance. He could see that the metal locking lever had been fused with an acid, but a hand-width beyond, into the wood of the door itself, he could see the weak point.

Crack! He lifted the stone again and slammed it down on the wood. The gap opened wide enough to force the blade of his gauntlet inside and widen it further. He gripped the new handhold, and strained. The door split vertically, and opened the inside of the Home to outside air. He was in.

Up ahead, he could hear whispers, warning of his coming.

. . .

Joshua stumbled to a stop. Three figures blocked the corridor ahead of him.

They were young—a guy his age and two slightly younger, a boy and a girl. They all held poles with spines on the tip.

Animal minders. Came the thought, explaining his question about the tool they'd pulled from his mind even through his *ineda*.

You are not of Rikna. I can't let you take them away from me.

Joshua tried to shake away the powerful thought. "I'm here to save their lives. Get out of my way."

The younger boy shifted position, moving closer to the right wall.

They're trying to surround me. I can't let that happen. He felt an echo of the battle Samson fought with the Cerik on the day Rikna fell. Only this time, his opponents held the weapons, and he didn't have claws.

But he moved instinctively to crowd the one on the right. The boy raised his pole and jabbed the spiked end in his direction.

Joshua swung his leg high and kicked it aside, moving even closer.

Don't touch him. That might just be the survivors' fears, but why risk it. But he was wearing his leathers; that ought to prevent skin contact.

The other two were closing in. The young boy tried to swing his pole back, but Joshua was already too close for that. He grabbed the pole and yanked it out of the boy's grip.

Joshua swiveled, swinging the pole like a club all the way around and clipped the boy on the head.

"Ahhk!" he screamed and fell. The other two jerked. Feeling the shared pain.

Don't stop. Joshua felt a battle lust surge within him.

Was that Samson? He didn't think, just moved his aim to the girl. He wasn't fighting a cutie—he was fighting the hive.

She read his intent, turning her face away from the swinging pole. He shifted his aim, catching her upper arm, and he heard the bone snap.

She shrieked in pain and collapsed.

Joshua turned his attention on the oldest, who had ducked back out of range.

The boy's face was impassive, not even looking at his hurt companions on the floor.

There is no room for two. Join us. Don't you realize that this is the only way we can survive!

Joshua's heart was pounding, and whether the surge of emotion he felt had somehow leaked from Samson or whether it was all his own, he was raging with the will to fight.

"You'll never survive," he screamed. "Samson will *flick* this place."

The boy was moving farther back, but the words felt as close as a breath. **We can stop Samson. If we can gain more minds, we can reach out to stay the Cerik who will come to *flick* us from the sky. Join us, and we can stop the Cerik from ever hurting us again.**

Joshua didn't know if they were right, but the corridor ahead of him was clear, and he had to check the baths.

Destiny

Samson stepped carefully through the corridor. Chairs, beds, brooms, even plates and dishes had been strewn in his path. They knew his weakness. They knew his blindness. A stumble would delay him. A simple injury, on top of his current trauma, could weaken his resolve.

But he knew the path. Dario had shown him the way, and he didn't need eyes to find it. The hive mind lived in U'tanse bodies, and those bodies needed filtered air to survive. They needed the power cell to live. And he needed it to kill them.

A little girl walked into the corridor from a side room. "Please don't kill me!" Another came to join her. "Don't hurt us." A third and forth came from the next cell. "Don't hurt us. Don't kill me."

It was enough to make him pause his steps. He could disregard their words. It sounded like a chant. And each of the girls held one hand behind her back. If he were still relying on his eyes, he might not have noticed the knives they were holding.

He was sure these were cuties that had been swept up into the hive with no resistance. There were six of them now. How many more were rummaging through the Home, hunting for knives?

How many little girls was the hive prepared to sacrifice?

Samson reached up and gripped the jawbone of the *haeka*. It slipped free of its clasp with just a click. The first girl he hit with the mass of bone had no warning, if that even made sense when talking about a hiver. The jawbone clipped her shoulder and sharp edges tore through the arm holding her knife. She screamed. They all screamed.

Samson kept moving, swinging the jawbone to connect with anyone who got in his way. They were shouting, "Monster! The monster is killing us!"

The *haeka* jawbone was dripping with blood when he got past them. He kept moving as quickly as he could. There was no joy in that battle. They weren't warriors, not even opponents—just a barricade like the broken dishes scattered in his path.

...

Joshua shook off the bloody image as he entered the Rikna baths, the pole still gripped tightly in his hand.

This was probably the oldest part of the Home—the Delense-built mud burrows on the shore of the dammed-up stream. Much later, the whole pond was roofed over when the complex spread out to cover the notch in the valley. But there was still a number of cells opened out to the water, not used by anyone except bathers and lovers. It had numerous places for people to hide.

He prepared to shout, to call to people he knew were hiding, when he saw her.

Perhaps he remembered her from when he was looking for girls. She was somewhere near his age—perhaps a friend of Sally's. Her tunic was covered with blood, where it had oozed out of her chest. Her hands were still clutched on the handle where she must have steeled herself and then plunged the blade into own her heart from panic at being taken over by the hive.

She lay in one of the shallow cells next to the water. Why had she chosen that spot? Why had she brought a knife in the first place?

Just thinking about it sent shivers through his body.

No time to think.

He threw his head back and screamed at the top of his lungs, "Samson is going to *flick* this place in just minutes! I know a way out! I know a way to safety! Follow me! I'm not going to wait for you!"

Several heads appeared from hiding places. He stepped up on a rock ledge at the water's edge. "No time to wait! Follow me now!"

He meant every word. If they followed him, they might have a chance. Waiting for them to make up their mind would kill them all.

He turned and walked past the suicide, pausing at the doorway.

Around the corner a handful of people appeared, he waved them on, and stepped out into the corridor.

Two of the hivers blocked his way. One was the first guy he'd seen, still holding his spiked pole. The other was female and looked a *lot* like Veronica. She said, "You have to leave them behind. They are Rikna. They are my people."

Knife behind her back. It felt like Samson, but he'd had that thought already, having seen what he went through.

The guy said, "You shouldn't stand in our way. You are already part of Samson's hive. You know it's not a bad thing. We're just trying to survive, and we need all the Rikna together to hold off the Cerik."

A rock whizzed past his head and hit the girl, knocking her to the ground. Her knife clattered on the floor.

Joshua moved, striking hiver's hand with his pole, twisting his own body around for a second strike his head just above the ear, knocking him aside.

An old man moved up beside him—a one-armed man. It was Frank.

"Don't let them talk to you. They'll tell you lies and half-truths to throw you off balance. Let's move."

"Right." He didn't look back, hurrying toward the rear entrance. He didn't even try to count how many followed.

But was the hiver right? Had he fallen into attachment with Samson?

...

The entrance to the power room was blocked by three naked women. Samson moved quickly, knocking them out and pushing them aside with his foot.

He snarled at the other hivers he knew were waiting just behind him, waiting until the moment when he was distracted to drive their knives into his back. "You made a mistake, insulting Omelia like that!"

The door was locked with a Delense code, but even if the hive had thought to change the code from the day he lifted it from Dario's mind, it made no difference. He drove the blade of his gauntlet into the door at the right height. Ceramic fractured, and his metal made contact with the internal lever. He pushed to the side and the door clicked open.

He was inside with the door closed behind him before the hivers could reach him.

He overturned the transport carriage and piled it against the door. They would have to dismantle the door to open it again.

It was just him, alone in the room with the power cell.

. . .

"Samson has reached the power cell!" Joshua screamed, as they streamed out the back entrance.

Sally looked back from her position leading a number of blindfolded cuties up the trail. He waved her on. She must have heard him, because she hurried even faster. Others in the group started running. Joshua waved his party on past.

"Go! Go! Get over that ridge before the place explodes. Move now!"

Panicked faces hurried past. How many of them even bothered with *ineda*?

He shook his head. Unless they moved faster, it wouldn't matter.

. . .

Samson shook off the nagging.

It doesn't matter if you change the settings on the power cell. I won't let your hand tap the white dot.

Samson tried to ignore the hive, chattering in his mind, trying to distract him, trying to make him set the cell's discharge rate wrong.

There were enough distractions he'd have on his own. He'd prefer to lock his mind behind *ineda* and concentrate on shutting out the hive, but he couldn't do that.

He knew people were reading his thoughts. He knew the Name's telepath was probably reading him as well. People cared what he was doing, and why he was doing it.

That had come home strongly a few minutes earlier when a thought opened up nearby, someone talking to Elizabeth. He didn't know the young man, although he was distinctly familiar. It had puzzled him, and even though the man's *ineda* had closed again, there was still a hint of his thoughts and actions making their way through.

This one had been following his thoughts all along. Samson sensed that now. For reasons of his own, this other one was fighting the hivers, too. Sometimes he was using Samson's own moves. Had be been following him long enough to have picked up some of his training?

How many others in the world had been following him? How many thought he was good? How many now considered him a monster. The hive had picked that out of his mind, making its captured cuties call him that. Only training had kept him from being distracted.

Bloody.

Samson snarled. *Yes, I know. But that's my fate, isn't it?*

From the day his parents named him Samson, he was destined for this end. He even studied his namesake in the Book. The original had suffered at the hands of an unfaithful lover, and he had been on guard against that—waiting out numerous temptations until Omelia arrived. She was true.

But there were so many things that had bent his course to this moment, waiting in a utility room, ready to bring down destruction on this place.

The *haeka*. Why had he killed it like the lion? Why had he saved the jawbone? Why had it been instinctively right to slaughter the knife-wielding cuties with the jawbone?

Perhaps his own mind tricked him into this, but it hadn't been his call to be blinded. Elehadi couldn't have even known of the Samson tale.

Even now, he was still in the thrall of the legend. The original Samson, blind and thought safe, had been brought to the hall of his enemies to be ridiculed—to be entertainment. Until he brought down the building on them all.

And I know that across Ko, others are monitoring my thoughts, watching me. Am I just to be entertainment for them?

Samson felt a pain in his arm, it flashed into searing heat. He clenched his teeth.

"No! You lie to me."

And his mind went silent.

. . .

Joshua stumbled on the trail, suddenly alert to his surroundings, now that Samson had clamped down with his *ineda*. Did that mean he was ready to trigger the power cell?

The top of the ridge was just in sight. Caught up in Samson's thoughts, he'd drifted into a daze. He should have been running.

He glanced back, and his spirit sagged. Elizabeth was behind him, helping a cutie make her way up the trail.

No time. But he turned back around, skipping down the trail and picking up the cutie from Elizabeth's hand.

"Come on—seconds now! I feel it."

Elizabeth nodded. "I'll be right behind you."

He carried the little girl a few paces, turned and saw that Elizabeth was still where he'd left her, panting, trying to catch her breath.

"Come on! Run! Your life depends on it."

She nodded and stumbled forward. It wasn't a run, but she hurried.

Joshua moved a few more paces and checked on her again. She was still coming, still seeing him checking on her.

He knew Elizabeth was exhausted, on the verge of collapse. It had been hard for her. Would she just give up if she were left behind?

But he couldn't carry her. The little one squirming in his arms was hard enough.

...

Samson was defiant. He shouted, "Enough tricks! You can't take my own muscles from me!"

He raised his hand to the control panel. Each inch was a struggle, and his hand jerked as the massed minds of the hive tried to take his control away.

But he had tricks of his own; invoking and dropping his *ineda*, reaching back home to touch the mind of Omelia for strength, resolving to stay true to his duty, no matter what.

A tiny part of his mind watched the trail of survivors seek the protection of the mountain ridge behind the Home, and that single mind that felt so familiar to him. He was almost there, if he could just hold out long enough for that one to make it...

But the angry hive started reaching into his body, reaching for his heart. Samson felt it flutter in his chest. There was no time.

...

Joshua screamed. "It's coming!"

The ridge was so close.

He wrapped the cutie in his arms and ducked his head.

He was just aware that Elizabeth had pushed up behind him and spread her arms when the world turned white.

Out of the Egg

He was flying—flying in a white, burning sky. Everything was hot and suffocating, and it was *burning* him. He was falling—falling toward the lava field on the Moon, where it would burn him up.

The swirling, confusing noise—a rushing noise that covered everything, abruptly stopped. He could hear his breathing. Or, was it his?

He remembered. He could open his eyes.

And he was staring at Sally as she looked at him.

She breathed out. "You're awake. I was worried."

He shifted, and everything hurt. "What? What's going on? Samson?"

She shook her head tightly. "Gone. The Home is gone. It's just a hot crater in the ground, still bubbling and steaming. It almost got you."

He tried to look up, but everything other than Sally's head leaning over him, was a vague white. "Where are we?"

"You and I are in one of the eggs. You're in here because of your injuries, and I'm healing you."

"Injuries?" he tried to feel his body, but she must have done something to him, because all he could sense was an unpleasant numbness.

She nodded solemnly. "Burns, broken bones, giant bruises from when you landed. Joshua, when the Home exploded, it sent you flying through the air and you crashed on the ground. I was afraid you were dead."

He remembered nothing. "Elizabeth and the girl I was holding—what happened to them?"

"Lucy came out of it with hardly any injuries. You protected her the whole way. Elizabeth ... didn't make it."

He tried to pull together that last instant before the world lit up.

"Elizabeth saved me, I think. When I yelled that it was coming, she stood behind me and protected me from the blast."

Sally's eyes oozed a trace of tears. "That was my grandmother, all right. She had severe burns. She must have died instantly. The places where the blast light reached you burned your leathers all the way through to your skin, but she took the most of it."

He felt a hurt, a deep loss in his chest. His eyes went blurry. "I wish I had known her. We barely exchanged a dozen words." And she had died for him.

Sally continued, "Other people had injuries, some burns and broken eardrums. But none as bad as yours."

He nodded. "Where are we? Where is the egg?"

She frowned, "We're right where you landed, on the other side of the ridge, hidden in the trees. The boat hasn't come for us. We don't know what's going on."

...

He wanted to know more, but the world drifted away.

And then, some time later, there was a knock.

He blinked as a puff of outside air caused the back of his scalp to sting. He blinked away the fuzziness. Sally had opened the clamshell egg, unsealing the inside.

She whispered, to a figure in the darkness. "What is it?"

"There's a small party of Cerik moving nearby. We might need to run or fight."

Joshua felt his mind clear up, and a lot of pain returned. But it wasn't in the same class as the torment Samson had endured.

Just thinking the name gave him a hollow echo. Samson's familiar mental presence wasn't there anymore. He shook off the feeling.

Sally climbed out of the egg and hurried over to where a group of people were standing. Joshua tried to get up as well, but it was difficult. His left arm was bound to his chest. A quick *look* showed an upper arm fracture, but Sally's work had already helped the bone to start mending. His whole left side ached.

He needed to know what was going on. Although it hurt considerably, he rolled over onto his right side and pushed up. Falling out of the egg was the better description, but he had one arm and two legs that worked, and he got to his knees, and holding onto the egg for stability, managed to stand.

The night air accentuated just how much of his leathers had been burned or torn off. The left leg and most of his chest were bare, except where strips of the leather had been used to bind his arm. Everywhere, open wounds complained of the raw air, but he was grateful he was unconscious when they were fresh.

He stumbled closer to the group.

"Six Cerik, I think. They're curving around the crater, trying to keep their distance, but they're moving closer." The man pointed in their direction.

Joshua tried to look and soon located them. He checked more of the surrounding area.

"Nomads," he mumbled.

Several people turned his direction. "What did you say, Joshua?" asked Sally.

"They're nomads. When the guards all left and flew home to Kakil, some of the Rikna Cerik workers broke down the side of the breeding pit and let the females out. There are several small groups now. Nomads. Several males and captive females escaping to the mountains."

"So, there are more of these groups?"

"Yes, but they're on the run. They're hiding out, just like we are."

One of the women said, "So, does that mean they're scared of us, too?"

"Maybe. If I were escaping before the Kakil returned, I'd steer clear if I heard any strange noises."

The man in charge set guards around the perimeter of their hiding place. "If Cerik get closer, make a noise—hit the rocks with a stick. Something distinctive, but that doesn't say 'prey' to their minds."

Another woman came closer and asked, "Sally, is your egg free? My daughter and I have been five hours without a shift in the eggs, and she's coughing."

Sally said, "No", but Joshua said, "Yes" at the same time. He said, "I'm up for now. I have to move around for a bit."

Sally sighed, "Okay." She nodded to the lady, who hurried off to take advantage of the filtered air.

She took Joshua by the free arm, "You. Come with me. I need to put more ointment on your burns."

She walked them over to a gap in the ridge and sat him down on a stone overlooking the red glow still radiating from the blast center. It was a little warmer in the protected spot, and she pulled a pouch from her pocket and began smoothing an oily paste on sensitive spots.

"Lucky you brought burn ointment." He gritted his teeth as she touched the wounds.

"Yes. It was just an impulse. Veronica had just mentioned making burn ointment, and it was on my mind. This is just a heavy airburn lotion, but it'll have to do."

Joshua thought of his sister.

"Oh!"

Sally asked, "Did I hurt you?"

He took a breath. "No, it's not that. I just had a thought. It's nothing."

"It didn't sound like nothing."

"Ignore me. I'm probably still dazed and confused."

Then he asked, "Did you find your brother?"

"Yes. I got him out, but now I can't find him. While I was working on you in the egg, apparently, Jack left with Hugo and Terry on some task. I hope they haven't run into any of those nomads."

He nodded. "Although, the nomads are likely to be more of a problem at the Base. Once they spread out and feel safe from Elehadi's reach, they're going to wander all over the mountains. It's going to be harder to keep the factory hidden. I wouldn't feel safe going for a hike anymore."

She sighed. "That'll be a problem. But I'm worried that something has happened to the boat. How will we reach safety? Hike the whole way back?"

"Wouldn't work. Even if we could avoid the nomads, could we carry the eggs? We need filtered air, or we'll all sicken and die quickly."

"How long will the eggs work?"

"I don't know. I didn't even know we had them before this rescue."

She adjusted his wrappings. "Well, it was cosy in there with you. I was sorry to give it up."

Joshua stared out over the crater. Clouds had rolled in, and he could see the red glow from the crater reflecting on them. "How long do we have before sunrise?"

"You're the better clairvoyant. You tell me."

Off in the distance, he could hear someone rap a stick on a rock twice in the distance.

He just shook his head. "Too tired."

She leaned up against him. "Just rest. I have more healing to do to you."

New Home

The buzz of a boat coming out of the clouds startled the camp.

"Is that ours?" someone asked.

"No!"

Joshua got to his feet. The low clouds swirled as a large boat lowered unsteadily toward a gap in the trees. It was definitely not the small boat that had dropped them off.

Someone yelled, "Run!"

Joshua saw more. There was a great tear in the metal along one side of the boat. He recognized it. "No! Stay put!"

He chest heaved, threatening to vomit mucus. His injuries and breathing raw air had left his lungs weak. He spit and then said, "It could be ours."

The boat edged down, breaking some tree limbs as it landed. The buzzing died away. Everyone could see the damage now.

Joshua coughed and said to Sally, "It's one of Kakil's transport ships. One that was damaged in the Rikna battle. Elehadi tried to salvage it, but couldn't."

She gripped his arm. "That's Jack."

They hurried over to where the man was getting out of the boat.

Her brother yelled, "Hurry. We need to load the eggs. Kakil is sending in guards at dawn. We all need to be gone by then."

Hugo came out and saw him. He waved. "Joshua, come here. I'll need help getting everything organized."

Sally helped him as he hurried and then began a coughing fit. Hugo helped him step in through the warped entrance.

He said, "Sorry you're hurt, but we need you to direct people. Have everyone load up on the right side of the boat. We'll need to stay clear of the tear in the hull. Everyone needs to find a place to hold on securely."

Joshua nodded. "Where's the other boat?"

Hugo grinned. "We'll talk about that later."

He hurried away. Joshua found a place to sit and Sally hurried off to help move the cuties who were still waiting in eggs or drugged.

"Find a place," he told the women coming in, "next to the back wall, where you can hold on when things shift."

He gave everyone roughly the same instructions.

"It will be shaky, like a rough quake. Make sure you have a place to hold on. Stay to the back side."

Soon the men arrived, two at a time, carrying eggs. Joshua hoped there would be room for everyone.

Jack arrived with his sister. They were both carrying unconscious cuties. For the trip, they were putting the helpless in the eggs. They'd be safer in there if the trip was too rough.

The noise of a crowd of people was something Joshua wasn't used to. Even at the Base, people didn't crowd together so tightly. In all, there were about fifty people who had gotten out before the explosion.

Finally, Sally and Jack sat down beside him. "That's all of them."

Joshua said, "I saw an unconscious man with them. Was he injured?"

Jack sighed, "I don't know. Three of our number screamed and went into convulsions when the Home exploded. We doped them up, just in case."

"You think they were hivers?"

Jack nodded. "That's the guess. They were trying to put some of their numbers with us, and take us over from within."

Sally asked, "Joshua said this was a crashed boat. How did you get it to fly?"

Jack beamed, "Hugo and Terry asked me to join them. Hugo had some papers that detailed exactly what was wrong with the three crashed boats. Patrick dropped us down in the landing field and we salvaged control systems from one of the boats and got this one flying. Hugo says it's hard to handle and the hull won't hold air, but it is structurally sound and he can fly us all out. I hope he's right."

They were just about to find out. Hugo closed the warped hatch, tying it shut with a braided rope of cloth.

Hugo and the man Joshua had identified as the leader of the group stood up together.

Joshua asked, "Who is he?"

Sally whispered back, "Otto. He was on track to be an elder, and just barely missed being shipped off to Sanassan. People trust him."

Hugo said, "We're leaving now. Hang on to something the whole trip. We will have a rough ride, and you will fall out that gap in the wall if you don't take care. Remember to keep your *ineda* firm and don't worry about where we're going or how you'll survive. The most important thing is to keep those thoughts locked up. Your cuties are drugged to keep those things away from the Cerik. Don't make us drug you, too."

Then Otto spoke. "We're all family here, and remember that we owe it to the ones who didn't make it to pull ourselves together and make certain we help each other. This is the start of a new age for us. Be thankful."

Hugo moved to the piloting station and started up the engines. With the hull breach, the noise was much louder than it had been in the other boat. They lifted and moved off. Wind whistled through the crack and people began to take the advice to hold on a lot more seriously.

It also got colder. There wasn't much of a view, just flickers of landscape through the gap in the hull. Joshua managed to close his eyes. Sally snuggled closer. One time, when there was a sudden shift, he looked up and was surprised to see Jack looking at them with a grin on his face. Sally had gone to sleep, her head resting on his least-damaged shoulder.

Daylight was leaking in when the flight leveled out and Joshua realized that they were somehow out over the ocean. Hugo must have taken a devious route, just in case they were being followed.

When they were still over the ocean after what he considered much too long a flight, he began probing with his *sight*.

They were indeed far from land, at least at his first scan. But soon, he saw that they were approaching a mountain chain. But he felt disoriented. The morning sun was from the wrong direction for them to have gone out over the water and then returned. This wasn't where the Base was located. It was somewhere else.

At times like this, he wished he had his mother's talent for flash comprehension. It would take him a long time to figure out where he was.

And the engine buzz began to change, shifting as they turned and approached the land.

People were waking up. Coughing began again in earnest. Too many people had been out in raw air for too long, and the boat ride hadn't helped.

They landed. Hugo killed the engines and untied the warped hatch.

Otto invited people to exit. "We're at our new Home. We're starting a new one."

One by one, the people able to move walked out. Joshua was startled to see Debbie, greeting them.

His mother was sending them into a open hatchway into a concealed Delense burrow.

"It's been abandoned for hundreds of years, at least, but we've gotten the lights and the air system to work, so you can start your healing."

Questions could wait, he realized, until everyone was unloaded.

By the time the sun was high in the sky, and everyone was breathing filtered air, Joshua got a moment's time with his mother.

Debbie fussed over his broken arm and complimented Sally on her work fixing him up.

Sally asked the question, "Where are we?"

Debbie smiled, "The Base wasn't the only hidden Delense facility we've discovered over the years. We just didn't have the people to activate it. Now we do."

"Why not just move them to the Base. You have the room."

"Two free U'tanse outposts is better than one. Or three, or a dozen. As a people, the more places to hide, the safer we are."

Sally frowned, "Maybe. But the more people, the more resources."

"We'll share resources, no doubt about that, but our biggest danger is leaking the information of our existence and our location to the Cerik. Joshua was raised knowing this. You learned quickly. But a random population from a Home—that's too big a risk. So we brought you here, to a place no one knows."

Sally quickly looked at Joshua and then back at his mother. "Am I to stay here, or go back to the Base?"

Debbie shrugged. "There will be some adjustments. Elehadi's sell-off removed too many men from your population, the Base and the factory have too many of them. We can swap people carefully, but we don't need to decide that right now. The Base will be needing to ship food, supplies, and equipment here for some time, until the new Home is self-sustaining. It will be easy to hitch a ride."

Joshua said, "I guess I'll be heading back to the Base."

His mother said, "Definitely. Your father has been agitated since you left. You're needed there. And you need to heal."

Sally asked, "What about the cuties? The ones we rescued first?"

"You'll help with that. You're the only Rikna native that knows all about the Base, and knows what secrets to keep. You've been reliable, and we'll need you to help smooth the conflicts that are sure to come up. Your insight will be needed on who to move. I think we'll need to keep families together, as much as possible, but it will be tricky to know who should move to the Base, and who to the new Home. I suspect you'll be traveling back and forth for a while."

Father and Son

It was relaxing to walk the spiral again, and he looked forward to a long, relaxing bath to rinse off all the dust, smoke, and burn ointment. He'd been promised a ride home in one day, but everything seemed to be running behind schedule. Sally even caught a ride back before he did. Jinger had reacted badly to the death of the hive, and she was needed urgently.

But he was barely to the maproom when Cyclops met him in the corridor and waved him into his private room.

"How well do you know Cerik?"

Joshua shook his head. "Not well at all."

"Well, fix that. Monitor some Cerik—hopefully a *rettik* in Elehadi's service. Learn the language. For now, just take a pencil and write down what I say."

Joshua sat down and prepared to write.

Cyclops relaxed in his chair. There was nothing for a moment, and then he said, "Stakka says, 'For your Name.'" Joshua started writing.

"Elehadi grumbles. 'I hope you have Graddik's thoughts for me.'"

"Stakka: 'He is pretending to be clever. He wants others to believe that his thoughts are open but he had meetings with his Second, with them both under *ineda*.'"

"Elehadi: 'He'd better find a place where no one can hear them, and then guard it well. There are spies everywhere. But you haven't told me what he is thinking. Your blood is safe from my anger.'"

"Stakka: 'His plan is becoming clear. The story he is speaking, and revealing in his public thoughts is this: Elehadi has betrayed all of the Names by his handling of the Rikna U'tanse. By putting great numbers of them in a *dul* with no escape, he pushed them into becoming Ferreer. He intends to seek an uproar at the next Face. Elehadi is too dangerous to remain a Name.'"

"Elehadi ruffs, 'Graddik will suffer for this. The Face is still many months away and I have my own story to tell. Our U'tanse took the blame for not handling the Rikna U'tanse correctly. They know this, and I will remind them.'"

"Stakka says, 'Graddik is telling his own thoughts about your U'tanse. It goes like this: The double-fingered one tried to preserve the valuable slaves, but when Elehadi's blunt-clawed actions pushed the slaves into becoming Ferreer, he saved his Name from disaster by destroying the Ferreer when Elehadi could not.'"

"Elehadi is hissing. Stakka steps back a few paces and kneels to the ground."

Cyclops tapped his fingers in impatience. Then he leaned forward. "Okay, now Elehadi calms down. He says, 'This is a dangerous tale. We have spent our time cultivating a loyal U'tanse that others of his kind could admire. Through him, they would come to revere the Name as they should. But Graddik's tale honors the slave and ridicules the Name. This could lead to even more difficulty with the slaves. I shall need to think more about this.'"

"Stakka says, 'Should we begin again with a new U'tanse?'"

"Elehadi says, 'Not yet. Let his absence be felt. Did he sire any cubs?'"

"Stakka says, 'I don't know. I will find out from our U'tanse spy.'"

"Elehadi says, 'Is this one loyal?'"

"Stakka says, 'He is loyal to his favored position, the extra food and the attention of his females.'"

"Elehadi says, 'Perhaps one close to him should suffer for being less loyal.'"

"Stakka says, 'It will happen as the Name directs.'"

Cyclops waved, "They separate. Stakka heads off in the direction of the Perch. Elehadi slips off into the bushes, stalking a *sendt*."

Joshua clenched his writing hand. He'd never written so fast before.

"How did you monitor them?" he asked.

Cyclops said, "One of the Ba slipped into Elehadi's protected hunting ground, invisible under the soil. The Ba listens, and since it comprehends the speech, I can listen to the Cerik speech through him."

"So we finally can monitor the secret meetings? But what about this U'tanse spy. He's in Kakil Home, probably. Did we know about him?"

Cyclops shook his head. "It's worrisome. It sounds like he's in a position of importance, maybe even an elder. We'll have to identify him as soon as possible."

"And Omelia. We have to warn her that Elehadi is interested in the child she's carrying."

Cyclops shook his head. "No, we don't. We don't reveal anything we discover with the help of the Ba. That's why you're here instead of Lincy. It's just you and me. And as soon as your Cerik language skills are better, I'll help you identify the Ba's thoughts. They are hard to detect. Do you understand the need for secrecy?"

He nodded. "If the Base is ever discovered, before acting Elehadi and Stakka will discuss what to do in secret. They can't suspect that we can listen in. But surely there's no one here at the Base who would let that information leak!"

His father sighed. "Even if we kept the Ba's involvement secret, we can't risk a failure of *ineda*—ours or our new neighbors. There is a spy at Kakil. Samson demonstrated a strong loyalty to Elehadi. We can't risk it."

Joshua nodded, although the idea that there could ever be a spy at the Base left a sour taste.

Cyclops took the notes Joshua had scribbled and placed them in an unmarked folder. "I suspect you want to clean up and rest after your trip. I'm glad to have you home, for more reasons than your sloppy handwriting."

The man put his arm around his shoulders and gave him a hug. Joshua appreciated the rare gesture. His father had difficulty expressing his emotions.

He hugged back.

"Dad?"

"Yes, son?"

"There is one other thing. Do you know of anyone who can see the future?"

Cyclops stiffened, getting back to business. "It was mentioned in the Book, but no one has that ability."

"Veronica had nightmares of girls and knives and a monster killing them. Days later, Samson fought that battle with little girl hivers. Then, she had a nightmare of me, flying through the air. And then the Rikna explosion tossed me through the air. Before we left on the rescue, Veronica was casually interested in burn ointments, and because of that, Sally had some with her when I needed it."

Cyclops sat back down and said, "The Book mentions that the half-brother of the Mother of us all had that talent. Why it would hide in our genes for so many generations before being revealed is a mystery. Are you sure?"

"No. I just think Very's nightmares need to be logged and considered."

"So do I."

Duty

Joshua made sure the third-level bath was empty before he went to his favorite spot, relaxing in the warm water where the pipes returned water heated by the machinery on the top level. He scrubbed the travel stains and ointment from himself and stretched out, with just his face above the water.

It had been the best talk he'd ever had with his father.

Hugo's secret had been the plan to recover the damaged boats. The destruction of the Home was the perfect cover, with no Cerik staying around to watch, and with the blast's shockwave providing an excuse for the missing machinery.

Cyclops and Hugo had worked long hours diagnosing the damage to the boats via their *sight*. Some of the damaged equipment could be scavenged from the boat crashed by Rikna's Name, but along with the eggs, the original boat carried several control systems that needed to be replaced. Both the transport used to take the Rikna refugees to their new Home and the other Kakil boat damaged by the crash could be made to fly and moved to hidden places where they could be repaired more completely.

As Debbie had hinted, the Delense had left a number of hidden facilities behind when they had attempted their bid for freedom. Cyclops told him he'd be told more as needed. Some secrets had to be parceled out bit by bit.

Cyclops was especially pleased that the Rikna's spare power cell, filled by the Name just prior to the Face, was found intact in the wreckage of his boat. They would have the power they would need to keep all three of their boats flying, at least for a while.

But as they talked, Joshua had asked more personal questions and had learned a lot.

Both Joshua and his sister were conceived in the Base with hardly any pre-conception advice from the other women. Since the earliest days of the U'tanse, the genetic fate of their race was in the hands of the women's council of each Home. At different times in their history, such things as gender ratio, and the genetic history of each young woman and her potential mates were carefully checked prior to match-up. They had all started from a single male and female and only strict genetic filtering had kept their gene pool viable.

But the Base was different, with a random population of people rescued and those Festival girls who could be recruited. There was no women's council, no generations of advice to pull from. Nor could questions be passed on to other Homes.

So with only her own training and the advice of a handful of other Festival girls, none with experience, Debbie had handled the genetic filtering herself, trying to conserve the valuable clairvoyance of herself and Cyclops in the mix. No one knew exactly how they would turn out.

And perhaps, it explained why they were so worried that he and Sally would start another generation with no training and no advice.

He had also learned the story of how his father lost his eyes. It was strange to think of his father, who seemed to be center of everything the Base did, as a man who had been an outsider all his life. Even now, the man thought of himself that way—separated by his *sight* and his secrets from the ordinary life of all his friends.

Joshua felt a warmth in his chest, realizing what it had taken from his father to reach out to him as he had. *I'll make you proud of me, Dad.*

A splash startled him. He pulled himself upright.

"Hey, don't get up," Sally said.

"What are you doing here?" he asked.

"Girls gotta keep ourselves clean, too." She smiled, "Oh, don't panic. Comfort is here to keep an eye on me."

The woman's voice echoed from around the corner. "Hey, I knew what Sally was up to when she suddenly decided to take a bath in the middle of the day."

Sally found a place to sit—close enough to admire, too far away to touch.

"I heard you were back at the Base," she said, "but when you didn't show up at the nursery, I was worried about you."

He lifted his left arm. "I'm fine. The arm is getting its range of motion back. But how is Jinger?"

Sally nodded thoughtfully, "Fairly well. She doesn't act attached anymore, but it's as if she doesn't remember much of her old life. When the hive died, it was pretty traumatic from the stories I heard. She scared the others."

She sighed, "I've know her since she was a baby. She's always been timid. I think she hooked up with her friends so tightly because she wouldn't have to face the world alone. It was a way of running away from her problems. When the hive appeared, it was perfect. Decisions were all made for her. Now that it's gone, maybe the memory loss is another way for her to run away."

"But she's acting normal?"

"Mostly. She takes care of Bella, but she knows her friends are dead, even if she can't remember the details, so she's always a little sad and subdued. But she talks to the others. She argues with Weelie, so that's a good sign."

"And the others—they must know that something has happened."

"We say, 'It's over now.' The older cuties get the standard explanation: Learn your *ineda*, and you can learn the secrets."

Joshua saw that she was a little tired. She slipped lower into the water to enjoy the warmth. He asked, "Which of them has family back at the new Home?"

She lowered her hair into the water, rinsing it. "Buster is going back, but Green's mother didn't make it. Karli and Kurtis have an aunt who wants them back. I guess the others will stay."

"And Jinger?"

Sally shrugged, making waves. "I think everyone who was a hiver and survived is going to be watched for a while. I don't think they want them to get back together either. Jinger will probably stay here. Those at the new Home will probably be kept separated."

He hesitated, then asked, "How is my sister doing? Any nightmares?"

"None that I've heard of. She's trying to get Ash to teach her how to draw."

He chuckled, "That's a change—she made fun of his drawing before. Weelie?"

Sally grinned and nodded. Then she asked, "Veronica is waiting for you to come back. Why are you waiting?"

He thought a moment. "I needed to get cleaned up. I didn't want to show up mangled and dirty from the rescue. I wanted to be just the same when I returned."

He sighed. "But maybe, that's not possible anymore. I lost someone, too."

"Oh?"

He nodded. "I was in Samson's head nearly constantly since even before the invasion. The hive even tried to confuse me into believing that he and I were a hive mind. That wasn't true, but I was there when he went to his death. To many people, he was a monster, a villain, but I knew what drove him to do the things he did."

Sally just listened, and he wasn't sure what she thought of the man.

He tried to put his thoughts into words. "Samson was driven by his loyalty to the U'tanse as a race, and also by his fealty to Elehadi. The Name forced those loyalties into conflict, for games of his own, but Samson walked that line, having to kill U'tanse hivers—something that not many U'tanse could do. The only thing that kept him at peace with himself was his faithfulness to his duty and the woman he'd waited all his life to meet. The one women he knew would be true."

Sally's mouth dropped open a little, as if she almost had a question to ask.

Joshua said, "He went to his death, feeling certain he was doing the right thing. When my time comes, I want to feel that certainty."

She said, "You will. I don't know about finding the one true woman, but…"

He interrupted, smiling, "I don't know. Not many available women around here. How is your training coming?"

She blushed, "It's on track. Comfort is helping me here, and my old teacher, Allison, is back at the new Home. They're working me through the steps."

She looked down at the water, tracing trails with her fingertips. "For now, they're teaching me how not to have a baby. Later, I'll learn how to do it right."

Comfort yelled, "Tell him the first rule!"

Sally grimaced. "No touching boys."

Joshua laughed, "I got the same advice about touching girls from my mother."

He looked cautiously in the direction of Comfort's voice and stretched out his arm. She grinned and stretched in his direction, until their fingertips touched.

Comfort yelled. "Hey, none of that."

Joshua settled back, content for the moment. He could wait until the right time. He was confident Sally was the right girl, if she had the patience to wait for him.

Comfort called an end to the quick mid-day bath, and Joshua watched Sally step out of the waters, enjoying every curve.

But he still had chores to plan and puzzles to solve. Cyclops had examined George's papers. The tenner was still on track to record every Cerik tale before he had to return the device to Elehadi. But George's secret log was still a mystery, written in code, notes about only certain of the tales—ones about the Delense and those about the time of expansion, when clans sought other worlds. What was George doing? Some private duty of his own, perhaps.

Joshua wondered, if he and Samson had ever met face to face, what would the giant have thought about him? He'd never know. But looking at the world through the giant's eyes had woken him up to a lot of things.

All a man has to look forward to, at the end, is how he has met his own duty. Samson had so much of his fate forced onto him. I've got a chance to make my own destiny, and I'd better do it right.

THE END

Cerik Terms

Cerik Term	Definition
'eeh	The bloodlust, a heightened sensual awareness.
Cerik	Literally, 'Hunter', the name of a race of predators
chitchit	A small predator from the Cerik home world that were used to root out burrowing prey. They were also used as pets.
conek	Tall slender trees, often used for construction of light-weight structures such as huts and decorative walls. Conek trees only grow at high altitudes.
dak	A substitute kill. Used when an honored soldier is killed. An enemy is killed, the blood drunk, and the kill attributed to the honored soldier.
dakka	A swamp-living prey, wide and flat in front with a long snake-like tail behind. Cerik like the taste, but since they live in the water, the Cerik hate to chase them.

Cerik Term	Definition
Delense	Literally, "Builder," the name of a semi-aquatic race of tool users. The Delense were enslaved by the Cerik in prehistory, and existed in a symbiotic relationship for thousands of years before they were exterminated by the Cerik.
dlathe	A broad shade tree, with many low-hanging branches. It was a favorite hunting Perch for Cerik.
dul	A traditional net used to hold a captured prey
erdan	The long wait. A semiconscious trance state when no prey were expected, but instant alertness might be required.
fenke dan	The meal, and the following period of torpor. In good times, a Cerik would eat once a day. Digestion has its own heavy demands and causes a deep lethargy that is not easily overridden.
Ferreer	A telepathic, hive-mind alien species that had inhabited several planets.
flick	To bomb an enemy with an overloaded TP core. Invented by the Delense to attack the Ferreer, the only race the Cerik could not attack directly face to face, it was also used in the fatal rebellion against the Cerik. It has the blast effects, but not the radiation, of a small tactical nuclear bomb.
Ha	The Ko Moon. Large with an elliptical orbit that brings large tides and triggers quakes and volcano eruptions.
Hae	Cerik mythology—the male spirit of the moon.

Cerik Term	Definition
haeka	Larger predator, sometimes known to capture Cerik cubs or nomadic females. Generally preys on runners in the foothills
hatsen	Mid-sized predator that feeds on small prey like *chitchits*.
hurru	A Perch. The rear talons of a Cerik efficiently gripped any branch large enough to hold them. The Perch of a Name was a ceremonial throne from which the Name ruled as he rested above all the others. It also came to refer to the buildings around it.
ineda	A telepathic block. This skill can be learned by any Cerik who needs to be a leader over telepaths. Before the arrival of the telepathic U'tanse, an ordinary Cerik who practices ineda was, by definition, a suspected thief.
janji	A freshwater fish that is edible by humans. The meat is chewy. More common in the north.
jenna	Common saltwater fish that can be digested by humans.
kadan	The anticipated kill wait. Like erdan, but with heightened anticipation that prey would appear any second.
katche	The "peace." During the Face, all clans are bound to refrain from clan-on-clan attacks, with the threat that all other clans would turn on the aggressor.
kede	A Broken Hunter. Any Cerik who is valuable even though severely injured. Surgery is unknown among the Cerik and it is up to the clan leader whether to support anyone crippled by injuries.

Cerik Term	Definition
kel	A common tree that is found near streams
klakr	The Cerik world's version of a triceratops. Twice the size of a Cerik. Large massive head with spikes and tusks. A spiked tail. Vegetarian, with easily offended sense of territory. Nearly extinct.
Ko	Literally, "all lands." This became the name of the Cerik home planet when they discovered that other planets existed.
Koee	Cerik mythology—the female spirit of the land.
La	Literally, "First," also referred to as "Named." The title of the leader of a clan, family or guild. A First was the only individual Cerik with a name. The First names himself when elevated to rank. All other adult males are addressed by their rank, and known unambiguously by their scent. Females and cubs are known by their scent and genealogy.
Larek	Literally, "Second," the second in command, and prime assistant to the First. Second is also heir to the First and can usurp his position with a physical challenge. In addition to the possibility of death in such a challenge, there are numerous social- and clan-level sanctions against a Second who endangers the clan by a challenge at the wrong time.
lulur	Large centipede-like creature with tubular body and a pair of legs per segment. Carrion eaters for the most part. Cerik disdain them and eradicate them only for sport.

Cerik Term	Definition
ooro	Coastal lizards that are a food delicacy, traded to interior clans
po	Flying reptile that nest in dlathe trees.
pree	To register personal satisfaction. Physically there can be a purring component, a salivating component, and/or a relaxing of the subdermal plates.
Rakladel	Cerik mythology—telepathic demon who could make a Cerik mindlessly crazy and who could not be killed.
ralak	Speaker. A clan-to-clan personal ambassador, with various levels of importance.
rettik	Literally "right eye," a close assistant, with status over other assistants. Often personal soldiers or bodyguards.
ruff	A territorial noise and posture, a threatening purr.
sendt	Literally, "Runner," a grazing herbivore that make up a dominant prey species for the Cerik. There are dozens of native varieties and several off-world varieties, prized for taste or for being skillful prey.
shash	A reed-like plant that grows along stream beds.
shillee	Long mid-sized lizards know for their erratic running path.
soso	A trade that both parties were happy with. "Fairness"

Cerik Term	Definition
ssitt	Literally, "Take the eyes." In battle among Cerik, the ritual death stroke was to take out the eyes of an enemy and eat them. Due to the tough skin of the Cerik, the most common death stroke in duels was a blow at the weakest part of the head, at the eyes.
tetca	Literally, "dance." A guild, an organized collection of Cerik workers with their own First, Second, and lower workers. A clan First will have many tetca First's under his direct command. Some common tetca: Rear Talon - Boat and spaceship pilots Telepaths; Scientists—nearly obsolete. This tetca came into being after the extermination of the Delense. U'tanse were better scientists than the Cerik by far and took over that task; Herders; Tale tellers; Ralak—messengers.
uuka	The ritual of submission where a Cerik lays face down, defenseless and awaits either a killing blow or the opportunity to swear allegiance to the new master.

U'tanse Terms

Over time, the original language of the U'tanse, English, has acquired a number of loan words from the Cerik, but has also added new terms of their own, or redefined old ones.

U'tanse Term	Definition
creeper	A bug, but the Ko varieties range from tiny crab-like species, to legless worms. Multi-legged varieties do grow larger, but many of those have their own Cerik names.
cutie	A U'tanse child old enough to walk, but too young to have come of age.
Festival	A trade and exchange of females between U'tanse Homes designed to reduce inbreeding. Over time, selected goods were exchanged also.
Home	A colony of U'tanse inhabiting a Delense burrow.

U'tanse Term	Definition
random	A person whose genetics was dictated by the random combination of the parents sperm and ovum, rather than having been controlled by the mother. A term of abhorrence, due to the history of birth defects whenever it was tried.
slurk	Monitoring thoughts or activities with salacious intent.
tenner	By policy, one in ten males is bred with no psychic abilities, in order to keep the U'tanse from drifting too far from the old human stock. In practice, tenners have proved superior in science, engineering and math.

Slave Races

A variety of species were conquered by the Cerik as they scavenged Star damaged planets. Most stayed on their home worlds. Only a few could survive the Cerik atmosphere and were valuable enough for the Cerik to make the effort to bring them home.

Species	Type	Value
U'tanse (Human)	Erect bipeds	Technically talented, and could design and repair tools.
Dadada (BaBaBa)	Radial symmetric turtles, triangles at birth, add legs as they age.	Young ones used as pets. Older ones as slow transport. Can carry heavy weights and understand spoken directions.
Uuaa (Wob)	Quadruped with long, multi-jointed arms and thicker hind legs for jumping.	Favorite pet of the Cerik because they jump the same way. Used to quickly climb trees and harvest fruits and nuts that the Cerik can't reach. Not vocal, but they can be trained.

The Ko Calendar

The Cerik have always lived by the moon. There are two types of cycles. One cycles through the phases, just like on the moon of Earth, but there is a more important cycle as well. Their moon, Ha, is in a highly elliptical orbit that brings it close enough to regularly trigger quakes across the globe. The Large Moon dominates the sky much more than Earth's full moon, regardless of which phase it is in. While the Cerik have noted that certain stars are in the sky following a "yearly" pattern, it makes no difference in their lives. With no noticeable yearly weather pattern, months, marked by the Large Moon, are the dominant measure of calendar time. On a day to day basis, the Large, Small, Full, and New moons make convenient markers even though these "weeks" can vary from 1 to 12 days in length.

The phases of the moon are slightly less than half of this month, with a Full Moon taking place every 24.4 Cerik days. Important days such as the Face are often marked by the conjunction of these 2 cycles, i.e., a Large Full Moon.

When the U'tanse arrived, Father began documenting what he could. There was a wristwatch, by which he determined that a Cerik day was slightly more than 20 Earth hours. A Cerik month was a little over 58 Cerik days.

The U'tanse set up their own calendar system, one that more closely matched the human norms. A Normal week was seven Cerik Days, with the same names Father and Mother were used to. Each Normal month was 5 weeks. There were 10 Normal months, which didn't quite match the Cerik year, but it was close enough. The month names were: January, March, April, May, July, August, September, October, November, and December.

Free U'tanse

U'tanse count birthdays and ages by the Normal year, which is only 80% as long as the Earth year. A 20 (Earth) year old would be deemed aged 25 on Cerik.

	Hours	Earth Days	Cerik Days
Earth Day	24	1.000	1.198
Cerik Month	1162.4	48.433	58.033
Normal Month	701.05	29.210	35.000
Normal Week	140.21	5.842	7.000
Cerik Year	6867.3	286.138	342.851
Normal Year	7010.5	292.104	350.000

The PROJECT Saga

Star Time

What if... Humanity gained the technology to move worlds?

What if... Captive humanity had to develop their psychic abilities?

Kingdom of the Hill Country
Henry Melton

In the Time of Green Blimps
Henry Melton

Captain's Memories

Tales of the U'tanse
Henry Melton

Free U'tanse
Henry Melton

Coming mid 2015, a new story of the **Project**

Coming early 2016, a new story of the **U'tanse**

http://henrymelton.com

Small Towns, Big Ideas

Adventure stories set all across the continent, from California to Labrador. High school aged heroes encounter an out of the ordinary event and have to take that step into the unknown. Teleportation, time travel, wormholes to another planet, Roswell aliens, alien nanobots, and even reality-bending conspiracies are just some of the problems they must solve.

Roswell or Bust — Las Vegas, New Mexico
Extreme Makeover — Crescent City, California
Falling Bakward — Chamberlain, South Dakota
Golden Girl — Oquawka, Illinois
Emperor Dad — Hutto, Texas
Lighter Than Air — Munising, Michigan
Pixie Dust — Austin, Texas
Follow That Mouse — Ranch Exit, Utah
Bearing Northeast — Churchill Falls, Labrador
The Copper Room — Canton, Missouri
Breaking Anchor — Lake Michigan
Beneath the Amarillo Plains —Amarillo, Texas

http://henrymelton.com

Come stay updated on U'tanse and other books by Henry Melton by visiting his website:

http://HenryMelton.com

Add your email address to his mailing list for periodic updates about book releases, book signing events and background information about his stories by going to:

http://henrymelton.net/2/email-list/

www.ingramcontent.com/pod-product-compliance
Lightning Source LLC
Chambersburg PA
CBHW020651030726
47498CB00002B/457